A Change
of Heart

Hugh Harris

A Change of Heart

The Dinkel Island Series

A Novel

Second Edition

TATE PUBLISHING
AND ENTERPRISES, LLC

Published by Tate Publishing & Enterprises, LLC
127 E. Trade Center Terrace | Mustang, Oklahoma 73064 USA
1.888.361.9473 | www.tatepublishing.com

Tate Publishing is committed to excellence in the publishing industry. The company reflects the philosophy established by the founders, based on Psalm 68:11,
"The Lord gave the word and great was the company of those who published it."

Book design copyright © 2015 by Tate Publishing, LLC. All rights reserved.
Cover design by Caypeeline Casas
Interior design by Deborah Toling

Published in the United States of America

ISBN: 978-1-68164-315-1
1. Fiction / Christian / General
2. Fiction / General
15.09.04

To Sharon, with love.

Acknowledgements

I am grateful to the people who listened to or read parts of this story as it formed in my mind and gave me the benefit of their reflections. Most of all I am indebted to my wife, Sharon, whose encouragement and skills in listening, proof reading, and editing enabled me to complete the book and whose sensitivity has informed my own understanding of the deep currents of the human spirit and of our eternal possibility for redemption by the grace of God.

Return of the Prodigal, by James A. Harris

Preface

Then the son said to him, "Father, I have sinned against heaven and before you; I am no longer worthy to be called your son." But the father said to his slaves, "Quickly, bring out a robe—the best one—and put it on him; put a ring on his finger and sandals on his feet. And get the fatted calf and kill it, and let us eat and celebrate; for this son of mine was dead and is alive again, he was lost and is found!"

Luke 15:21-24 (NRSV)

This story takes place in 1983-85. Some features of that time include these:

- Telephones had rotary dials or push buttons. Cell phones were available but too expensive for common usage, so telephone booths were prevalent.

- TV was received via antennas; cable TV was not widely available outside metropolitan areas.

- Laptop computers did not yet exist in general usage.

- Manual and electronic typewriters were common in offices and business settings.

- Popular among smaller and less expensive automobiles were the Chrysler Mini-Vans and K-Cars, the Plymouth Volare, Toyota's small Tercel, the Honda Accord.
- Video cameras and VCRs were available and growing in popularity.

1

Impressions

*P*astor Edward Heygood arrived for his first Sunday at the Dinkel Island Wesleyan Brethren Church as the steeple bell pealed its monotonous invitation. Its *clang-a-clang, clang-a-clang* seemed to say *come to church, come to church.* Ed pulled into the pastor's reserved parking space near the main entrance. His wife, Sally, reached into the backseat to straighten Billy's collar and give him and Angie some last minute instructions. At ages eight and five, they seemed to be taking the move into a new church and community as a playful adventure.

"You both look so nice," she said. "Remember, we want to make a good impression and make some new friends here today."

They got out of the car smiling self-consciously toward a small group that had gathered to welcome them. Suddenly the church door burst open, and a middle-aged woman rushed toward them with outstretched arms and a huge smile.

"Oh, here you are already! I'm Sarah Jones, and I just want y'all to know how glad we are to have you at our church."

Right behind her came a more subdued, slightly younger man whose smile embraced them before he even spoke. He and Sarah quickly took over the welcoming process. Sarah moved toward Sally and the kids while the man spoke to Ed.

"Pastor Heygood, I'm Jim Swank, your lay leader. It's good to meet you. Please forgive me for not being here to greet you when you arrived Thursday."

"That's okay about Thursday." Ed shook Jim's outstretched hand. "It's good to meet you, and please—just call me Ed."

"You got it! Now, let me introduce you to some people."

As Ed turned to follow Jim he gave his wife a 'see you later' glance. Sarah launched Sallly and the children off on a search for Sunday school classes. As they disappeared, Ed weighed his impression of these two people he'd just met. Sarah was charged with energy—an obvious take-charge type of person. Jim seemed to have a more subtle leadership style. Ed liked him instantly.

Jim's whirlwind orientation tour of the church quickly ended up in the office where Ed had cartons of books stacked up. He had begun to settle in on Saturday, so he was surprised to find that his files and papers had been pushed aside. In their place now were the treasurer, education chairperson, and Sunday school superintendent who were busy with their official Sunday morning duties.

Ed felt offended at the disregard with which they had seized what was supposed to be his work space. *Easy*, he said to himself. *Every church has its customs—no need to get into turf issues right up front*. He picked up a hymnal and a copy of the worship bulletin, spoke briefly to the men occupying the office, and asked Jim to introduce him to the organist. *There will be plenty of time later to deal with how the office is used.*

The sound of organ music triggered a timeless sense of comfort within Ed as he and Jim approached the sanctuary. Jenny Tyrone was rehearsing for the worship service. As they entered the back of the room she stopped playing and turned to sort through some music. Ed saw her as a woman of striking appearance who exhibited an air of aloofness. He wondered if she was used to consulting with the pastor about music. He decided to approach her with a gentle firmness that he hoped would win her trust and cooperation.

"It's nice to meet you in person," said Ed, extending his hand toward her. Jenny remained seated and reached over the organ to accept the handshake. Ed went on, "I believe you told me you've been organist here for a couple of years. I'm sure you know what music the folks like to sing, so I'll be relying on your to help me get started."

"Yes, I do know something about how people at Dinkel Island like to worship, and I will be happy to help you any way I can. Pastor Prentiss followed the lectionary and gave me a list of his sermon topics two months in advance so I could plan the services and hymns. Will you be doing that?"

Ed felt a wave of fear that he might easily make a fatal mistake in this delicate conversation. He hadn't been in the church a half-hour and was already treading carefully. "Well, I don't usually use the lectionary. You see, I feel God leads me into certain areas of preaching and emphasis, especially as I get into my work in a church. I try to be open and responsive to that. I like worship to be an experience of inner freedom that finds expression outwardly in words and music. I've been accustomed to choosing my own hymns, but I'll welcome your help. I'm sure we can work together. Let's talk about it this week."

They agreed to meet on Tuesday morning and parted politely. Jim sensed the friction that Ed felt. "I'm sure you're going to like working with Jenny. She's really good—took over when the old organist retired. She does like to take charge. Just let me know if I can help iron out any wrinkles."

"Thanks," said Ed.

During the morning service, Ed became aware that Jenny's idea of worship was much more formal than his. Her musical skill was excellent, even exciting. The people sang out with enthusiasm, and that fueled his spirit. He had tried not to change the service too much, so it was more formal than he wanted, but he was used to that from First Church in Richmond where he had just completed five years as an associate pastor.

After the service, people shook hands and chatted with Ed as they left the building. He felt overwhelmed. Besides his years as an associate pastor, he had been a student pastor during seminary. This was his first full-time assignment as pastor-in-charge of a congregation. He wanted to make a solid, positive impression to launch his work at Dinkel Island.

Attendance was good—about 150 people—and as they spoke with him, he wondered, *How many of these names and faces will I be able to link up next week?* Several people thanked him for singing the "old fashioned hymns—we don't sing them enough." Several made comments to the effect, "I enjoyed your talk, Reverend. Sam used to really make us laugh, but you're all right, too." Ed felt optimistic about the day and breathed prayerfully, *It's in your hands, Lord. Bless these people.*

A facet of his congregation Ed knew nothing about as yet was the after-church lunch crowd who met at the Seafood Pavilion. Affectionately dubbed the "Brunch Bunch," these were mostly people who were active in leadership and didn't eat breakfast because they were in a hurry to get to church on Sunday mornings. Their gathering on this Sunday was filled with airing out their impressions of the new preacher.

Some felt blessed, others did not. Those who did had grown tired of Sam Prentiss's endless jokes and constant surface frivolity. After six years they had wanted some depth in their preacher that Sam seemed to lack. Ed's message had seemed to promise that. And they liked the hymns. In fact, just about everyone agreed about the hymns. Most had grown tired of stately music all the time. It had felt good to sing some things that had the ring and feel of childhood memories to them.

Those who weren't sure about the blessings were mostly those who had grown into the habit of coming to church to be entertained by Sam's wit and sparkle. Some of them hadn't been in church for years until he came along. They were insiders now, and a change of preachers wouldn't make them leave, but they weren't about to call themselves "blessed" either.

Ed would soon learn that Dinkel Island was a place where nothing you experienced was, in reality, what it seemed to be. Not really an island at all, the town was located on a small peninsula on the Virginia shore of the Chesapeake Bay. It was surrounded by water on all sides at high tide, but the rest of the time it was only water-bound on three sides. The side where the highway entered the town was simply an uninhabitable marsh that bordered Crabber's Creek with a drawbridge over it; hence the designation, Dinkel "Island." The characteristics that applied to the name of the place also carried over into much of the nature of life for those who lived there.

∾৲৹

As the Heygoods left the church, Ed asked Sally, "How ya doin', hon?"

"I'm okay."

He could read an expression of uncertainty underneath her smile.

"What do you think of the church?"

"It's different, being a small-town church, but I liked your service, and the lady at the organ is really good."

"That's Jenny Tyrone. I think she's been used to running the music program so I'll have to be careful not to step on her toes."

"Yes, you will." Sally seemed pensive a moment then went on, "I thought the woman who met us when we arrived—Sarah—was a little bossy. Hope we don't have to deal with her very much."

"Actually, we'll probably hear from her a lot. Jim told me she's head of the Women's Association."

Sally raised her eyebrows. "Other than that," she said, "I thought things seemed a little…well, artificial."

"Artificial?"

"I mean, it was like everybody put on a false face to make a first impression, and I wondered what they are all really like."

"Oh! I guess we'll find that out in due time."

"I like my Sunday school teacher," said Angie.

"I like that bell! It's loud!" said Billy.

The topic of conversation changed when they drove past a storefront with a peppermint-striped awning over the entrance.

"Oh, look," shouted Billy, "An ice cream store. Can we have some, Momma?"

"Let's turn around and go back, honey," said Sally. "I don't feel like fixing left-overs for lunch, and this would be fun. We need some fun after all we've been through in moving."

"What, ice cream for lunch?" said Ed with a mock expression of disdain.

"I'm sure they have more than that in there. Besides, what's wrong with ice cream for lunch, anyway?"

"Yeah!" shouted the kids.

"Okay, okay, you win." They made a U-turn and went back to experience their first taste of Dinkel Island outside the boundaries of the church.

Inside the shop they were surrounded by peppermint. The wallpaper was the same as the awning outside, and the proprietor wore a peppermint-striped apron. She was a slightly plump, middle-aged woman with fading reddish-brown hair in tight curls all over her head. She had rose-rimmed glasses perched atop the bridge of her nose.

"Welcome, Preacher," she said with an enthusiastic smile when they entered the store. "What a surprise to have y'all come to my store right after church."

Ed remembered the curly hair and rose-rimmed glasses among the blur of faces that he'd seen when greeting worshipers. "Well, you're one of our church members. I remember talking to you."

"I told you my name this mornin', but I'm sure it ain't took yet in yer brain. I'm Polly Allmond, and this here's my ice cream parlor. Glad y'all come by."

Polly would have nothing less than hugs for everybody, and then she went back behind her counter and said, "What will y'all have today?"

The children started to name the ice cream they wanted, but Sally said, "I see on your menu board that you have snack lunches. So, let's see—"

"Ain't got all that stuff on there right now. People don't come in here to eat lunch much now we got that McDonald's up the street. But I can do some real good hot dogs and chips."

Ed and Sally looked at each other. Sally said, "That's great, and then we'll have some ice cream afterward."

There were no other customers in the store, so Polly got a chair and asked if she could sit with them while they ate lunch. "This place used to be hoppin' on a summer weekend.

"You say that McDonald's up the street is new?"

"Yep! Opened up last summer. I can't even get teenagers to help out here no more—not that I need 'em now. I shoulda moved over onto Beach Drive when they gussied up those beach-front businesses couple years ago."

"Sounds like there are some growing pains here in Dinkel Island."

"Place is gettin' awful big, but worst part is the new stores comin' in from other places and puttin' the rest of us out of business."

"I'm sorry to hear that." Ed said.

"I guess the beach draws lots of people to town," said sally as she got more napkins to clean up some mustard Billy spilled on the table.

"Yep, in the summer, it's a whole different place rest of the year."

"I'm sure it is," said Sally as they finished their hot dogs and ordered their ice cream.

When they'd finished eating, Sally spoke for all of them. "We'll definitely be back for more of this!"

The Heygoods spent a busy afternoon unpacking and getting settled in the parsonage. That evening as twilight muted the sky and the tree frogs began to sing, Ed and Sally relaxed on the patio. A dog barked somewhere in the distance, and a car accelerated, but Ed noticed the absence of a constant traffic rumble in the background.

"It sure is quiet here compared to Richmond," he said.

"I could get used to this!" Sally closed her eyes and rocked in her chair. "This afternoon you asked about my impressions of the church. I forgot to mention one of my biggest impressions."

"Oh? What was that?"

"That huge stained glass window in the sanctuary. I liked the way you used it in your sermon."

She was referring to a prominent window with a plaque under it that read "Return of the Prodigal." It featured a father joyfully embracing his broken, penitent son who had obviously suffered a lot. In the shadows it showed an older son who was clean and well groomed, looking on with disdain.

In his message Ed had said, "God is our loving heavenly Father. Even when we've been openly hostile to him, God's is big enough to give us another chance. God always believes in us and calls us beyond our failings and sins. He calls us to new efforts and growth. Of course we always have the jealousy of the older son in the background, but God is larger than that, too."

Ed had closed his thoughts saying, "What are you letting God love you out of—or into—today." It had been a very effective message.

Sally's words and the evening atmosphere brought thoughts to Ed's mind. *That window reminds me of my relationship with my own dad. I really hurt him when I went to work for a competitor of his. We almost got over that, and I turned around and went into the ministry. Forgiveness has been hard for him.*

Ed closed his eyes and reminisced.

"You gettin' sleepy, hon?" asked Sally.

Ed opened his eyes. "Not really. I was just thinking about how much strife my dad and I had to overcome about my going into the ministry."

"He sure had his heart set on you taking over the store!"

"Yes, he did. I've always felt bad about crushing his dreams for me, but God had a bigger vision for my life. I believe he's beginning to understand that. God heals all wounds if we give him a chance."

They sat on the patio enjoying Dinkel Island's refreshing summer night a little longer and then went to bed.

Ed didn't know it yet, but there was a man in worship that morning whose personal story was also stirred by the stained glass window. He was Stan Grayson, a freelance artist from Norfolk who had been divorced for two years and had recently moved into a small cottage at Dinkel Island.

Stan had noticed the window's power on his first visit back in the fall. It tapped into his own grief over his fourteen-year-old son, Marty. Until the divorce he and Marty had been close. They had kept that closeness while Stan lived nearby in Ocean View. Dinkel Island was eighty miles away, which created an emotional chasm.

Stan traveled around to art shows, most of them in Northern Virginia and Maryland. Dinkel Island provided easier access to those places. It also cost less to live there. Plus, his home now provided an inspiring view of Tranquility Bay and that provided atmosphere for his nautical paintings.

As he had gazed at the window during Ed's message that morning Stan realized he had been running away from his father's sternness all his life. He really didn't believe the man could ever express enough positive emotion to reach out and hug anyone.

He wanted to believe in a God who could love him in spite of his failures and upheaval. Sometimes he just wanted to believe in God—period. Ed offered him hope, and he wanted to hear more. Stan's emotions were charged as he left the church and went home to pack for an art show trip. He went out a side door.

2

A Pastoral Challenge

*T*here are some people a new pastor gets to know quickly, and at Dinkel Island one of those was Clara Jasper. At age sixty-seven she had compiled a long history of pastoral care. Her many chronic conditions, taken individually or as a group, were severe enough to render her at least 85 percent disabled.

Ed came to know Clara in July. He found her house on Third Street, in a section of town known as Vacation Acres. The neighborhood consisted of small frame bungalows, an assortment of large shade trees, tall pines, dogwoods and an abundance of honeysuckle. Ed stepped into the fenced yard that featured more weeds than grass, then walked past overgrown shrubbery to the front door. He knocked loudly.

"Don't knock the door down! I'll be right there!" The voice behind the door sounded sharp and irritated. It seemed an eternity to Ed before the door finally creaked open then caught against a small chain inside.

"Who do you think you are, and what do you want?" barked a gruff voice whose owner was invisible inside the shadowy opening. "Make it quick! I ain't got all day. I ain't even s'posed to be up at all."

"Uh...are you Clara Jasper?" Ed stammered, shocked by the greeting.

"I am. So what do *you* want?"

"Well,"—Ed tried to smile and sound relaxed—"I didn't mean to startle you. I'm Edward Heygood, your new pastor, and—"

"Oh, thought you was some fool salesman."

Ed felt uneasy. "I understand you've not been well lately. I just came to get acquainted."

"Humph! Lot a good that does. That other one didn't do no good," retorted Clara, still keeping the door blocked by the chain.

"Look, maybe I've caught you at a bad time. Why don't I come back later, and I'll call first to see if it's a time that suits you."

"No need fer that!" Clara suddenly slammed the door then jerked it open and motioned him to come in. The house was stuffy and close and smelled of stale, cooked cabbage. She wheeled about and practically fell into a chair just inside the door. She was a large woman, clad in a blue bathrobe with floppy slippers on her feet. Her hair was tousled, and Ed could see she had been in bed. Her face was flushed, with small, wire-rimmed glasses, which she constantly pushed up, set on the bridge of her nose.

Ed left the door open, with only the storm door closed, just in case he wanted to leave quickly. Stepping past Clara he sat on the couch in front of the picture window where she pointed, saying "Sit over there!" Searching for something in the room around which to establish a basis for conversation, Ed took in his surroundings. Between the Victorian couch, the two wing-back chairs on either side of it, and the fireplace across from it framed by floor-to-ceiling book shelves, lay a dark-green carpet. On this carpet was a marble-topped coffee table with curved legs that held assorted magazines.

Ed noticed a mantle full of pictures, one of which must have been Clara and her husband in their early years. He was startled by the sound of a door slamming in the back of the house. The ensuing heavy footsteps produced a man of medium height wearing a mechanic's uniform.

"That's my husband, Phil," Clara said. "I called him to check by when you knocked because I seen you through the window and didn't know who you was. Can't be too careful, you know, especially someone who's sick, like me." As she spoke, Phil sank into a recliner beside the fireplace.

"This here's the new preacher," said Clara. Phil started to get up to shake hands but glancing at Clara, thought better of it and sank back into the chair. He produced an old pipe from his pocket, scraped out the bowl with a pocket knife, and then proceded to fill it with fresh tobacco. He struck a wooden match against the abrasive material of his overalls. Amidst a flurry of puffs he lit the pipe, producing an aromatic swirl of smoke that floated above his head. As though oblivious to all of that, Clara began to fill Ed in on all her woes. Phil never said a word. His facial expression didn't speak either but seemed to be a study in controlled emotion.

Clara left little doubt what was going on inside of her. She was an angry woman and very much afraid of just about everything and everyone. Ed would have liked to ask a few questions to get a glimpse of her inner self, but she never gave him a chance to speak. She raced through descriptions of her acute arthritis that made her joints swell and ache. She had medicine for this, but it didn't help.

The only thing that helped was lying down. And then there were the headaches, severe at times, that she'd begun to have when her boys were teenagers. Though that was years ago, she still had them nearly every week. She talked about her frequent intestinal distress and about the pain she sometimes got in her chest that the doctors (who weren't any good these days) said were just nerves—from stress.

"Stress, indeed!" she said. She hadn't anything to cause her stress, except those doctors. She made a few allusions to the church, and things she used to do there, but quickly assured Ed she was too sick to go anymore. Then she complained about the people who didn't visit her regularly—after all she'd done for them—especially the members of the Women's Association.

The monologue stretched on for nearly an hour. Several times Ed tried to inject a comment when Clara paused for breath, but she quickly recovered and charged in even more rapidly with a new thread of her tale. Phil went through two bowls of tobacco in his pipe. He didn't seem in a hurry to get back to work. Finally Ed was able to squeeze in a word, saying that he really did have to leave because he had promised to get something done at the church. It was a lie, but he felt worn down and desperate to escape. She'd had several complaints to lodge against Sam's ministry, so he figured she'd be getting started on him next. He offered a brief prayer and then shook hands with Phil as he went around Clara to the door.

"Well, you didn't say much," said Clara as he opened the storm door. "Tell me about your family and where you're from."

"Another time, Clara. I really have to go now. I'll be praying for you, and we'll visit again soon. Okay?"

One day in early August, Jim Swank invited Ed to go fishing with him. It was a hot Tuesday morning, already near ninety degrees when they started out at ten o'clock.

They set out from a place that had intrigued Ed ever since he arrived at Dinkel Island. The building was rustic, with a sign that read, in large faded letters, "Pappy's Place." There were faded circles on either side of the sign that had once held soft drink emblems. Another sign advertised bait for sale. Inside were several tables with chairs around them, and a counter with beer and soft drink taps behind it. A rack on the counter contained bags of assorted chips, crackers and nuts. Pappy's Place was a Dinkel Island icon.

Jim introduced Ed to Junior Hawkins, who owned the establishment, and bought some bait. They went out to the slip where Jim kept his boat and stowed their gear. Jim had Ed cast the lines off from the pier. They slowly backed away from the slip, and then started out toward the open water, keeping their wake down. Once they cleared the channel marker, Jim opened up the engine and the boat picked up speed, taking the swells with a rolling motion. Ed was thrilled by the beauty of Dinkel Island from the water. The sky was a cloudless blue backdrop against the green trees and white buildings. It looked almost like a postcard. When they reached a suitable location, Jim cut the motor and got the gear out. "We'll toss the lines in and drift here a few minutes and see if there's any activity."

Ed used the fishing trip as an opportunity to ask some questions about things in the town and church. He told about his visit with Clara Jasper and asked Jim what he knew about her.

"I was wondering if you'd run into her yet. She's really a tough old bird, hard to get along with. Patty and I sometimes wonder how Phil puts up with it."

"Well, I'm glad I'm not the only one who reads her that way. I've really been having trouble visiting her. I've been there twice, and both times she just seemed to ventilate so many feelings, yet she never lets me get a word in. I don't know how to deal with her. She's different from anyone I've ever met."

"I can understand that. I've never met anyone like her, either."

"I just wish I knew more about her past. She seems really hurt and angry, and I wonder why."

"Well, I do know this much. She and Phil were quite poor for many years. It seems he had trouble holding a job, and they had those young boys to raise. I think the struggle took its toll."

"That's probably part of it," said Ed.

"She used to be really active and involved at church during those years," Jim went on. "I've never heard what it was, but it seems something happened at church that made her mad, and she never came back."

"And you don't know what it was?"

"Nope! But I do know this— she *is* quite active at the town bingo games. Never misses a Thursday."

Ed was shocked. "You're kidding!"

Jim shook his head. "If she can go there she ought to be able to go to church. She complains all the time about people from the church not visiting her enough."

"I know. She said that to me. It sounds like she's crying out for something. I sure wish we knew what happened. I'll bet it would answer a whole lot of other questions."

3

A Load of Care

As October cooled the air at Dinkel Island, Ed found his pastoral load increasing. It all began with a phone call in the middle of the night. He fumbled groggily for the phone and turned on the light, which woke Sally.

"Hello?" he said, more as a question than a greeting.

"Pastor Heygood? This is Gwen Taggart."

Ed realized the voice belonged to the teenage daughter of one of his church families. "Yes, Gwen, what is it?"

"Daddy asked me to call and ask you to pray for Grandma."

"Sure I will. What's going on? Where is your dad?"

"He and Mama have gone to the hospital with Grandma."

"Do you know what's wrong?"

"I'm not sure, but I think she's really sick."

By now Sally had pieced together what was happening and who he was talking to. She asked to speak to Gwen. Ed handed her the phone and bowed his head momentarily in prayer. He felt an urgency to respond.

"I think this is really serious," he told Sally. "I'm going to go to the hospital." She nodded that she understood. He dressed quickly and then drove to Potomac City.

Arriving at nearly four in the morning, Ed found Maude's daughter, Karen, and her husband, Kenny, pacing nervously in the waiting room.

"They think she's had a stroke," said Karen amidst a spurt of tears. Ed sat down with her and Kenny. He could sense their tension as they awaited further word about her mother. Ed offered a prayer and as he finished the doctor came into the room. He told them Maude had, indeed, suffered a stroke. She was now in the intensive care unit.

The morning light was breaking over Dinkel Island as Ed walked in the back door of the parsonage. It was seven-thirty in the morning. Most people in town were stirring about by this time. Some would be cooking bacon and eggs, while others shaved and dressed for a busy workday. Some would be catching up on the morning news.

Ed felt out of sync with the world. He was tired and ready to crawl into bed. Yet he couldn't. He had appointments in the office beginning at nine-thirty. Sally was busy getting the kids off to school. Shaking off his fatigue, he showered, shaved, and fixed breakfast. Sally kissed him goodbye as she rushed out the door to catch her ride to the high school where she was substituting.

Ed sat at the table alone for a few moments. He felt overwhelmed by all that had happened so suddenly. When he finished eating, he cleared his dishes, started the dishwasher, and brushed his teeth. Then he paused to give thanks and ask God to heal Maude and comfort her family. Finally, he grabbed his briefcase and headed to work.

The next day Ed went back to the hospital where he found Karen in the ICU waiting room.

"Hi, Karen. How's your mother?"

Karen broke into tears for a moment. "I'm sorry. Its all been too much at one time. I'm not sure how Momma is. She looks terrible in that bed with all those tubes, and she cries a lot."

"Did she speak to you?"

"No, Dr. Burton says her speech is affected. So is her left arm and leg."

Ed listened while Karen spilled out some of her feelings. He offered encouragement and support, and prayed with her, then went in to speak to Maude. He took her right hand in his. "Maude, this is Pastor Heygood. I've come to visit with you for a moment." He felt her squeeze his hand. She moved her head slightly, opened her eyes a little, and attempted to speak. The sounds were weak and unintelligible. "If you can't talk right now, that's all right. I know it's hard to express what you want to say. Right now I want to pray with you, okay?"

Maude squeezed his hand again. He prayed that the Lord would be with her, comfort her, and lead her beyond the shadows of fear.

"Lord, in the midst of our deepest pain, we know you as our Shepherd. We know you will provide every resource we need, if we trust you. Heal Maude's mind, body and spirit. In the name of our Lord. Amen."

As he concluded the prayer, Ed felt some of the tension recede from Maude's hand. He promised to return soon. In the waiting room he spoke again with Karen. She was going to stay until the next visitation time. Ed prayed with her and then left the hospital.

At seven thirty-eight that evening the parsonage phone rang again. The Heygood's had just finished watching a television show. Sally had Angie in the bathtub while Ed played a game of Sorry with Billy. The caller was Jim Swank.

"Ed, I hate to bother you tonight. I know you've had your hands full with Maude's stroke and all, but I'm afraid I have another situation for you."

"Oh?" Ed felt himself tense up. "What's going on?"

"It's Mary Stone. She just died a little while ago."

Mary was a ninety-three-year-old widow who lived with her son, Norman, and his family. Ed knew he would have to call on the family. Mary had been taken to the funeral home, so he headed there. To all appearances the family was taking her death well, and they did not seem to be open to much pastoral care. Ed prayed with them and said he would visit again the next day.

Nobody could remember the last time Norman had been in church. He let everyone know he had resented his mother's church activities when he was young and that he could get along quite well without God or the church. If he could have found a way to have this funeral without a minister, he would have done so.

Ed understood the situation but hoped he could so handle the funeral that he might put at least a crack in Norman's oak door of resistance. This made doing the funeral more stressful than it would otherwise have been. Ed worked hard at trying to find out enough about Mary to make the occasion a meaningful tribute to her life. This, along with keeping up with Maude and her family, filled his week with stress. The last thing he wanted after the funeral on Thursday afternoon was a call about another crisis, but that's just what he got.

This time it was Rufus McCorkle, a seventy-five-year-old retired merchant in a nursing home in Potomac City. Not many people did well with nursing homes, but Rufus seemed to know how to make the best of it. So it was a real shock to Ed when Rufus had another heart attack and was at Nor'easter General.

Ed felt terrible telling Sally he had another emergency that would interfere with their family life, but he felt he had to go see Rufus. The nursing home assistant administrator had called, and she sounded like there was not much hope. Ed had begun to feel the effects of the stress these constant emergencies were having on Sally and his family. He understood when she blew off some steam.

"Is that what life at Dinkel Island is going to be like—you running someplace for someone all the time while we have to make do without you? If that's the case, maybe you'd better stay here and do this job by yourself. I don't think we can take it."

Sally's tone, if not her very words, brought distress to Ed's soul. Now he not only felt stressed from the workload, but angry and hurt by the effect on his family. He cursed as he hung up the phone but knew he had to take care of this need, too. His mind told him it wasn't always going to be like this, but his fears tried to overrule his mind. It was a good thing the drive to Potomac City took awhile, because he was able to cool off by the time he got there. He went straight to the hospital and looked in on Rufus, who was unconscious. He offered a prayer, which he wasn't sure Rufus heard. Then he stopped in to check on Maude, who was now in a private room and beginning to regain both her speech and her hope.

By the time he'd done all this, Ed was exhausted. It was getting dark, so he stopped at a fast food restaurant for some supper and then went home. Sally apologized for the way she had spoken to him on the phone. He had long since forgiven her, knowing how unfair it all sometimes was in the craziness of the ministry. They went to bed and made love deeply and passionately.

Rufus died in the night and the funeral was held on Saturday. Somehow Ed knew, as he finished at the cemetery, that one of his roughest weeks in the ministry was ending. There had been two deaths and a stroke and a lot of family and personal stress. His faith and stamina had been tested, but he had gotten through it. He wished there was a way to spread these things out, but that's the way it was—things came in bunches. All of this had come just as Ed and Sally had been feeling content and relaxed with the pace at Dinkel Island.

4

Not So Fast!

Ed's headlights seemed to grow dim as he drove along the foggy seashore road with heavy rain pounding against his windshield. His car threatened to hydroplane at any moment. He was late getting to the funeral, which for some reason was being held in his own home rather than the funeral parlor. That was bad enough, but he'd had to go to Potomac City on another emergency call, and he didn't want to be late getting back.

Complicating matters was the truck behind him. It seemed to be coming up much too fast for the conditions, its bright headlights glaring in his mirrors. Ed didn't want to go too fast and lose control, but it seemed the truck was running right up on his bumper. His whole body tensed as he pushed the accelerator harder.

Glancing back in his rearview mirror again, Ed suddenly panicked. The truck was coming at him faster, no matter how hard he tried to lengthen the distance between it and his car. He glanced to both sides. There was nothing but muddy banks, bushy trees, and puddles of water that seemed to be getting deeper. He was sweating. He'd never felt so out of control. Trying to accelerate even more, he instinctively hit the brakes.

There was another huge truck in front of him! He was rapidly coming up on it and realized there was nothing he could do. Then his right front wheel hit a puddle causing him to swerve out of control. He tried to correct by steering in the direction of the skid, but it only made things worse. His car skidded sideways. He was about to be crushed between the two trucks, neither of which seemed to do anything to avoid a crash. As he heard the noise of the truck bodies beginning to crunch in the sides of his car, he felt himself shaking, and pain shot throughout his body.

"Ed! Wake up, Honey! It's ten o'clock. You've been asleep here in the recliner. Don't you want to go on to bed?"

Ed opened his eyes to see Sally standing beside him, shaking his shoulder. Suddenly he remembered. It was Saturday night, and he'd meant to only catch a brief nap so he could get into his study and put the finishing touches on his sermon. As the nightmare faded from his mind, he realized how much pressure he'd been under. His whole body ached with fatigue. The funeral for Rufus in the morning along with the intensity of the other situations during the week had left him feeling restless and anxious. He hadn't been able to clear his mind enough to really work on the sermon.

"You've been sleeping," said Sally. "You seem exhausted. Don't you want to come to bed now?"

"Uh...sure. What time is it?" Suddenly Ed bolted into an awareness of his plight. "Gosh, it's late. I was too tired to work. That's why I came out here—to rest for a while. I didn't mean to fall asleep. I still don't know how to pull my thoughts together for tomorrow morning."

Sally massaged his shoulders. "Why don't you come to bed and get your sleep? Listen to your body. If you get up early, I'll bet the ideas will flow much better. God isn't going to let you go through a service without something to say tomorrow."

Ed rubbed his eyes, and felt the tension leaving his body. He believed in living by faith and trusting God to come through when he was pushed beyond his limits. Sally was challenging him to live by what he preached. "You know," he yawned, "I think you're right." He got up and went to bed.

At four thirty, he awoke with thoughts racing through his mind. He showered and dressed then went to his study where he paused to ask God's guidance. Alert and rested, he was soon deeply involved in a whole new direction. By the time he left for church, he felt better about his message and the service to come than he had any of the Sundays since he arrived at Dinkel Island.

Jim Swank greeted Ed as he arrived at church. "How ya doin', preacher?"

"I'm feeling great, Jim. How are you today?"

"Man, you've been through a tough week. I wasn't sure you'd be able to get things together today. Been praying for you. If there's anything I can do just say the word—except preach, of course!"

"Thanks, Jim. Everything's under control. Just keep the prayers going, okay?"

What had occurred to Ed in the early morning hours was that he was not isolated in his exhaustion from the week's events. His role in dealing with them had been unique by virtue of his position, but everyone in the church knew the various people involved. They had all felt the weight of sadness, sickness, and grief coming so close together. Ed had realized his function was not to carry the load for everyone but to simply find his strength in the Lord and point others toward that same source.

Ed wanted to portray his joy that the suffering and pain of disease and physical deterioration wasn't the last word—that God in his mercy wanted each person to find eternal fulfillment and satisfaction at his right hand and that finding it began with his Spirit as a resource in such times as this. That was the whole thrust of what had come to him at four thirty in the morning.

Ed rooted his message that morning in words from Psalm 23 and 2 Corinthians 4. "Grief is hard," Ed declared, "and all too frequent a visitor in our lives. Today we're all feeling grief over the deaths of Mary and Rufus, and Maude's stroke. We all probably feel uncertain, even a bit afraid, and those are natural feelings. We need to acknowledge them.

"God gives us a special promise in the image of a shepherd seeing his sheep safely through a deep ravine on the way toward higher ground and green pastures. '*Even though I walk through the darkest valley, I fear no evil; for you are with me; your rod and your staff—they comfort me.*'

That promise comes alive for us even more in Paul's words: '*We are afflicted in every way, but not crushed; perplexed, but not driven to despair; persecuted, but not forsaken; struck down, but not destroyed; always carrying in the body the death of Jesus, so that the life of Jesus may also be manifested in us.*'"

"We all go through that 'valley of the shadow of death' whenever we have to live for a while in the state of loss. It's not just the loss brought on by death, as real and personal as that is. We may go through other losses that are even more devastating, and we need the hope that God is with us in these difficult times. They are the turning points that can make us or break us for a lifetime."

"Such losses are devastating, they shake us to the roots of our being. They leave us feeling utterly alone and defeated. It's important to go through these feelings, hard as the journey may be, because they bring growth. We are always more—our lives involve more—than grief or loss, and that 'more' is where we need to come out, with God's help.

"By seeking God in the deepest part of ourselves, we are saved from being crushed, driven to despair, feeling forsaken, or destroyed. In other words, we have *HOPE* in capital letters, and that's enough to get us safely through anything. The key is in the inner walk of faith we cultivate when all is well, so we'll thrive and grow, with God's help, when times are tough."

The sermon was one of Ed's best efforts, and he knew he'd connected with many people. As the congregation filed past him at the door, Ed engaged each person in a tidbit of personal conversation. Many of the comments were deeper than usual.

"Thanks for talking to us so honestly about things that have happened this week," said an older man.

"Your words intrigued me, and I'd like to talk to you more about this sometime," said a young divorcee with two kids.

"I guess I never thought about what I felt as grief when I lost my job," said Fred Klingson as he shook Ed's hand. "I'm not sure I know how to find God's help, but I think I believe you when you say he wants more for me and wants to help me overcome the loss." The response at the door was somewhat overwhelming. Ed felt warmed and gratified by it.

As the last of the worshipers filed past, Jim Swank stepped up with an older man Ed hadn't seen before. The man wore a joyless expression. Dark eyes set under bushy eyebrows were complimented by long, thinning silver hair combed straight back across his head. His wiry build suggested he had once been strong and formidable. He wore a dark pin-striped suit with a starched white shirt and a dark red-and-black striped tie. He did not seem to have been moved in any positive way by the service.

"Ed, this is Harper Jauswell. He usually spends the summer with his sister up in Michigan. This year he's a little late coming back to Dinkel Island."

"I'm happy to meet you," said Ed, reaching out to shake hands. "I believe I saw your name on a list of our oldest members, and I've been wanting to get acquainted."

Jauswell returned the handshake but with a gruff, gravely reply. "Don't be so fast there, young man. You don't know whether you're going to be happy to meet me or not."

Ed was taken aback by the hostility in this stranger, but he recovered quickly. "That sounds like a challenge!" He laughed. "But I'm sure we'll be friends."

Harper scowled, turned abruptly, and stormed out the door without another word. Jim called after him, "See you next Sunday, Harper." He turned to Ed. "I wish I could say his 'bark is worse than his bite,' as the saying goes, but I'm afraid sometimes he can be really hard to get along with." Jim shuffled his feet awkwardly. "I'm sorry he didn't seem to be impressed with you, but he'll get over it." He slapped Ed on the back. "Anyway—don't let it bother you. Harper gets kind of vocal sometimes, but he really isn't here much anymore. He'll be going to Florida in January."

"Well, I'm not gonna lose any sleep over that guy. God loves him, so I'll try to do the same. Overall, I'm very impressed with the congregation and I look forward to the things we'll do together."

Jim seemed relieved. "I think you did a great job today. You certainly helped me with my grief, and I think most folks would say the same."

"Thanks," Ed replied. "I worked hard on this, and I appreciate your opinion. I hope I can do as well learning to deal with Mr. Jauswell."

Franklin Harper Jauswell III had deep roots in Dinkel Island. His father had helped with the original layout of the town and in later years had founded the Liberty Savings and Loan Company. Harper had gone to work at Liberty after college, rising to become its president and later its owner. He had served two terms as mayor of the town. Harper was a hard-driving man who seldom used more words than necessary to express a thought and who prided himself on being difficult to get along with.

In his few short months at Dinkel Island, Ed had noticed the Liberty S&L office across the street, but he hadn't gotten to know anyone there, so he didn't know it was owned by Harper. He had noticed the Jauswell house. The large, three-story, white frame Victorian home with dark-green trim, round turret with curved windows and a pointed roof, slate shingles, numerous gables, and a porch that wrapped around the building. It sat on a flat lawn with large oak shade trees and a boxwood hedge marking the distinctiveness of the property. There was no place else like it in the town.

"Fanny!" Harper shouted in the general direction of the kitchen as he stomped in from the garage. "Fanny, it's time to eat!"

Fanny had worked for the Jauswells for twenty years. She had felt especially close to Harper's late wife Annabelle, who had related to her as a caring person, not just as an employer. Annabelle had enabled Fanny to like herself and enjoy her work. When she died, Fanny stayed on out of loyalty to her and out of fear that if she left, Harper might see to it that she never got another job in Nor'easter County.

When Harper yelled at her, which was frequently, Fanny wished she hadn't stayed on, but she dutifully responded, making no ripples to incur his wrath. She knew his ways, and even before he yelled, at the sound of his car in the drive, she had gotten the meal ready to serve. As he hollered for her now, she appeared almost before the sound of his voice faded. "Humph!" he grunted. "It's about time."

Since his wife's death, Harper had developed the habit of spending a good bit of each year away from home. From June to September, when it was hot and humid in Dinkel Island, he went to his sister's in Michigan. She was widowed and needed someone to see to her affairs. He found the change of climate pleasant, and he even enjoyed the sense of family cohesiveness, though he would never admit it.

During January and February, when the winter at Dinkel Island was at its worst, he went to Orlando where he stayed with his other sister, Hattie, in a condominium he owned there. This schedule left him in Dinkel Island for the most active seasons of the church year—Lent, Easter, Thanksgiving, and Christmas. It also put him in town during the times when major administrative decisions, like budget planning, were made at the church. He was practically a lifelong member of the official board and the finance committee.

As he ate lunch, Harper thought about this new preacher. The man seemed a little too self-assured to suit him. Maybe it had been a mistake to stay longer in Michigan, though the extension had been brought on by his sister's ill health. It seemed this man had everyone looking up to him, and that could spell trouble. He might lead the church into some program or expenditure that was unwise. Between now and New Years, he would have to have a few serious talks with some of the more dependable leaders in the church.

Sally was quite complimentary toward Ed's service after lunch. When the children went into the family room and she and Ed were doing the dishes, she said playfully, "Now, don't let this go to your head, but that was a mighty good message, Preacher."

"Oh, 'preacher' is it! My, how formal we are. You sound just like Jim Swank."

"Well, I could sound like someone worse, you know."

"Yeah, I guess so. Jim's a good guy. And thanks for the compliment. Just about everybody had something to say as they left this morning. I mean more than the usual stuff, like 'I sure enjoyed your talk.' I don't know if waiting until this morning to pull it together made a difference or not, but I did seem to connect with people better today. It's a good feeling."

"By the way. Who was that man you and Jim were talking to after everyone else had gone. I don't think I've seen him before. He certainly didn't seem too friendly. Was he a visitor?"

"Oh, that was Harper Jauswell. He's one of the oldest members of the church. Seems to be away a lot. Just got back in town this week. You're right. He doesn't seem too pleasant. In fact, he seems to have a very negative disposition. I don't know. Maybe his underwear is too tight or something!"

They both laughed, and then Ed went on to tell her about Harper's conversation and his comment as he was leaving the church. "Seriously, it's almost like he was giving me a warning. Jim sort of shrugged it off, but I don't know."

"Maybe it's just travel fatigue. Maybe he's not as bad as he seems. So far everyone we've met has been delightful. Well, almost everyone."

"Maybe so," Ed replied. "But you know, that's one of the paradoxes of the ministry."

"What is?"

"That everything can seem to click together so well for so many people, then just when you feel good about yourself and your ministry, up pops a discordant voice to say, 'Hold on there, Preacher.' It's like even when you're on target, you're still off."

Sally stepped over to Ed, and they hugged. "Lighten up. Don't take things so seriously. You're the man I love. You're still first on my list."

He pulled her closer and felt the excitement as their bodies sent messages of love and comfort beneath their words. "And you're first with me, too. Keep pulling me down off that pedestal. I love you."

5

The Brunch Bunch

September and October were the months for budget and program planning and church leadership selection. All of that had the potential to be volatile within a congregation, especially since it all had to be completed and gain final approval by mid-November. Ed had hoped to step back and let the people lead during this time. He became anxious, however, when he realized he would be responsible for translating whatever they did into action come January. The fact was, he felt a need to control something he really couldn't control, and that gnawed at him on the inside.

Early in September some rough edges had begun to show up when Steve Tyrone, the finance chair of the church asked Ed to drop by his car dealership for a conference. Ed went over some of his concerns and asked Steve when he could call the finance committee together. Steve said, "Right now's a rough time for me, closing out the eighty-three models and stocking up on the new ones. Give me a couple of weeks, and maybe we can get together."

By mid-October Ed felt anxious as he realized the deadline was just a month away, and he still hadn't heard anything from Steve. Two weeks later, Steve's voice had surfaced again.

"By the way, Preacher," said Steve"I guess you've been wondering when we were going to get this budget together, so I know you'll be relieved to hear that we met Thursday night and did it—all except for your salary, that is. We wanted to go over that with you before we get it all typed up."

Ed was dumbfounded. He stood a moment and looked at Steve. He had never heard of a finance committee just meeting privately to do the church budget without the pastor present. He felt responsible for the administration of the church, including budget planning. Steve's actions left him feeling put down and rejected, though intuitively he knew better than to take this personally.

Steve gave him a handwritten draft of the new budget. He seemed to sense Ed's anxiety. "We don't want you to feel left out, so we wanted you to go over this before we type it up. Just bring it to me at my office later this week, and I'll have my secretary do the rest."

Studying the sheets, Ed saw that the figures included all the new amounts requested for denominational support. "We always take all the denominational askings," said Steve, pointing over Ed's shoulder. "And we decided a five percent increase for most things would put us in good shape. Of course, you'll have to get the pastoral relationship committee's recommendation for your salary. I tried to reach Don on the phone a couple of times this week, but he's been out of town."

Don Upton, Vice President of the Dinkel Island branch of Nor'easter National Bank & Trust Co., was chairman of the pastoral relationship committee. His committee had met with Ed in mid-September and agreed on a small salary increase of $100 per month for the next year. Ed didn't feel he could ask for much more in his first year and was pleased the committee offered a raise at all. "Well," said Ed, putting the papers on his desk, "it's good to have someone with your skills working on the budget. I'll get it back to you tomorrow."

The rest of October went by smoothly. Colorful foliage began to thin into a brownish-gray skeletal backdrop. The Heygoods became much more sensitized to the smallness of their two-mile-long island community. The crisp morning air became fragrant with cloud banks of wood smoke that soon blew off toward the mainland. Seagulls seemed to proliferate as the afternoon sun baked the sandy shores and reflected with startling clarity from the foamy whitecaps. The family quickly fell in love with the beauty and charm of fall at Dinkel Island.

November came and went with a refreshing calmness that made them glad they had escaped the traffic and tangle of Richmond's frenetic pace. Even the annual meeting at the church went off without a hitch. Ed's next encounter with discordant voices within the church community came just after Thanksgiving. It all began when Harper Jauswell decided to favor the Brunch Bunch with his presence on the first Sunday in December.

"Hey, look who's here! We've been wondering when you were going to drop by," said Jack Reilly as Harper came into the Seafood Pavilion. Jack ushered him to the backroom where the group always gathered. Most of the Brunch Bunch were there, and they jumped up to greet him.

"How's your sister doing?" someone asked. "She's much better now," said Harper. "What have y'all been doing with yourselves lately?"

Before anyone could answer, Jack came into the room. "The buffet's open, folks," he said. "We've got fresh oyster stew." Everyone was abuzz with small talk as they lined up and selected their food at the buffet table. Each of the round tables could seat six people. Harper sat down with some of the regular attendees. He turned to Polly and said, "What do you think of the new preacher?"

"He's no Sam Prentiss, but I like him a lot. And he has a darling family."

"That's true," said Myrtle McCloy.

"But does anybody really *know* him? I mean, I don't see him here, and I'll bet he never shows up."

"You know, that's true," said Grover. "I have wondered why he and the missus don't come by and eat with us sometimes."

"Now, Grover," said Myrtle, "maybe they don't know about this wonderful group. Has anybody invited them yet?"

They went on like that for a while, good-naturedly tossing around the virtues of the Heygoods. Hearing the conversation behind her, Barb inserted her own view. "We have to give them some time. After all, they're city folks and don't really understand yet about small town ways. But they're good people, and they'll learn. We need to give them our support."

"I'll go along with that," said Polly.

"Well, I don't know," said Harper, frowning and shaking his head. "The man seems a little too uppity for me. I think we gotta watch that he don't try to change our church too much. We've got a good thing going here. I just don't want no city preacher to mess it up."

"He's right about that," said Jack. "He does seem to have some different ideas. We just all need to try and show him the way. Maybe it would help if we did invite him and his family to eat with us one Sunday."

They all agreed and went on with their meal and other topics of conversation. But Harper still wasn't satisfied that they really understood the danger he saw in Ed Heygood's leadership in their church.

6

Downright Worrisome

*T*he joyful sounds of Advent and Christmas soon drowned out the voices of the Dinkel Island inner circle. Ed found himself enjoying the traditions of his new parish and remarked frequently that the people really had a Christmas spirit that was refreshing and inspiring.

Among their traditions was collecting food, clothing, and other items for a needy family. That sounded good to Ed, who didn't know the criteria for selecting the recipient family. By longstanding, although unspoken Dinkel Island tradition, this had to be someone whose moral qualities were above reproach—a family who could be shown to have made every effort to avoid eligibility.

It was further expected that the recipient family would turn the corner in their needy condition once Dinkel Island Wesleyan Brethren Church's generosity had been bestowed upon them. Such rigid qualifications made it extremely hard to find a target family. A couple of years, in fact, they had found no one on Dinkel Island worthy enough for their gifts and had sent them to the Salvation Army's collection booth up in Potomac City.

Such was not the case this year, however. Harper suggested they help Jimbo, his handyman, whom he said had been working hard and going through a rough time with his family. He brought this up the second Sunday in December when he again showed up at the Seafood Pavilion to eat and chat with the Brunch Bunch.

His idea hit receptive ears immediately. Jimbo and Barney Jinks had been Jake Dobbs' two helpers back when he was building boats out at Lighthouse Point. When Jake died, they both had trouble getting work. Eventually Barney got settled in with Horace Backelder's construction company and went on to experience new levels of contentment and satisfaction, not to mention financial security.

It had not been as easy for Jimbo whose skills were nearly invisible because he was black and people thought of him as simply a helper. The truth was Jake had seen his ability to grasp the finer points of boat-building early on and had taught him electrical wiring, as well as how to read blueprints. Jimbo had been a hidden asset for Jake who provided him with food, a small cottage on his land where his family multiplied around him, and enough spending money to meet a few simple needs. It was Jake's support of Jimbo that made him more visible in the larger community.

The white islanders adopted Jimbo and his family as their self-proclaimed model for successful race relations. "Y'all wouldn't have no trouble with them blacks over there at Stumpy Cove (or wherever it was they were addressing) if you'd just do like we do over at Dinkel Island. Blacks and whites get along just fine in our town." And of course, they did, because it was all a closed system. It was clearly understood that black outsiders weren't expected to settle within the limits of the town since it would upset their delicate racial balance.

When Horace hired Jimbo along with Barney it didn't take long until a stir began among his regular men. They came to him one night to see if they couldn't "work something out." The result was giving Jimbo less carpentry work and more menial tasks, like cleaning up and emptying trash. Jimbo soon discovered he could do those same things for a lot of people, so he spread his talents out and became the town handyman. That seemed to work out for everyone. Jimbo retained his level of acceptance and affectionate kidding from the white folks. They kept a dependable person for odd chores and maintained their reputation for racial balance and harmony within the community.

Harper Jauswell saw a crisis looming over Dinkel Island, namely that the "city preacher" might disrupt some delicate "balances." He decided to direct the church's Christmas benevolence toward Jimbo and his family. To help the issue along, he amplified some of Jimbo's actual needs and spun a story that sounded convincing to the good-hearted Wesleyan Brethren Brunch Bunch. When they adopted Jimbo and his family as their needy folks, Harper silently congratulated himself for his astute social engineering.

All of this was unknown to Ed Heygood. He didn't know the inner workings of the selection process. He didn't understand that one, and only one, family could be helped in any one season. In fact, he was so pleased with the apparent willingness of the congregation to reach to a black family that he wrongly assumed a purity of motive he could transfer to other needy situations, should they occur. And one did occur.

Ironically it involved Barney Jinks who had a little too much Christmas cheer over at Pappy's Place one night and got hold of one of Horace's bulldozers he'd loaned Pappy's Place for spreading oyster shells in the parking lot. Barney went on a rampage and managed to sink the dozer in Tranquility Bay, taking a piece of the pier with it. Horace might have been inclined to find some way to keep Barney on and work out some settlement on the damage, but a few influential voices in town demanded that Barney be fired. Horace conceded to the pressure.

Ed got involved when Barney came by the church office. His family was angry at him. They were running out of food and fuel. In the aftermath of his disastrous night on the town nobody would give him a job. Ed knew he needed counseling. The whole family needed help in understanding what was going on, but that was not the immediate need. The immediate need was food, fuel, and gifts, which translated into hope.

"You know, Barney, I think we can help you," said Ed after hearing the story. Barney had been honest with him. He had accepted responsibility for what had happened. He desperately wanted to make amends and go forward. An idea ran through Ed's mind that he might be able to help him find a job. Maybe he could put in a good word with Steve or someone. But first he *knew* he could give him some food and maybe some financial assistance. The rest could be tackled later.

"Come with me." Ed led Barney down the hall to the room where a huge cache of donated food and other items had been amassed for Jimbo's family. "We've been collecting this for a needy family, and I know we have much more than we need. I'm sure nobody would mind if we spread this out a bit to help you, too."

"Now, you better be sure, Preacher. I don't want to take nothin' if it's gonna git you in trouble. But if you can spare something, we sure would be obliged."

Ed questioned him a bit, found out his daughter had run off and left two children for him and his wife to raise, and how hard it was going to be if they didn't have Christmas gifts. "Here's a couple of boxes. You pick out what you think you can use, and I'll be back in a few minutes."

As he went down the hall to the office, Ed prayed. He felt settled in his spirit and made a decision. Opening his bottom desk drawer, he pulled out a small metal box with petty cash in it. Jack had just refilled it Sunday, and he counted through the bills. There was a hundred dollars there. It would be enough to get Barney some fuel for his house until something else could be done. He put the money in his pocket and walked back down the hall.

"Here." Ed handed Barney the folded bills. "This will help you with fuel and whatever else you need for a few days. I want to have a prayer with you, and then you go on home. We'll see about some of your other needs in a day or two."

"I really want to thank you," said Barney as Ed helped him carry one of the boxes out after the prayer. "Me and the missus gonna be in church Sunday, too. You can believe it."

When Ed told Sally what had happened, she was *not* sympathetic, which threw him, since she was generally a very sensitive, caring person. "It's not that I don't think you should have helped him, honey, but shouldn't you have cleared it with someone first? I mean, what if someone objects? Look, this man already has a whole town angry at him."

"Yeah, but that's all the more reason the church should help. I mean, it almost seems sinful to lavish as much stuff as they've collected on one family. I just believe when they find out the whole picture, they'll be glad we had another place to express our generosity this season. After all, that's what Christmas is really all about, isn't it? This is the birth of Jesus Christ, the Savior. If we weren't open to what that means we'd never have collected all this stuff in the first place. Nope! I don't think we'll have any trouble over this."

The next day, when he told Jack he needed to have the petty cash fund replaced and why, he was proven right. Jack didn't seem a bit upset. He wrote him a check on the spot. Then Ed called Steve and asked him if he needed anyone in his shop just now and told him about Barney. Steve had already heard about the incident but agreed he could use some extra help if Barney could handle mechanical work. He said he'd give him a try.

When the angelic voices of the children's choir sounded out the joyous news that Christ was born during the Christmas Eve service, Ed felt deeply moved. He was happy to be serving a church with such a warm and generous heart. He couldn't be in a better place. What he couldn't hear a couple of days later were the not-so-angelic voices when Harper got news of what had happened from Jack. They were in Jack's office, and the customers outside in the dining room felt the walls shake when Harper thundered, "*The hell you say!*"

"Quiet, Harper! I've got customers out there. Keep your voice down!"

"Yeah, yeah," Harper responded, getting a grip on himself. "This is just what I was afraid of. This man's goin' to ruin us. We have to get rid of him—get us another preacher, somebody who understands country folk."

"That's a little extreme," said Jack, "don't you think? I mean, he just didn't know. He meant well."

"Now, don't you go getting soft on me."

"You know me better than that. Here's what I'm gonna do. I'll talk to Jim and get him to kinda let Ed in on some of the facts of Dinkel Island life in a friendly but firm sort of way. Jim can handle that. We just have to educate this man."

Harper went along with it, but not because he liked the idea. He was ready to stomp on Ed Heygood and get rid of this city preacher and save Dinkel Island Wesleyan Brethren Church from liberalism and apostasy. It was, in his mind, a holy cause, and he set out to do his part in it.

The New Year arrived with little local fanfare. The very next day Harper Jauswell was on the train out of Richmond headed for his condo in Orlando. December had already been winter enough for him. He couldn't get away soon enough. He said his good-byes to Jack and Barb Reilly, who had driven him to the Amtrak station, boarded the train, and settled into a coach seat. The car seemed to be filling up fast, and he hoped nobody would take the seat next to him. He put one of his suitcases there just in case then slouched down into his seat and closed his eyes. The trick seemed to work. Soon the train was rolling south, and he had his seat to himself.

Pulling up on the release button under the armrest, Harper eased his seat back into a more reclined position and shut his eyes again. His mind wandered back over the events of recent weeks at Dinkel Island. If it hadn't been for the onset of cold weather, not to mention the money he had tied up in the condo, he would never have left at such a crucial time. This new preacher really bothered him. He was a little too independent, and too many people seemed to get hooked by his apparent faith and enthusiasm.

It was true—he *had* really been there for Maude Taggart and her family, but then that was his *job*—that's what he was *supposed* to do. The real issue had surfaced when he took it upon himself to give money and things they'd collected for Jimbo to that no-account Barney Jinks. As far as Harper was concerned, that was blatant, raw misuse of pastoral power. It would be nearly Easter before he got back, and he hoped Jack and the others would be more alert to what was going on and keep the lid on Heygood. He trusted them about half-way, which was good for him. That's about as far as he trusted anyone. In fact, he only trusted himself about 90 percent. That's how he had done so well in business— by not letting himself get soft with people. He knew it wasn't going to be an easy winter. In fact, it was going to be down-right worrisome.

7

Lillie Plume

Unknown to Harper, another Dinkel Islander was headed for Florida that same week. Stan Grayson had learned early that you go where the sun is to find the money in the winter. This was his second year of traveling to Florida for the January and February round of art shows and expos. Last year it had saved his business. He hoped it would do the same this year. He had sent notes announcing his itinerary to customers and others who had signed his book the year before, so he hoped for some repeat business.

Stan left Dinkel Island early Monday morning. The day before, which was New Year's Day, he had gone to church. He had begun doing that more often since the new pastor arrived. Pastor Heygood seemed to be someone who might be able to understand the deep sense of isolation and loneliness that Stan felt deep inside. It wasn't that he didn't know a lot about what was going on inside him—he did. He had been trained in social work and had been a counselor with troubled boys before his foray into art. But somehow when it was your own stuff that needed to be aired, self-help wasn't enough. That was one of the problems with living in a place like Dinkel Island. There was nobody there who seemed to function above a very shallow surface level.

Last September during one of his shows in Northern Virginia, Stan had been placed next to a flamboyant female artist named Lillie Plume. It was obvious just looking at her work that she had some natural talent, but was short on training and technical growth. She freely admitted that she used a lot of shortcuts in producing her work. She readily told her customers she didn't waste time on such things as a final varnish. She just applied acrylic paint (which she said is just plastic after all—so how much protection does it need?), snapped the canvas into a ready-made frame, put a title and a price on it, and her painting was ready to sell. Lillie even admitted to her customers that she was more interested in making money than being artistically creative. Her personality was bubbly, flirtatious, and winsome. That plus the fact that she underpriced everybody else, overcame the technical deficits of her work. As she herself said, she made money at art and did it by sales volume and hype.

Ordinarily Stan would have paid very little attention to someone like Lillie. Everything about him and his work seemed contrary to her. He was more of an introvert, so he didn't bounce around pulling people into his display like a spider with a web. He spent meticulous, sometimes even painful time with his paintings. He studied and researched his subjects and tried to portray an authenticity both of feeling and physical representation in his work.

While Stan did occasionally work in other mediums, like Lillie, he was mainly an acrylic artist because the paint dried so much more quickly than oil, and watercolor was so much more delicate and unforgiving. He carried an easel and paints with him and often worked during the shows, but he suspected that cost him sales since he tended to get so engrossed in what he was doing that he appeared snobbish or disinterested. He wished he could change and become more aware and flexible.

Interestingly, it was this very difference between them that seemed to bring Stan and Lillie together during the days of that particular show. One afternoon a young boy came by and started watching as Stan worked on a painting of a harbor scene.

"Is it okay if I sit here and watch?" the boy asked, flopping cross-legged onto the floor beside the easel. "I've been trying to learn how to paint, and I like boats. I like the way you're making yours. Can you show me how to do it?"

Mental images of his own son flashed through Stan's mind. How he had hoped he could have shared moments like this with Marty, but his son was absolutely unresponsive to his efforts. In fact, since the divorce, Marty seemed to be so aligned with his mother that he and Stan could hardly relate at all.

"Sure you can," Stan heard himself saying. "What's your name?"

"Tommy."

"How old are you, Tommy?"

"Eleven—well, almost twelve. My birthday is in May."

"How long have you been painting, Tommy?"

"A couple of years. Hey, is that oil paint you're using?"

"No, it's acrylic. Do you know what that is?"

"Sure. You mix it with water. I've tried it, but I can't make it work. It all gets hard and dry before I can mix the colors."

"Ah, a common problem. You should have seen the first one I did. I had to throw it away. Here, watch how I'm doing this." Stan proceeded to demonstrate his method of mixing colors on a disposable pad, and keeping them moist while he worked with the canvas. "Do you think you could do that?"

"I could try," said Tommy, "but I think I'd need one of those pads like you're using, wouldn't I?"

"Well, sure. Listen, I have another one over here that's only half used." Stan handed him the pad and said, "Why don't you take this with you and give it a try."

"You mean it? You're gonna give me this?"

"Sure, why not. You know…one artist to another. Okay?"

"You bet!"

That was the beginning of an unusual relationship between artist and boy that existed only for that one brief show but had a profound impact on Stan's soul where he ached so much for his losses. It also opened the way for another kind of sharing Stan hadn't experienced in a long time, something that touched another part of his inner self. Lillie noticed and admired the relationship that developed between artist and boy. Not only did she not work during her shows, she also lacked the patience to teach anyone, least of all a child. Putting her competitiveness aside momentarily, she went over to tell Stan she thought he was doing something really great with Tommy.

"Do you do things like that very often with kids?" she asked after introducing herself.

"Not really," Stan replied. "In fact, this is the first time. He seems to be a cool kid, and he's really interested. He's going to bring me some of his work tomorrow."

"That's cool. I wish I could do that. I guess I'm not a real artist. I mean, I don't really have any training. I just taught myself."

"Hey, that's all right. I'm self-taught, too. Talent's more important than all the pedigrees in the world."

"Do you really think so?"

"Sure. Take your use of color, for instance. You can learn theories about color from books and classes, and you can learn about contrast and how to mix colors. But your colors are vibrant and exciting, and they sell your work. That's something from within you—the way you feel your world—that you share through painting and nobody can teach you that. You have to have it inside."

"Yeah! Yeah, I like that," said Lillie. "That's the way I think of it. Maybe not in such good words, but that's it. Hey, I like you, Stan Grayson."

Stan laughed and felt a little embarrassed. "I like you, too. I'm glad you came over and got acquainted. I guess I should've done that myself."

"Oh, I'm used to other artists not talking to me." She winked. "I scare the starch out of 'em! I think they're jealous because I make so much money. I guess knowing how to do that is my natural talent. I really would like to learn more about painting, though. It just seems like I never get the time."

From that beginning the conversation between them grew. By Friday Stan and Lillie were talking to each other freely. Friday evening they did something different. Instead of one watching both displays while the other went to eat, and vice-versa, they both put up Be Back Soon signs and went to supper together. Stan hadn't been with a woman in a long time. He'd looked a lot and felt a lot of deep inward longing, but he'd been hurt so badly in his marriage and divorce that the pain had been too great for him to feel free. Somehow Lillie was different. Her effervescent personality teased him, and something in her eyes and voice caressed his spirit and he felt a tingly sensation with her. She was five years younger than him, but that didn't seem to matter. At supper they decided to go to a movie together when closing time came around. That's when things just sort of got out of control.

The movie was a comedy, and they caught the late show, so it was after midnight when they came out. Like school kids, they had begun to hold hands in the theater. As they walked into the parking lot, there was a chill in the air. Stan put his arm around Lillie's waist, and he felt her body respond. When they got to her car and he opened the door for her and then, suddenly, very naturally, their lips met. The kiss was warm and tender and sent thrills charging through both of their bodies. The chemistry between them ignited, and they kissed again. Stan felt lightheaded and looked longingly after her as she drove away. Then he turned and walked to his own travel trailer. He went to sleep wanting Lillie's closeness to linger.

All day Saturday there was an electric kind of warmth between them. They wondered if others noticed it and kind of hoped they didn't, yet really didn't care if they did. Lillie lived in an apartment in Alexandria. She had married while still a teenager, but it had been a stormy, unsettled union. One day she simply packed her things and moved out. For a couple of years she continued her office job but began to notice how happy and carefree some of the artists and crafts people she saw at the mall shows seemed to be. Talking to them she picked up pointers and some encouragement to try painting herself. With her talent, a real flair for color, and a good head for business and salesmanship, she quickly found her way into a whole new way of life. She had soon been able to leave her office job and do her painting full time.

On Saturday night Lillie invited Stan to her apartment. The chemistry exploded. He spent that night and the next two nights with her before he returned to Dinkel Island. The experience had been traumatic. He knew he didn't love her in a sense of deep commitment, yet he was very much attracted to her. They had shared their nights out of deeply repressed sexual needs. Since that weekend they had been together a few times and had shared increasing phone calls. When Stan told her about the show circuit in Florida, Lillie was interested. Just before he left on the trip, she called to say she had contacted some promoters and she would be there, too, part of the time.

Stan was both thrilled and troubled. He really didn't know much about her and felt a kind of shame inside because their relationship had become sexual so quickly. Yet the more he tasted of it, the more he felt he was falling in love and wanted to be with her. Something was happening that could change his whole life, and he was afraid. It was like being caught between two powerful forces, each tearing at him emotionally. He wasn't sure he could hold himself together. He knew that he and Lillie would be together in Florida, and he longed for it, yet fought it at the same time.

It was this inner struggle he wanted and needed to share with someone. He knew he should see a counselor, but his schedule kept him moving so much he put it off. That's why he wondered if Ed Heygood, who seemed emotionally connected to the human spirit, might be able to at least hear him out and help him clarify things. He wanted to trust Ed and reach out to him, yet somehow he hadn't quite crossed the line and spoken to him.

8

Clara's Letter

*B*ack in Dinkel Island, winter, with its vacant starkness along the beachfront, brought more adjustments for the Heygoods. Compared to summer's bustling energy, walking along Pleasant Beach on a blustery winter day with a brisk, cold northeast wind coming in off the water, chilled them to the bone in spite of their heavy coats. Even the sand was cold and lifeless. The leafless trees in the municipal park. The town hall with its clock tower seemed to shiver in the aura of the sky's grayness. Billy said it seemed to him it must be like living on the moon. They all agreed and felt drawn to the warmth of home with a new passion.

Snow came the second week in January, and it hit hard. Thick clouds began to build in solidly over the bayside community on Tuesday. By daybreak on Wednesday, a sheet of ice was glistening on the landscape. The precipitation soon turned to snow, accumulating five inches before tapering off in the afternoon and then changing back to freezing rain that left a glaze across the landscape. Everything in town came to a stop, including church activities.

The wintry slowdown gave Ed a chance to turn his attention to some old boxes of files and papers he had found in the back of the closet in his office. The contents were mostly old annual meeting reports, miscellaneous correspondence, budget sheets, and lists of church officers over the years. Since the statistics that mattered from past years were recorded in the association files, he started to throw these things out. A musty envelope fell out of the box. His curiosity piqued, he looked inside and was shocked at what he found.

The envelope contained two letters—one from Clara Jasper to Reverend Elwood Richards, who had served the church from 1953-58, and the other was his reply. Skimming quickly over them he discovered there had once been a house behind the church which had apparently been the parsonage. Ed figured the congregation must have rented the house to Phil and Clara when the new parsonage was built. Since there was no house there now he assumed it had been removed when they built the current education building. His mind clicked back to his first visit with Clara where she had been so rude and harsh toward him and his thinking that there had to have been something behind her behavior that was related to the church. Here was evidence that his suspicion had been right.

September 23, 1954

Dear Reverend Richards,

I hardly know what to say first in this letter except that I was shocked last night when someone told me you had the audacity to double our rent to pay for those pamphlets you hand out in church.

You had absolutely no right to do that because the old parsonage doesn't concern you in the least. The ones who send preachers here decide a house isn't fit for a preacher to live in, so that relinquishes any right whatsoever you might have had. If the house isn't fit for a preacher to live in, certainly it isn't fit to double our rent to satisfy a whim of yours. The idea of those pamphlets is yours. You receive wages and I think you should pay for them out of your own pocket if they're so important.

Ed paused in his reading. Obviously the letter was written out of a high degree of anxiety and stress. Apparently someone had told Clara the church was going to raise her rent to pay for worship bulletins. So in her mind the pastor was behind it. *Was he?* Ed wondered as he read on:

> My husband works hard for his small wages. We have lots of doctor bills for me from when I was in the hospital with surgery last year. My children need dental care again, some of them need another polio shot, and we just had to go through preschool shots earlier this month. We try to pay our bills and send four children to school, one just starting in for the first time this year. My husband's wages don't go up, but our expenses do.
>
> We don't even have any money to spend between checks. Reverend how would you like to raise and provide for a family of six on half your salary?
>
> I don't want your sympathy. I'm just letting you know our circumstances. We're going to pay $5.00 a month for our rent just like always. You can pay for your own expenses for the pamphlets. You can afford it. We can't.

There was more to the letter, explaining how Clara had managed to make do in the dilapidated house, but Ed stopped reading there. He leaned back in his chair and closed his eyes, feeling the weight of her pain. He wondered, *How long had she been going through this struggle?* Unpleasant encounters with Clara flicked through his mind as the thought occurred to him, *Is her constant ill health and antagonism toward the church one of the results?* In a way he was sorry he had found the letters, yet in another way he hoped they would help him understand and relate better to Clara.

His curiosity turned now to the pastor's reply in a letter dated five days later:

September 28, 1954

Dear Mrs. Jasper,

In answering your letter, I must first of all assure you that I did not ask that your rent be raised and that there has evidently been some misunderstanding. I don't know who you talked to, but apparently they failed to listen closely to what went on at the board meeting last month.

The bulletins you mentioned were one small part of a request I made to be included in next year's budget under the heading of office supplies. I suppose the confusion came from the discussion about our income from the church and rent of the old parsonage. To my knowledge, however, no one ever tied the increased office expenses to your rent. Instead, it was decided to challenge the congregation to meet a slightly higher budget next year.

I am very much aware that your family does not have a high income. I am quite sympathetic to you in that regard and would never go behind your back and try to harm you in any way. If anything, I wish we in the church could help you with spiritual strength to face the trials I know must come your way.

Please accept my apology for this misunderstanding. I would suggest you show this letter to whoever came to you with this story so you can set the record straight. Also, I am not aware that Mr. Harper Jauswell is in any way involved in trying to raise your rent. The motion he seconded in the meeting had only to do with authorizing the office expense fund in the budget. I hope this misunderstanding can soon be straightened out.

Yours in Christ,

Elwood Richards

Pastor

Ed started as he noticed Harper's name. He hadn't seen that in Clara's letter. He grabbed her letter and searched—no, it wasn't there. *Now where did Elwood get that reference?* Ed wondered. As he put Clara's letter down, he dropped the second page. There on the back was a postscript he hadn't seen:

> P.S. I know the official board didn't pass this. You had the idea, and Harper Jauswell seconded it. You should both be ashamed of yourselves. I would be if I did something like that.

Wow! No wonder Richards was so careful to explain what the issue was about and Harper's role in it.

"Harper Jauswell!" Somehow this man seemed to crop up in the background of things at the church, yet he kept a low profile. Ed saw him at church Sunday mornings, but that was it. He must have been much more active in the days before his retirement. Two things seemed to stand out as immediate needs. First, it would be a good idea to talk to Jim Swank about all of this and see what else he could learn. Second, he needed to visit Clara Jasper again and listen with more sensitive ears for the hurts she must still harbor—and with an ear toward helping her heal those wounds.

That evening Ed told Sally about the letters. She didn't seem as concerned as he felt about it. "Why do you feel you have to do something about this? It's something out of the past that was probably settled long ago."

"Well, I just wonder if there's some current anger or distrust rooted here that might explain some of Clara's attitudes and maybe even her physical symptoms now. I don't feel I have to react and *do* something, but I also don't feel I can ignore it. I guess I just wanted to hear myself talk about it with you so I could get some perspective on it."

"I can understand that. I'm glad you did. Do you feel better about it now?"

"Yeah, except that rascal Harper Jauswell seems to be in it somewhere, and he never makes me feel settled. But I need to let go of that, too. After all, he's in Florida and really doesn't seem to be around much when he's here. It seems he was a lot more involved in the past."

"I think you're giving him too much power over you."

"Maybe so. I think this is something I just need to file away in my 'that was interesting,' mental file drawer."

That didn't prove to be so easy, however, when he talked with Jim Swank the next week. He had put it out of his mind, yet somehow it just sort of surfaced in the midst of their conversation.

"Did I tell you I found some old papers in a box in the office closet? Just a bunch of old records and stuff, but it seems there used to be an old parsonage right behind the church. Was that torn down when the education wing was built?"

"Gosh,"—Jim chuckled—"I haven't thought about that in years. There was lots of dissention about that house for some time. Tearing it down to make room for the education wing was one of the best decisions we ever made."

"There were a couple of letters among those papers," said Ed. "One was from Clara Jasper, who lived in that house once. Apparently there was some misunderstanding about something in the budget. She thought the church was going to raise her rent, back when she and Phil were going through tough times. It seems she thought the minister at the time and Harper Jauswell had conspired against her."

"Oh yeah, I remember the stories about that. And you know, as I recall, it turned out Harper really was at the center of the whole thing."

"You're kidding!"

"No! I think what happened was Harper didn't like the pastor..."

"Elwood Richards."

"Yeah, I think so. Anyway, it seems Harper thought he was, as he put it, 'getting out of hand.' Whatever that meant. So he fastened on a budget item and called Clara and told her the pastor was going to raise her rent to cover the budget increase. She apparently believed him but also didn't trust him, so she put it out that the pastor and Harper were in it together. It caused quite a stir."

"I guess it would have!"

"But the good part was it made us see how bad the house really was. We did a little looking around and realized it wasn't fit to live in. The problems with that building were way past fixing! As soon as Clara and Phil moved into a house of their own, that incident made it easy to sell the idea of tearing down the old house to make room for the new building. I guess that whole issue reveals one of the darker undercurrents of Dinkel Island Church that we'd really rather not think about. In the long run, I think we grew through the whole thing."

"I can understand that, but I can't help but wonder if Clara and Phil might not have grown through it. You know, there's a lot of bitterness in that woman, and it may be what keeps her from ever being really well. It might explain why she can get out to bingo during the summer but shies away from church. The more I think about it, the more I believe some healing is needed there. And some prayer."

"I'll be honest with you, Ed, I don't know much about all that. I guess that's your department."

That statement seemed shallow and disappointed Ed. As a school principal, he thought Jim would have had more sensitivity and savvy about the deep currents that go on under the surface of people's lives. He thought about this as he walked back to the church. Maybe that inherent insensitivity was something he would have to deal with in more dimensions than one during his time at Dinkel Island.

9

Twists and Turns

*S*tan Grayson entered Florida heading for a mall show in Tampa. He felt refreshed driving through green surroundings after a couple of months of wintry, brownish-gray landscape in Virginia. It wasn't just the warmer climate that had Stan excited; it was also the prospect of being with Lillie again. They planned to link up in two weeks at the Broward Mall show.

They had been together a few times for brief dates since that weekend when they met, and each time they felt closer and more intimate. They had begun sharing stories about shows they'd been in and people they knew in common, which led to sharing their itineraries and the discovery that they could rearrange their commitments so they could link up in January. As the time had drawn closer, Stan had grown more impatient to be with her.

The Tampa show went well and as soon as possible afterward he struck out for Fort Lauderdale and his link-up with Lillie.

Stan felt young, energetic, even a bit nervous—almost adolescent. It was six o'clock Sunday evening when he drove into the parking lot and over to where some of the artists were already forming their rigs into a little community. For this and the next few shows, he and Lillie would be traveling and working with a touring association run by some promoters.

Even though he was very much a loner, Stan did hook up with this group occasionally. He got his assignment and pulled his rig around. The association had rules for neatness, a system for security, and procedures for handling trash and other matters. Artist's rigs had to be completely self-contained. The quality of work and of exhibit and conduct were all factors covered by the rules so that artists working with them generally made money and enjoyed being together.

Finally, as dusk cast a reddish glow over the sprawling mall structure, Stan walked toward the main entrance and saw Lillie standing there, waiting for him. *Gosh, she's beautiful*, he thought. She'd let her auburn hair grow longer and as a gentle breeze caught it, the strands billowed back across and behind her right shoulder. She was slender and just an inch and a half shorter than his own six feet. Even in an old, light-blue t-shirt and denim shorts, she looked gorgeous. He became excited just looking at her and wondered how far their relationship would go. About that time she turned, seeming to sense his approach. Their eyes met. Spontaneously they moved together across the remaining twenty yards until they were locked in an embrace. As they kissed Stan wondered why they had waited so long to see each other.

"It's so good to see you," he said, stroking her cheek and brushing her hair back along the side of her head. "I've been itchy, just waiting for this moment."

"Me, too," she said, kissing him again and then stepping back in her characteristic, teasing way. "Darn it, Stan Grayson, I told myself all the way down here that I wasn't going to fall in love with you, but you know what? I think it's useless!"

He kissed her again. "Yeah, I know what you mean. I feel the same way." They slipped their arms around each other's waists and walked together almost as if they were one person, back to the encampment and Stan's RV. There they ate supper and shared a rapid flow of conversation about all the things they'd each been doing since they were together.

"Hey, Lil, it's getting late. Where are your things? We need to get you settled in before the mall closes and its set-up time." They got her minivan, unloaded her clothes and personal things, then drove his truck and her van up to the unloading area, and went into the mall for the set-up meeting. Stan was a little shy in introducing Lillie to everyone because he'd never been with anyone around this group. Everybody in the gypsy-like setting seemed really excited to meet her, and they both felt quickly accepted as a couple. When assignments were made, the show director picked up on the situation and changed Stan's site so he and Lillie could be next to each other. Then they unloaded their things, set up their displays, and at nearly midnight, walked back to the trailer.

Stan and Lillie spent the rest of January and most of February living, working, and traveling together in Florida. It was exhilarating. They found time to go to the beach, to visit Sea World and Disney World, and to share some long walks and long talks. They found a lot of common ground in their experiences, feelings, and goals. At the same time, they were different enough that there was a sense of contributing something to one another that each felt had been missing, yet that made each feel more complete.

They grew closer than they had dared imagine. Finally just before leaving to return home Stan took her to a small seafood restaurant he had found nearby. He had on a white polo shirt, chinos, and a navy blazer he rarely wore but kept for unexpected occasions. They asked for a table with privacy, which wasn't hard to find since it was past the normal supper hour. The waiter brought them a bottle of Chardonnay and some assorted breads.

They ordered salads, and the restaurant's signature grilled sword-fish dinner with garlic mashed potatoes and a vegetable medley. The candle on their table glowed in the dimly-lighted atmosphere. Lillie had a radiant glow about. They sipped their wine and nibbled at their salads, talking in hushed tones. She had on a bright flowered dress with a deep V neckline, and wore a necklace of colorful polished stones on a silver chain with earrings to match. Stan couldn't take his eyes off of her.

When the waiter brought the entrée, they backed off a bit and busied themselves eating and just reveling in the moment. During their last show, Stan had slipped away from his booth to take a break and made a visit to a jeweler whose work he admired. He found a ring he liked and bought it. This wasn't a traditional gold band with a diamond set but a silver band with a colorful fused glass structure that included a small diamond in the center. After they finished their entrée the waiter brought the check. Stan gave him enough cash to cover the bill and a tip, and he disappeared. That's when Stan moved closer across the table toward Lillie.

"Lil," he said, taking her hands in his, "this is a really special night. I love you so much. You've opened a whole new part of myself to me, and I've found in you something I never even knew could exist between two people—a deep entwining of our souls. I…I don't want to go on like this—just seeing you once in a while or on a road trip. I want to share life with you from now on with intimacy and commitment."

Her eyes glowed with deep warmth as he opened the small box containing the ring and placed in on her finger. "Honey, I want you to marry me. Will you?"

She looked almost startled by the suddenness of his proposal, but then reached over and softly touched the ring and looked back into his eyes. Stan said, "I know it's not a traditional kind of engagement ring, but neither you nor I are traditional type people. I wanted to get you something truly special that would express my appreciation for your uniqueness."

Lillie grasped his hands in hers warmly and leaned toward him, kissing him deeply, and then pulled back. She seemed to cry and laugh at the same time. "Oh, darling, you know…I…I… Listen to me. I'm stuttering. I said I'd never let a man get so close to me again, but…oh, darn it, of course I will! I love you, and I need you, too. I haven't felt this, well, complete—I guess you could say—ever in my life."

They got up from the table and melted into each other's arms. After a long embrace and another deep kiss, they stepped back, suddenly aware of where they were and that the few people in the restaurant had begun to applaud. Their faces flushed, and then they laughed and took each other's hands as they dashed for the door. Outside Stan said, "I don't know what I would have done if you hadn't said yes. I don't think I could leave here and go back to being a lonely bachelor again. I need you—we need each other."

"I'll let you in on a secret. If you hadn't asked me, I think I would have asked you." With that, they went back to the RV to revel in the intimacy of having just become an engaged couple.

Back in Dinkel Island, the snow melted, and the weather seemed to gradually mellow. When they first moved there, Ed wondered what winter would be like in such a summer-oriented place and how they would get through it. Now he knew that the summer-oriented idea was just that—an idea—not something based on fact. Dinkel Island really was a four-season place. Summer did bring a resort-like atmosphere along Beach Drive, at the Grande Hotel with its golf course, at the campground and the Yacht and Supper Club, and of course at the Wedding Pier. At the same time, fall had been exhilarating with its variety of colorful leaves and wind-blown changes in temperature. Then winter had turned out to be special, too, with its brief time for sledding and ice skating. Each season so far had been different and exciting. Ed wondered what spring would be like.

On a quiet Monday morning in late February, Ed sat down in his office and took stock of his ministry at Dinkel Island so far. He had mixed feelings about the turn his life had taken with this move to Dinkel Island. After seminary he had felt charged up and anxious to get into the nitty-gritty of ministry. Moving into an associateship had put some of that energy on hold, but it had allowed him and his family to live a more relaxed life. Now he was definitely into the full swing of ministry. He thought back over the events of the past eight months. Summer had been a honeymoon time where everyone bent over backward to be friendly and accepting. During that time, by the grace of God, there had been few emergencies within the church family.

Thinking about it now, Ed decided the honeymoon had ended that first part of October with Maude's stroke and the deaths of Mary Stone and Rufus McCorkle. Something bothered him. *What difference does it make that I'm serving here? Where's the pattern in my ministry—something to launch me into a second year?* He felt depressed. "I gotta shake myself out of this," he said.

One thing that had happened during these months was that he became more intentional than he had ever expected to be in planning his worship themes ahead of time. He really appreciated Jenny's skill as a musician and her dedication to the job of organist/choir director. She had a lot of energy and needed to be authentically involved, so Ed had found himself looking ahead at blocks of Sundays, mapping out sermon themes he hoped to cover, and then sharing with her the process of selecting hymns and planning liturgy. This was making him more liturgical than he'd been comfortable with before, yet Jenny was bending more his way with the hymn selections. Somewhere he had read that an exciting, meaningful worship service needed to involve a variety of emotional movements so that when it was all put together the worshiper left with a sense of wholeness that was enhancing to his life.

That's it! Ed thought as he looked at the worship calendar. *Easter will be late this year.* He still had a week and a half until Ash Wednesday and the beginning of Lent. He snapped his fingers and said aloud, "Lent is the time to get my ministry off dead center."

He picked up the phone and dialed. "Hi, Jenny, this is Ed. Do you have a moment?"

"Sure, I was just looking through my music for some Lent and Easter ideas. Do you have any suggestions?"

"What a coincidence! That's what I'm calling about. I've just been sitting here trying to figure some way to make this season a little more meaningful or unique. Of course, I don't want to step on any toes or scuttle any cherished traditions—"

"Oh, don't worry about that," Jenny broke in. "We *need* a little shaking up around here. Keeping everything just the same as it's always been is one of our problems, at least as far as I'm concerned."

"Don't get me wrong, I'm not planning to do anything outlandish, like painting the sanctuary purple."

They both laughed. "Now *that* would be a sight!"

"Seriously," Ed went on, "I notice it's been several years since you all had anything special during holy week, you know, like several nights of informal services with a powerful speaker or something like that."

"No, we haven't. That doesn't sound like such a bad idea. We could get in some special music talent and even invite different community groups on different nights. What do you think?"

"I think that sounds like a plan. Let's both do some thinking about it and get our heads together sometime next week, okay?"

Jenny agreed, and they hung up. Ed was beginning to feel some energy moving through his veins. He wondered who he might bring in as a speaker. *I need somebody with energy—somebody different enough to draw in a crowd.*

That thought was still in Ed's mind as he went to the March meeting of the Nor'easter District Minister's Association, which was being held this time at Trinity Church in Potomac City. These meetings were a time for the district supervisor to pump up the ministers to accomplish the program of the district and connection. They were also occasions for the pastors to stay connected with each other. That was what Ed looked forward to most of all. The host church always served a lunch at the end of the meeting. As he sat down at the table, he found himself next to Jay Sommers, a young pastor who served the Stumpy Cove Circuit.

The fare was the usual church dinner—a gelatin salad, ham slice, boiled string beans, mashed potatoes, roll, and dessert. As they waited to be served, Ed mentioned the holy week plans he and Jenny had been discussing. He asked Jay, "Do you know anybody who is really different or exciting that you'd recommend as a speaker for several nights?"

"That depends on *how* exciting you want to get."

"What do you mean?"

"I mean your program sounds pretty traditional, which it probably needs to be here in Nor'easter County. It sounds like you have some possibilities for music that will probably appeal to the people. Now, are you ready to break some traditions with your speaker?"

"Tell me more."

"Well, I'm thinking about Hew Sterling down in Norfolk. Do you know him?"

"No, but I've heard of him. Isn't he the guy who dresses like a clown and specializes in children's sermons?"

"That's part of it," said Jay. "He also uses puppets and magic, and while he does bill his ministry as an appeal to children and families, he really aims his message toward adults—especially those who have given up on the church, thinking it's full of hypocrites and outdated ideas. He's really very effective."

Ed pondered the idea for a minute. *I've heard of Hew all right,* he thought. *I've heard him called the "Karny King," and the "Sawdust Savior."* Ed realized, of course, that those kinds of remarks usually came from insecure people who were threatened whenever anybody questioned or tried to alter the institutional forms and traditions they'd come to rely upon. *Jay just might have an idea here, but would the people accept someone like Hew?*

"Have you ever used him yourself?" he asked Jay.

"Yes, as a matter of fact, I have. The setting was different, though. We had him in at Stumpy Cove's summer family program two years ago. Some of the people were a little shy about it at first, but it really worked out well, and we've been talking with Hew about doing a follow-up sometime. I think you could make it work with the right kind of build-up. That's why I suggested it."

Ed was encouraged with this response, but he wasn't too sure how to expect the Dinkel Islanders to take it. He brought the idea up with Jenny the next week.

"Hey, that's a really good idea. I'd forgotten about it, but I do remember some of the excitement I heard from down in the county when he was at Stumpy Cove. I never thought of having Hew Sterling here."

With Jenny's encouragement, Ed contacted Hew and found he could come in April. He suggested, however, that they plan the program a bit differently. Instead of a traditional holy week thing with evening services, they could start with a Saturday program for families. They could follow that up on Palm Sunday morning with a special adaptation in the morning service, and then have two more sessions Sunday and Monday evenings. The Saturday program, weather permitting, would be done outdoors. At the next meeting of the official board, Ed and Jenny presented the idea. There were a few questions that generated a fair amount of discussion. When the vote was taken, the board agreed unanimously to go ahead with the idea. Ed was surprised and set right to work making arrangements.

Jim Swank came by Ed's office the next morning to talk about the Palm Sunday program. "I'm not opposed to this, you understand, but you really did kind of drop it on us out of the blue. We would probably have all felt a little better if you had talked to us about the idea before the meeting."

This was the first evidence Ed had seen of a power struggle among the Dinkel Island constituency. Jim had always seemed so open and up front. As he listened to him now he realized he hadn't returned that courtesy.

"You know, you're right, Jim. Gosh! I guess I didn't think I was acting in a vacuum. The idea to bring in Hew Sterling came up through another minister on the district—who, by the way, had a fantastic experience with him right here in Nor'easter County. Like we said at the meeting, Jenny and I had been working on Easter worship ideas and were looking for something different. Somehow it just all evolved. I hope there aren't a lot of people who feel I was heavy-handed."

"I wouldn't say there was any big problem, but you've been here long enough to know by now that there are a few people who kind of need to be on the inside whenever decisions are made—especially if they involve strong breaks with tradition. But I guess that's nothing new to Dinkel Island, is it? I'm sure all churches have the same situation. I'm just mentioning it so you'll know to run things through informally in the future. You can always call me or Jack Reilly. Either of us can help smooth the way."

After Jim left, Ed felt puzzled. He wondered, *Did I just hear a warning to keep my place?* That was a troubling thought. He could imagine what his place might be—preaching, Bible study, visiting the sick, praying for people, and doing weddings and funerals. Jim had shocked and disappointed him with his visit. He had felt he had a friendship growing with him, as well as a pastoral relationship of trust and support. Now he wasn't so sure.

～✺～

Ed's secretary, Louise James, knocked on his office door: "Are you real busy? You have someone here to see you."

"Oh? Who's that?"

"Stan Grayson and his fiancée. They would like to talk to you about getting married."

Ed was surprised when he looked at Stan. He had talked with him briefly a couple of times after church and had thought he would come by sometime to talk with him more deeply. Stan always seemed kind of shy and perhaps a bit troubled. The man who stood before him now was a transformed person. There was a light in his eye, a smile on his face, and an assurance in his voice and movements. And the woman with him was beautiful and had the same kind of presence. Ed reached out his hand to Stan. "It's good to see you. I don't believe I've met your fiancée. In fact, I wasn't aware that you were engaged."

"Let me introduce Lillie Plume," said Stan, with a flourishing gesture. "We've just been engaged a couple of weeks, so you haven't had a chance to know about it. We're looking for a house, and we'd like to get married on May 5, if that will work for you."

Ed checked his calendar. There was nothing special noted. "That's fine. What time?"

"Two in the afternoon," answered Lillie. "And," Stan chimed in, "we're both a little unconventional. We'd like to know what we have to do to use the Wedding Pier. That's such a cool place."

"To be honest with you, I don't know. I haven't had a wedding since I came here last summer, and I've wondered about the pier myself. I'll do some checking and let you know what arrangements you have to make. For now, though, if you have the time, we can do some preliminary preparation."

Ed took down some basic background information and had them fill out some standard forms. When they finished he got them to talk informally about themselves. He was fascinated as

Stan and Lillie went through the whole scenario of how they met. They seemed well suited for each other, at least on the surface.

"I should have asked this first, I guess," said Stan. "Lillie and I have each been married before. We've each been divorced. You don't have anything against marrying divorced people, do you?"

Ed understood the question. Times were changing and thinking had broadened a lot about marriage, divorce, and remarriage. Still there were some pastors who refused to marry anyone who had been divorced. But Ed was not one of them.

"My answer to that is you both seem to have grown a great deal through whatever experiences you've had. I trust we'll share some of those things in our next session or two. I certainly have no right to limit your right to another chance with marriage, and I wouldn't think of it."

Ed's reply brought their conference to a warm and positive conclusion. After a brief prayer, they left. Ed called the town hall to find out about using the Wedding Pier. Ann Streible answered. Basically, she said all he had to do was clear the date on the Wedding Pier calendar, which she could do for him right then.

"You say May fifth?"

"That's right."

"Well, you're in luck. That's the first date the pier will be available this season. It's only used from May through September. I'll put you down and see that the canvas gets put up in plenty of time."

"Thanks. I'm kind of excited about this. It will be a different kind of experience." As he hung up, he thought to himself that this was turning out to be a rather lively spring season. Just a few weeks ago, he had been feeling a bit depressed. It must have been the winter doldrums.

10

―◆―

Parachute Preacher

*A*pril dawned on a Sunday morning, just two weeks away from the great Palm Sunday Weekend Spectacular. Ed was excited and increasingly anxious about whether or not Dinkel Islanders would accept this innovative idea. The plan was to have an outdoor gathering at 3:00 p.m. at Tranquility Bay Campground. This was the largest expanse of open area in town, and an open area was needed—not only for the crowds they expected but because Hew Sterling, dressed as a clown, was going to drop into the scene by parachute at the beginning of the service. The theme for the weekend was "A Message from Heaven."

"It may sound a little corny," Hew had said, "but believe me, the unchurched people who have some pretty rigid ideas about God will sit up and take notice. And that *is* who you're trying to reach—*the unchurched*! Trust me on this one. They won't stay home in front of the TV *this* Saturday afternoon."

After his talk with Jim back in March, Ed became aware that there really was a core of informal leadership exerting influence over the church's affairs from the background. He didn't know everyone who was involved, but he did know who some of them were. The list included Jack and Barb Reilly, Sid and Ann Streible, Polly Allmond, Don and Jill Upton, Al and Sarah Jones and, of course, Jim and Patty Swank. Jim and Patty were the ones who amazed him. He'd felt they were close, yet they had never mentioned that they were part of a group who often met after church at the Seafood Pavilion and discussed church issues. It was like there was a built-in polarization between these lay leaders and whoever the pastor was—like they set up a game for the pastor to play, called "Find the Key." *Well*, Ed thought, *I'm beginning to find the key, and it's unlocking a door into a dark, hidden compartment of this congregation that I'm not sure I really want to explore.* As all of this unfolded, he told Sally about it.

"I can't believe you didn't know there was an informal leadership structure to the church," she said. "We've both seen this before. At First Church Dr. Bradford was always dealing with people he called the 'backseat drivers.' How come you didn't look for those people here?"

"I guess I just took all of that for granted there, but now it's my church and my problem to deal with."

"So what are you going to do about it?"

"I honestly don't know. I've been thinking about trying to take it head-on. What do you think?"

"That sounds reasonable, but how do you do that? I have a suggestion. I'd be willing to go to the Seafood Pavilion after church this Sunday and see what happens. Maybe the great secret group will open up and not be so secret after all."

"Yes, that's what I mean by taking it head-on. I need you behind me. I need to know you understand what I'm dealing with and that we can talk it out. You know, the ministry is very isolating. I thought I had Jim to talk things out with, but now I don't know. In the long run, we only have each other, I guess."

"You can say that again!"

"Wouldn't it be great if we just had some way to relate socially to some people outside the church—people we could relax and explore life with?"

"Yeah, *in this burg*? No way! You can't even go to the bathroom in a town like this without somebody noticing what you did and how many times you did it and then writing it up in the 'Social Notes' of *The Island Sentinel*."

"It's not *that* bad," Ed laughed, "but you're not far off."

As Ed discovered who some of the Brunch Bunch members were, he made it a point to call on them pastorally and try to get some feel for what was going on. These conversations alerted him to the fact that he was perceived as trying to be the Lone Ranger in this matter. The fact that he had worked the idea out with Jenny first, and then brought it to the full board within a matter of days hadn't meant a thing, it seemed. He decided to form a Palm Sunday committee to do the planning and carry out the program.

He asked Jim Swank to suggest some people for the committee. He suggested the Reillys, Sid Streible, who worked with Barb, and Ann, who worked at the town hall. Then there was Polly Allmond, who in spite of her gushy personality knew the ins and outs of planning community events. And Sarah Jones had to be asked, to keep from offending her, and to get the support of the women. So this became his non-spectacular committee for the Spectacular.

Surprisingly, things really did go fairly well in their work together. Ed had attended a seminar on the Capital City District about reaching unchurched people. He dug out his notes and shared them with the committee.

"That sounds great," said Polly, "for the big city, but this is a small town. We know everybody. Except in the summer when the tourists come in, everybody either goes to church or they don't want to."

"Well, that's not so different," said Ann. "That's what we're talking about. I know lots of people who never go to church—*anytime*, summer or winter. Some of them live right on our street."

"I'm sure Ann knows this, too, but as a real estate agent, I can tell you there are a lot of people who have come to Dinkel Island in the last two years who are permanent residents, and I don't mean retired people—especially since Crabbers Creek Acres opened up. I think Ed's right. There *are* a lot of people we could attract to our church if we just tried. People are disoriented when they're new in a place. And often they're shy, too. They need someone to reach out with a helping hand. Why can't we help them find their way to church just like we do to the grocery or the drug store?"

"Okay," said Polly, shaking her head and throwing up her hands. "I guess you're all right. I'm just a simple, small-town person. I don't know about all these things. But I will go along. I'll do whatever I can to help make it a success."

Everyone thanked Polly for expressing herself and for being flexible and helpful. They decided the key to the event was publicity. Hew had suggested a colorful set of posters that could be placed in businesses around town to get attention. They discussed that and decided to print a small, colorful flyer that could be mailed to everyone in town. They would then place large posters around town to further flag people's attention.

It wasn't long before Jack broke in with a concern about money. "It's wonderful to come up with these kinds of plans," he said, "but how are you going to pay for it? You know, we're a small church, and our budget is hard-pressed as it is."

Jim Swank answered Jack, "So far we're looking at something in the neighborhood of $500 to $600, and we've got $600 in the budget for evangelism. That's why it's in there. Even if we go a little over, it won't hurt."

"You know as well as I do," Jack protested, "that what's written on paper doesn't mean anything unless we have the money. I still say we should go easy on this. Why are we in such an all-fired hurry? Why can't we just do the usual things for Palm Sunday this year, then we can plan ahead for something like this next year?"

It was Jim, again, who responded and held sway. "I don't think anybody here is 'in a hurry,' as you say, Jack. The thing is, we've come this far, and I think we ought to do this *now*. And if we're putting things in the budget we don't intend to spend, then maybe we ought to be more honest and make what we print say what we mean."

Jim looked Jack straight in the eye as he spoke. Everybody else looked away. It was a put-down, and they knew it. Ed caught the tension and felt it needed some ventilation or it would get stored up inside Jack and explode in some other direction at some later time. He also knew this wasn't the time or place to deal with it. He perceived that this whole thing had turned into a power play that could directly affect his future ministry. So he stayed in the background and let Jim take charge. The committee moved on with planning, and everyone took on some specific responsibility to carry it out—except Jack. He said paying the bills was all he had time for.

When April 14 rolled around, it became clear that the campaign to publicize the Palm Sunday Weekend Spectacular had worked. Bernie Sloan was Jewish, so he couldn't be appealed to on the basis of Palm Sunday, but Jim got Don Upton to talk to him and Bernie agreed to let them use the tent camping areas as a gesture of public relations. As people began arriving, Ed had a moment of panic. *I wonder if we'll have enough room.* The cars poured in. They had roped off an area in front of a make-shift stage (which was a hay wagon with a platform built on it to get more height).

Jim had gotten the sound equipment from the high school and set it up.

The Women's Association had a large blue-and-white striped tent they borrowed from the funeral home. They used it to sell soft drinks and snacks, and to maintain a first aid station. Jenny got the Mammoth Baptist Melodaires Chorus to come in with their gold robes and the Harmony Hubbies Quartet from Stumpy Cove to provide special music. The members of the men's Bible class took on parking and ushering. They handed each person or family a card to fill out and leave on their chairs when they left. Getting enough chairs together was accomplished by borrowing extra folding chairs from Bailey's Funeral Home, Mammoth Baptist Church, and St. Simon's Episcopal Church.

The most difficult part of the set-up was the mountain Hew had asked them to build. Steve got Horace Backelder to bring in several dump truck loads of sand, which were dumped beside where the platform would be to form a mountain. They built a stairway of two-by-eight planks, each about three feet wide. On the flattened top of the mountain, they laid down two sheets of plywood for a platform.

As the crowd gathered, Jenny played tapes of gospel music through the PA system. At three o'clock the Melodaires led the assembled congregation in singing a stirring hymn. Then Hew Sterling made his spectacular entrance parachuting from an airplane, dressed in white clown face with a white suit and gold-and-blue trim. Lighted flares emitted colorful smoke that streamed from his heals. It was a spectacular sight. He landed exactly where a large X had been marked out for him behind the speaker's stand. His helpers rushed over and assisted him out of his parachute rig and then folded it up as he stepped around in front of the crowd, who were applauding wildly.

He waved and went straight up to the mountain top where he held up his arms. His voice boomed through a portable microphone. "Hey kids, come on down to the foot of the mountain!"

And they did, scores of them, surging forward through the crowd, pulling against the restraining arms of protective parents. They started to climb the mound of sand.

"Whoa, there!" thundered Hew's voice through the speakers. The children in front stopped and looked up at him. "I don't want you coming up the mountain because there are too many of you, and somebody might get hurt. So just take a seat on the ground."

They looked a little uncertain, but then everybody found a seat, and they all looked up expectantly. Hew went on with his object lesson. He held up two wooden panels that he called God's Message Boards. These, he explained, were like the ones God gave Moses on a high mountain a long time ago. Those were made of stone and God had a message from heaven on them. He told them God's message was that we're all in this thing of living together. We need each other. And we need help from someone bigger than us. When we're small, that comes from our parents, but when we grow up, we have to remember to look to our heavenly Parent, the one who designed life and wants us to like ourselves, and who we are, and what we're doing here on earth. When people didn't listen to the message God sent, he did things a different way. He got into the body of a man, just like he, Hew, was in the costume of a clown. Then he came down from heaven just to show everybody how special they are.

"Did you ever see anybody jump out of an airplane before?" Hew thundered.

"*No,*" came the collective response.

"Did you ever think that was something you might want to do some day?"

The response was a mixture of yeses and nos swelling up from the children.

"When you think back and remember what you saw today, think about God sending a message from heaven. He sent it though a man, his own Son, Jesus, and he's still sending it today. That's what this is all about. That's what Easter is all about. That's why we have churches and people who do things to help others. Isn't he a wonderful God?"

"*Yes!*" The children cheered as Hew came down from the mountain, took time to hug them, and sent them back to their families. Then he climbed up onto the platform and sat down while the Harmony Hubbies sang a medley of gospel songs. After that, Hew made a brief talk aimed at the adults.

"How many of you are new residents here but don't have a church you attend regularly?" Hew asked as he finished his message. Numerous hands went up throughout the crowd.

"How many of you are old timers here but don't have a church that you attend regularly?" Another set of hands went up, although some were raised haltingly.

"Now, how many of you are old timers or newcomers here and *do* have a church you go to regularly?" Still another group of people raised their hands.

"Now, those of you who are in the last group, look around and find somebody in the first two groups and get acquainted. Then take them to church with you tomorrow! If you don't have a church and don't get invited to one, come on over to the Wesleyan Brethren Church in the morning. I'm going to be there, and I'd love to see you. And remember, nobody should miss church on Palm Sunday!"

Hew gave the people some time to get acquainted and do some linking up. Next they received an offering while the Melodaires sang. After that they sang a hymn, pronounced the benediction, and everybody went home. It was just about the biggest thing to ever hit Dinkel Island. It truly was a Palm Sunday Weekend Spectacular.

The program was over, and the crowd completely gone by 4:30 p.m. It took a crew of stalwart Wesleyan Brethren parishioners until sundown to clean up everything except the sand mountain, which Horace said he'd have his men clean up on Monday. Many of the cards they had handed out in the beginning were crumpled and smudged, but they did salvage about forty-three that were clearly legible. These they planned to use as a basis for follow-up contacts.

Ed was overwhelmed by the turnout and the excitement level of the crowd. They estimated that over 500 people had attended. The day had a show-business flair to it, yet at the same time there was something really genuine in the tone of what was said and the way it was received. He could clearly see that you could reach people of all ages if you aimed your message toward children and got on their level of seeing the world. He didn't know if this was anything like what Hew had done for Jay Sommers at Stumpy Cove, but if it was, he understood now why Jay was so positive about Hew Sterling.

He also knew this could turn into a horrible flop if he and the folks at his church just let this weekend be something cool and special but made no effort to follow up. They had opened a door to something that would require a terrific amount of energy. He began to doubt whether they had enough energetic people to do all that would need to be done. *Or will they expect me to do it?* Ed thought. He sensed that his own fatigue was beginning to take over and color his reaction, so he tried to put the whole matter aside and enjoy the rest of Saturday just being with his family.

11

Steamed Reaction

Stan and Lillie spent much of their time during March and April making their debut as a couple in Dinkel Island. He had been invisible in town on his own, but with Lillie by his side, he found that people seemed to notice him, and he began to feel more a part of the community. Their warmest reception was at the Wesleyan Brethren Church when Lillie was able to attend on a few Sundays.

"Dinkel Island is a cool place," she told Stan. "I think I'll like living here."

Barb Reilly at Beach Realty helped them look for a house. "What exactly are you looking for?"

"We're not really sure," said Lillie, "We do know we want working space for both of us, and it needs to be separate from our living area. I have a small inheritance from my father's estate, which we can use as a down payment. It's not a lot—fifteen thousand."

Barb raised her eyebrows and frowned. "You're right, that is *not* a lot for a down payment, *but it's okay*. We can probably find something that will work with that."

During the next three weeks Barb, Stan, and Lillie visited several homes in a modest price range but found nothing suitable. Then Barb remembered a unique piece of property on Beach Drive, right behind the Seafood Pavilion and across the street from the Grande Hotel. It was a frame building with a shop facing the street. Upstairs and to the rear of the shop was an apartment with living space. The way it was landscaped, you could hardly notice the restaurant from the living quarters.

Lillie fell in love with the place right away. In fact, she envisioned something she'd never really considered before. Instead of just a residence and studios, with a lot of trips out of town, perhaps they could turn the shop into a small gallery, with their studio areas in the back. This way they could be more selective about their out-of-town trips and concentrate on a more settled life. The best part was that the price was right.

Stan and Lillie talked it over and decided to take it. Barb did all the paperwork and helped them find financing. Closing would be in late June, which gave Stan and Lillie time to work on arrangements for opening the gallery. They were already living in Stan's place so they would just continue that a few weeks after the wedding then move into the new place.

On Palm Sunday weekend, Stan and Lillie had planned to do a show in Alexandria. The Friday before Lillie spotted one of the colorful posters about Hew Sterling's appearance at the campground the next Saturday. It was a colorful poster, showing a man descending from the sky with a parachute, and had a blow-up of his head in clown's white face. It intrigued her.

"Look, honey," she said, showing it to Stan. "Doesn't this look interesting? And it will be right here at the campground next Saturday."

"Yeah, I got a flyer about it in the mail from church. It's being put on by the Wesleyan Brethren Church, you know. I guess I figured we'd be too busy to go, so I didn't pay any attention to it."

"This is *your* church, isn't it? Gosh, for a church to do something like that is really different. I've always been fascinated by airplanes and hot air balloons and skydivers, although I have no desire to be a balloonist or skydiver. You know, I'd like to see what this is all about. I wish we were going to be here next weekend."

"You're *serious!*" said Stan, realizing there was an awful lot about Lillie that he didn't know yet. "I had no idea you'd be interested in something like this. You know, that show in Alexandria is marginal. I mean, it doesn't usually do much for me. I don't know about you. I've just been doing it each year to keep my hand in, so to speak. If you'd rather stay here and do this and work some more on getting the place set up to move into, heck, I'm all for it. We're not hurting *that* bad for money right now."

"Sometimes you have to think about more than money. Yes, I'd like to cancel out and stay in town next weekend."

So it was that Stan and Lillie were a part of the Saturday crowd at the campground for the Spectacular. They found it to be an exciting and novel approach. "If I'd known church people could unbend and do something like this, I'd have started going a long time ago," said Lillie. She wasn't alone, with similar comments heard throughout the crowd.

"Yeah, it's great," said Stan. "Of course, I like the church the way it is. I really go there for some peace and perspective, and I love that big stained glass window they have. Pastor Heygood is a pretty good preacher, and sometimes he says things that really make me think. But you should have heard the guy who was there before him. He was *funny!* He could get you started laughing when you came in, and you didn't stop until you left, and you always took some kind of thought away that stuck with you."

"Maybe that's why Pastor Heygood went in for *this* program. It makes a lot of sense, you know. I mean it would be hard to take the place of someone who's really skilled at using humor. You would have to do something spectacular to get people's attention away from the other guy so they would give *you* a chance. I'd say this guy's pretty smart, and he's doing something to break away from the aura of the other pastor."

"Hey, you're really something, you know? I mean all that hadn't occurred to me. I guess I've been too wrapped up in my own world, excuse me, *our world*, lately."

"I know, I have too, but I notice things like this. You know, if this guy has anything up his sleeve to follow this with, he just might end up making *me* a religious person again."

When Hew asked people at the end of the event to hold up their hands if they were newcomers or had no active church affiliation at Dinkel Island, Lillie held hers up.

"Why are you doing that?" said Stan. "You've got a church here with me, don't you?"

"*Shh!*" Lillie responded. "I'm still a newcomer, and I like people. I'd like to see who else is new and maybe get acquainted with someone."

That was a point where Stan and Lillie differed. She was much more outgoing. Stan actually didn't have many friends since he stayed to himself. He didn't know why, it just had always seemed to work out that way. He wasn't against people being outgoing; in fact, that was one of Lillie's qualities he really liked. So he decided to follow her lead on this, and maybe they would actually get acquainted with someone new."

"I'm glad to see someone else near me hold up their hand as a newcomer," said a voice from behind them. "My name is Cheryl Drew."

Lillie and Stan turned to face a young woman with brunette hair and sunglasses who had a personality just as warm as the sun. She was holding out her hand. "Isn't this something! I've never seen a church put on something like this before. This is great!"

They gave Cheryl their first names, and Lillie agreed with her assessment of the event. "I've lived here a couple of years, so I guess I'm one of those old timers he was talking about who is supposed to get acquainted with you newcomers," said Stan.

"Then you two aren't married?"

"Well, not yet," Lillie replied. "Our wedding is three weeks from now. We're getting married at the Wedding Pier."

"Wow! That's cool. I've wondered what that would be like. I've never seen a wedding there."

"Then you're invited," said Lillie.

"Just like that?"

"Sure, just like that! Why not?"

"Gee, I wish Bob could have been here with me today. I told him we would meet some great people out here. But he had to work."

"Where does he work?"

"I'm sorry, I didn't finish introducing myself. Bob is the new pharmacist at Dinkel Drugs & Sundries—in fact, he's the new owner. It's the drug store at the corner of Bank and Seashore, right across the corner from the church that put on this program. I want to go to that church tomorrow."

"We're going there tomorrow. Maybe we could meet and sit together"

"I didn't know Dinkel Drugs had someone new," said Stan. "I guess I don't go in there often enough to know there had been a change."

"Bob's actually been there a year. He started as a new partner after he finished pharmacy school last year, and then this year Mr. Barnes got sick and decided to offer Bob the store. He was able to borrow enough money to get started buying it and has taken it over, but we've got a long road to travel to get on solid ground."

"So, I take it you two haven't been married long."

"Right! We just got married last month. Bob came back to Richmond where I lived on his days off, so I didn't move in until after the wedding. It's really a *different* place to live for me, but I'm sure I'll learn to like it. Of course, I'm looking for a job because I had to give mine up. This does *not* look like a really easy place to find work."

"I can imagine," said Lillie as the offering was being announced, and the Melodaires were beginning their offertory number. "See you in church tomorrow."

"Can you beat that?" Lillie said when they were driving home. "To come out here and meet a new friend. I really like Cheryl."

"Me, too," Stan replied. "You know, I've never been real good at forming friendships. Maybe it's because I've been hurt by people too much. But I can learn from you, so I'm game if you are."

"I understand," said Lillie. "Gee, just think. We came out here hardly knowing anyone, and already we've made a new friend!"

Harper Jauswell was steamed. Here he was arriving in Richmond and had no one to meet him, no way to get home to Dinkel Island. *Wait until I see that scoundrel Jack Reilly.* Here he'd tried to build this man up into a real leader, and what did he get for his efforts? Just some limp excuse about having to stay in town to keep an eye on things. *What things? What in tarnation was going on back there, anyway?* That just proved once again that when *he* went away, everything went haywire. Jack was vague over the phone and said he had to leave and was sorry he couldn't pick him up. *Well, what about Barb—why couldn't she come pick me up?*

As Harper got off the train, collected his bags, and went out of the station, he saw three cabs standing by. "Daggone it," he said to himself, "that will cost a fortune, but what choice is there." He hired a cab in spite of himself. His first thought was to go to the bus station, but he hated buses, so he told the cabbie to take him to Dinkel Island. It wasn't as if Jack had left him no alternatives.

He had said he would be glad to pick him up Sunday afternoon, but Harper was never one to change a scheduled trip if he could help it. So here he was taking a cab home.

The cabbie pulled out from the station and picked his way through city traffic until he was finally out on the open highway heading east. It seemed to take a long time, and the meter was running, which irritated Harper. He never paid much attention to how long it took with Jack and Barb, but this just seemed to be way too slow. He challenged the driver, "Just where do you think you're going? I didn't say give me a tour of Eastern Virginia. I said take me to Dinkel Island, and I want you to get me there the quickest, cheapest way, do you understand?"

He began to wonder if Jack not showing up had something to do with the church and that new city preacher. *I told Jack to keep an eye on that man!* He knew Jack wouldn't let him down. *I'll bet that scoundrel Heygood is up to something, and Reilly had to stay there to keep the lid on him.* He'd soon be there and take care of things. If Heygood had stirred up something, he'd make sure he paid for it. Harper vowed that. With that settled in his mind, he cooled a bit, leaned back, and closed his eyes as the cab drove eastward across rolling hills. Tired from all his travel and worry, Harper fell asleep.

He awoke sometime later, conscious that the cab had slowed down. He saw that they were nearly there, but traffic was so heavy they'd practically come to a stop.

"What's the problem? Is the drawbridge up?"

"I don't think so. There are plenty of cars coming this way, so it must be down. Maybe there's an accident."

Somehow that didn't ring true for Harper. He didn't know what it was, but he sensed an almost electrical charge in the atmosphere.

As they crossed the bridge, he noticed that traffic was bumper-to-bumper toward Lighthouse Point. He was tempted to have the cabbie take him over there but kept his senses and had him go directly to his house. Begrudgingly he paid the man, then, almost as if he suddenly changed personalities, leaned back toward the driver's window and handed him an extra five dollar bill. "You've had to put up with a lot, so stop and get yourself something to eat on me before you leave town." He didn't know why, but every so often he would just do something like that. It was usually after he'd been really tense over something, and it seemed to help him relax and feel better about himself.

Fanny greeted him as he walked into the house. "Welcome home, Mr. J. How were things in Florida?"

"Humph! Ain't you got nothing else to do besides stand around starin' at an old man comin' home from a trip? Have that boy to get my bags in here!"

"Jimbo's already takin' them up the back stairs. Is there something special you want for supper?"

"Supper! My God, woman, it's only two thirty, and you're thinking about supper. I don't care. Fix anything you want. Listen, what's all this fuss about over at the campground today? I couldn't hardly get into town for all the traffic."

"Oh, it's *excitin'*, Mr. J. You'd be proud of your church. They're havin' this parachute preacher come in to speak to kids and families and stuff. Just about everybody's going who don't have to work."

"What *parachute preacher*? What are you talkin' about? You're not making any sense."

"I don't know too much about it, but you'll be able to find out more tomorrow because I hear he's going to be doin' somethin' special in your church."

"Tomorrow, my foot!" Harper thundered. "I'm going over to that campground and put a stop to this nonsense right now. Churches don't have no business fooling around with parachutes and campgrounds. Probably some stupid idea Heygood brought with him from the city."

"Oh, no sir. I heard they done the same thing down the country couple years ago."

"I don't care where else they do it. We ain't doing it here. I suppose if some idiot jumped off a bridge, you'd do it, too, just because somebody else did it in Potomac City."

"No, sir." Fanny hated it when Harper got like this. She felt abused by his attitude and his words. Many were the times she just wanted to walk out, but she needed this job.

"Now you get in there, and get busy on that supper, you hear me? I'm going out to put a stop to this nonsense, and I'll be back shortly."

"Yes, sir," Fanny said as she turned toward the kitchen.

Stopping the nonsense at the campground, Harper soon found out, wasn't as easy to do as it was to talk about. Traffic had thinned by the time he got there, but he had to park along the road clear back at the Marina. This in itself made him furious, but it didn't stop him. He left the car and began to walk toward the campground. As he got closer he could see the stage, and some kind of mound of dirt or sand, and he heard some gospel music. Then he heard an airplane engine above. He looked up and saw a figure leave the aircraft and begin falling toward him, with some kind of colored smoke coming from his feet.

"Oh no, it's one of them sky jumpers!"

Harper was dumbfounded as he watched the man descending. As he neared the ground, Harper ducked, sure he was going to crash straight down on him. Suddenly there was a *pop*, and the chute opened. The jumper had a cross painted on the underside of the chute and seemed able to control it perfectly. He landed in a cleared place just ahead of the cars in front of Harper, right next to a speaker's platform. Two men ran out and helped him out of his chute then folded it behind him while he went up on top of the mound and called the children to him in a loud, booming voice. It was all too much for Harper. He leaned against a pickup truck to catch his breath then made his way back to his car and drove home."

"Did you stop it, Mr. J?" Fanny asked as he came in the back door.

"Too late," he gasped. "Ain't feelin' good. Some fool almost landed on my head with a parachute. Had his feet on fire! I'm going to bed. Forget supper. You can go back to your apartment if you want."

Harper got a good night's rest, and when Fanny fixed his breakfast on Sunday morning, he was already up and dressed for church. He was feeling in no mood for a lot of backslapping foolishness this morning. He decided he would just walk down to the church when the bell rang for the worship service and then go in and take a backseat and see what all this fuss was about. Surely they couldn't do any parachute acts inside the church, and, thankfully, he hadn't heard that they were moving out into some field permanently. So he read the Richmond Sunday paper, and then walked to church, timing himself to arrive about five minutes after the service started.

He could hear them singing a block away and there were a lot of cars lining the street. He got inside in time for Heygood's pastoral prayer. The place was really packed. In fact, there were some people he'd never seen in town, much less in church, and some he had sworn that if they ever stepped inside, the rafters would crack. And there were absolutely no seats. People were standing along the wall behind the pews.

"Glad to see you, Harper," whispered someone. It was Don Upton, handing him a bulletin. "I'm sorry there are no seats left. Isn't this great!"

Harper was about to tell him how great it was when a young woman on the pew just in front of him and to his left stood up and said, "Here, you take this seat." He started to object but decided if she was fool enough to give it up, he wasn't going to argue. So he sat down right next to another woman he had never seen before. She was holding hands in church, of all things, with a man he thought he had seen around the church sometimes.

About this time Ed stepped back up to the pulpit. "It's time for the children to come forward." He seemed to be looking for something as the kids came up. There were an unusually large number of them. "I know you're all looking forward to seeing Message Man again today, and I know he's here somewhere, but I can't seem to find him." As he talked he looked behind the pulpit. The kids giggled. Heygood looked up again and held up a piece of wood. "Here's his message board. Look what it says: Look behind you."

They turned and looked back the aisle just as the door behind Harper opened again. In popped this same man he'd seen falling toward him yesterday with *two live animals*, a lamb and a goat, tucked under each arm and his powerful voice booming. "*Blessed is he who comes in the name of the Lord.*"

The door slammed against the side of Harper's pew as Hew entered. Harper, startled, jumped up and came down on Lillie's leg, pinching her thigh against the hard wooden seat. She yelled, "*Ouch!*" He looked around at her. The people nearby looked at him. Suddenly the fire flared within him. Harper jumped back up, slammed the hymnal down on the floor, and made for the door. The sharp sound of the hymnal completely disrupted the service, and now all eyes were on Harper. Dead silence gripped the room, except for Jim Swank who, when he turned and saw what had happened, said "Oh, crap!"

"*Jim!*" barked Patty. "Your language!"

Lillie turned to Stan. "Who was *that?*"

"I have no idea," he replied as everybody recovered from the shock of this momentary interruption. Then they went right on with the service as if nothing had happened.

12

Accountability

$\mathcal{E}$d was shocked by Harper's actions. He knew the man had been in Florida and this was the first time he had seen him since Christmas. Because of his gruff exterior during their brief encounters, Ed had inquired a bit about him. He heard about Harper's efforts to control things in the church. Some spoke of him as having almost "ownership" of the place. And of course there were the letters between Clara and Elwood Richards that implicated Harper in some behind-the-scenes manipulation. Yet Ed had to admit that he had not personally experienced anything with the man that would substantiate any of that.

Harper's protest wasn't the only one Ed would have to deal with, but it was the only one on Sunday. The service actually went very well, and Harper's interruption was all but forgotten, as was Jim's expletive. Hew used the lamb and goat to tell the story from Matthew 25 where Jesus said his Father would separate the sheep from the goats in the last day, and people would be known for what they had done to help each other. He invited them to come back for the evening service when he would do some magic tricks with palm branches. He used the Palm Sunday imagery in his message for the adults, likening it to the excitement they had all experienced the day before when he jumped out of the airplane. Later in the day, Hew discovered that there was a voice at Dinkel Island calling for him to be "crucified," or at least sent packing. In the service Sunday night, he said he would continue Monday night by focusing on the victory of our faith that overcomes all voices and forces that threaten to undo us.

It was a high experience, and Ed was elated. He went to the office Monday knowing that he would have to deal with Harper yet feeling very confident. He wasn't prepared for the phone call he received from Randolph Adams, pastor at Mammoth Baptist Church.

"Hello, Ed?"

"Yes."

"This is Randy over at Mammoth Baptist. How are you today?"

"I'm doing fine, thanks. How are you?"

"I called to say that was quite a program y'all had over at the campground Saturday—very impressive."

"Well, thank you. We appreciate your church loaning us some chairs. It was something really different, and we're hoping it proves to have been a good thing to do."

"Yes…uh, it seems to me we ought to sit down and talk some. Have you got time today?"

"Sure, I can make some time. When did you have in mind?"

"Let's say lunchtime. Maybe twelve thirty, over at the coffee shop in the Grande Hotel?"

"Well, I'd like to," Ed replied, "but that's a little expensive for me for lunch…"

"Don't say another word. I understand. In fact, I feel the same way, but there will be three of us. Herbert Grimme from St. Simon's is really the one who set this up and somebody in his church owns the hotel, so he said the lunch would be on him."

"Oh, really? Listen, what's this all about?"

"No need to go into that right now. We'll see you at twelve thirty. Okay?"

"Okay."

As Ed hung up, he began to rerun the conversation in his mind. *This had to be about the Palm Sunday Weekend Spectacular. That's all it could be. But why? Was Harper Jauswell somewhere in the background of this call? Nah, he didn't want to get paranoid over this, but he decided he really needed to talk to someone about it.* Sally was at work, and he wasn't sure where anybody else stood on the issue, so he decided to ask Louise what she had heard about the weekend.

Louise James was a forty-five-year-old mother of three boys, all teenagers, and had been secretary at the church for five years. Her husband, Milton, had his own electrical contracting business in town and was a Dinkel Island native. Louise had come there when they were married. While Milton wasn't very active in the church, she and the boys were. She'd had a secretarial job with an insurance agency in Potomac City for several years, and then as the boys grew older, she felt a need to be closer to home.

When Sam Prentiss needed someone in the office part time in 1979, Louise applied for the job. She started out working just two mornings a week, which had grown now to five three-hour mornings weekly. Her rapport with the people and her history in the church had proven invaluable to Ed on many occasions. She had been especially helpful recently as Ed had become more curious about Harper, and some of the tension he felt with the Brunch Bunch.

When Ed asked Louise what she thought about the weekend program so far, she replied, "I think it was terrific, and my boys were *impressed*. By the way, so was my neighbor, Jan, down the street. I've been trying to get her to come to church for years, but she never would. You know how it is when people have been out of the church for a long time—it's real hard for them to start back. But this program seemed to strike her differently. I suppose it was because of the emphasis on families and kids and the fact that it was outdoors. Anyway, she was there Saturday, but she didn't come Sunday."

"Good! I'm glad she was there Saturday. Do you think we might have a chance to reach her through the church now?"

"That's anybody's guess—but I'll tell you, what we did this weekend sure didn't hurt any. I think Dinkel Island needed something like this to get us excited."

"I hope you're right. What about Harper and the disturbance he created during the service yesterday morning. What do you think is going on with him? How do you think people feel about all that?"

"Personally, I think people understand Harper. Like I've said before, he's been hard to get along with ever since his wife died, and even before that. It seems to me like if he doesn't think up something himself, then he tries to put it down. I don't know what's going on with him, but I'll tell you this much. I sure feel sorry for him, especially the way he jumped up and then sat down on that poor lady next to him—Lillie, the one whose wedding you're going to do."

"Gosh, I didn't realize he actually *sat* on her! I'll have to check on her and see if she's all right."

"I think she is. It just startled her. I mean, can you *imagine…*"

Ed chuckled. "Yeah! Listen. Let me tell you what's on my mind. I've just had a call from Randy Adams. He and Herb Grimme want me to meet them for lunch today. They sound really urgent about it but won't tell me what's going on. You've known these men longer than I have. What do you think?"

"Well…I hate to dampen your enthusiasm, but I think it probably *is* about the program this weekend. My other next door neighbor, who belongs to Mammoth Baptist, said even though their choir had a part, their minister wasn't on the program and some people felt what we did wasn't fair to the whole community."

Bingo, thought Ed. He thanked Louise for her insights and went into his office to think this through. No sooner had he sat down than Louise had another call for him, this time from the district supervisor, Wesley Goodman, in Potomac City.

"Hello, Ed, I'm calling to see if we might get together and talk some things over…maybe today, say around lunch time."

"I'm sorry, Wes, but I already have a lunch appointment today. How about later in the week?"

"That's okay. How about tomorrow?"

Ed checked his calendar. "That'll be all right. What time and where?"

"Come to my office around noon. I'll treat you to lunch at one of my favorite places."

"I'll be there. Is there anything I ought to know about or bring with me?"

"No, I'll talk to you about it tomorrow. See you then."

Ed wasn't sure exactly what was going on here, but he was beginning to feel like a target. First there was all that trouble with Jim Swank, who seemed to have so much anxiety about the program that he even cursed during worship when Harper blew off. Then there was the resistance from Jack Reilly, who wouldn't do anything except write the checks, yet who made sure he was always on the sidelines. Then Harper on Sunday. Now a call from two community pastors and one from his district supervisor. He *knew* what this all had to be about.

Anxiety beginning to take root, he called Jay Sommers in Stumpy Cove. "Jay, how ya doin'? This is Ed Heygood up in Dinkel Island."

"Hey, Ed! I've heard great things about your weekend. It's going pretty well, eh?"

"I think it is… I mean, it seems to be doing what it was targeted to do on the one hand, but on the other hand, I seem to be getting an awful lot of flak around the fringes. I'm even getting some of it from my congregation. Tell me, did you have that kind of trouble after your experience with Hew Sterling?"

"Oh, gee, Ed… I'm not sure now. There were so many positives about it, but I'm sure we had some negatives. I just can't remember that right now. Why? This stuff you're getting isn't really serious, is it?"

"You see, I don't know. I mean, the other two Protestant ministers in town have called me and almost demanded that I meet them for lunch today and at *their* expense. Then I had a call from Wes Goodman, and he practically insisted I meet him for lunch tomorrow. What do you make of this? Is that how Hew Sterling affects people?"

"Professional church people, yes, it is. I recall now. I did have some trouble with the Baptists down here. It seems they thought we should have made this a community-wide ecumenical effort. In other words, they wanted to control it. The trouble with most of those things is they get watered down so much to keep everybody happy that they lose their power. That was exactly what we didn't want. My people stood behind me on that, so I simply laid it out and stood on my position. They got over it."

"That sounds like good advice."

"Now that other thing—with Wes. I know I didn't have any trouble with him. I can't imagine him having a problem with your program. I've always found him to be very open-minded. I expect that has to do with something else and it just happened to come up at the same time."

"Thanks, Jay, you've been helpful. And thanks for putting me onto Hew. He really does a superb job. He also left us with a lot of follow-up to work on, which is where I want to turn my attention next. By the way, we have over forty cards with possible prospects from either new residents or people without an active church affiliation. If we get just a fourth of those folks to become part of our church in the next few months it will have been worth it all."

As Ed hung up he felt more confident and assured. He felt he could hold his own with the other two ministers. So he settled into some work that had piled up on his desk and put the Weekend Spectacular on hold in the fringes of his mind.

When Ed met with Randy and Herb, the weekend program came charging back into the center of his mind. Jay had been right on target about those two. They complained that this had not been a true community-wide effort. Ed assured them he was not using this as a way to proselytize their members. They even admitted that they had picked up some new people in church Sunday because they had been there Saturday and had spoken with people in their churches. As far as Ed was concerned, that was now a closed subject, and he believed they understood that.

Handling Harper wasn't going to be as easy. Ed decided he would take someone with him to reduce the chances that Harper might twist things around to his advantage later. He called Jim Swank, who said he could get away about three-thirty. They went to Harper's front door where they were greeted by Fanny, who ushered them into a spacious room, filled with antiques. It felt polished and lifeless, almost like a museum. Ed wondered what the room had been like when Annabelle was living.

Suddenly Harper blustered into the room. He expressed no greetings or courtesies, just pure, unbridled anger. "Now see here, Heygood, it's about time I set you straight on a few things, or you're going to have one hell of a rough time in this town. There are some things I ain't goin' to stand for, and one of them is having some rotten, good-for-nothing city slicker come into my church and turn it into a field circus with sky jumpers and such. Damn it all, I've poured most of my life and a pile of my money into that church to make it what it is today, and I'll be darned if a sorry jerk like you is goin' to come in here and tear it up."

Both Ed and Jim were taken back by this onslaught. Ed's temper boiled, and he struggled to control it. He felt the adrenalin rise up his spine and out into his arms and chest.

"Now, Harper, I didn't come over here for this kind of conversation. In the first place, I take exception to your language, and I think you owe both Jim and me an apology. Second, it's not *your* church! It's not *my* church! It's not *Jim's* church! It's *God's* church! And if I understand anything at all, God inspired people like you to put your resources into building it in order for it to be a springboard from which the good news of a gracious God and a forgiving Savior can be taken to people in terms of how they live, spoken in a language they can understand. If a man coming down on a parachute gives children and families the idea that God has a message for them that is real, then so be it. What good is a message all wrapped up in religion and locked up inside the doors of a church, only for people who already know what it is?"

He could see the emotion taking its toll on Harper, who was getting red in the face and beginning to wheeze. He began to sputter and yelled hoarsely, "G-g-g-get out!"

"Yes, sir," said Ed, "we're leaving. I'm sorry we've all been pushed to the point of such bluntness. I'll talk to you later." He and Jim, who was pale and looked shocked, and who hadn't said a word, stepped out onto the porch. Harper slammed the door so hard the oval glass in it rattled.

"Whew!" said Ed. "I'm sorry it had to go that way. That's really hard on everybody."

"Yeah, I don't think I've ever seen anybody stand up to Harper like that. I hope you know what you're doing. He's a powerful man."

"So is God powerful, Jim, so is God. And if I have to be on one side or the other, it sure will be God's side."

Inwardly Ed was shaking all over. As the adrenalin rush subsided, he began to wonder if he should have said so much or said it so forcefully. Jim wanted to know what to say when people began asking questions about what had happened, because he was sure Harper would use the grapevine to turn people against Ed.

"Tell them what you saw, Jim. Just tell them what happened, and leave it at that."

∾◡∾

On Monday night Ed was pleased with the way Hew Sterling brought the Palm Sunday Weekend Spectacular to a strong conclusion. It seemed like over half of those present went forward at a call for penitence and commitment. Everyone left feeling excited about their church and their faith.

The next day Ed talked with Wes Goodman. Sure enough, Harper had called him and said Rev. Heygood was causing a serious split in the church and needed to be reprimanded. In fact, if at all possible, he should be removed. He said he could get enough signatures to launch a transfer effort if necessary.

"What's going on down there, Ed? Dinkel Island has always been such a quiet, solid place. I can't understand what this is all about."

Ed wasn't sure where to begin or just how much to go into, so he said, "Wes, it's just some of the most exciting and powerful stuff I've ever seen. Hundreds of people turning out for a special Palm Sunday weekend program, lots of prospects to be contacted among new residents and unchurched folks, and a lot of anxiety among the lay leadership as they deal with issues of chaos and forward movement. I think we've finally pulled free a little from the aura of Sam Prentiss. A few people who loved Sam's humor and used it to manipulate a lot of people behind their backs are beginning to feel challenged. It's probably the best thing that could happen to them or their church. And, for the record, I definitely am *not* requesting a transfer." Ed hadn't really planned what to say. The words just seemed to roll out,—and it was okay. Wes seemed to appreciate what he was hearing.

"I'm not going to ask you any more about it, Ed. I think you've been straight with me, and as far as I'm concerned, you're on the right track. Sam Prentiss really does have a strong charismatic pull with that personality of his. It sounds like we made the right choice for someone to follow him. You just hang in there, and you can count on my backing."

Ed felt good about the way things had gone these two days. His next task was to tackle the full board and bring their emotions out into the open. He did that by calling a special meeting for Friday night. When the meeting time arrived nearly half the board members were present. Notable by his absence was Harper Jauswell.

Jim called the meeting to order and explained that they were having this unusual session because a lot of emotional energy had been built up during the course of the Palm Sunday Weekend Spectacular, and the weeks leading up to it, so it was necessary to ventilate some of the pressure. The members glanced around the room at each other looking puzzled.

"A church is more than a place," said Jim. "It's like a living organism. When it gets too much emotion built up inside it can get sick or explode. Our church is a healthy organism, and we want to keep it that way. We want this meeting to be a healthy opportunity for everyone to express themselves. Whatever questions or concerns you might have, please feel free to bring them up, and we'll answer them and deal with those issues. If you have joys to celebrate in all of this, please share that, too, so we will have wholeness to this process. Anything you have to say is welcome on the table for discussion. Nothing is out of bounds. We don't want any of you to go away tonight feeling like you didn't have a chance to be heard."

They went around the table, giving people a chance to speak. Ed picked up on a lot of different emotional issues. Some people were still basking in the excitement of the weekend's thrilling and unusual program, while others were still trying to deal with the unusualness of it. Some voiced fear that their church would change so much they wouldn't feel comfortable in it anymore, and others expressed joy that it finally was changing. One person was honest enough to admit she really did miss Sam, yet admitted she felt bad about hanging onto him. No one expressed displeasure with Ed's ministry or suspicion of his motives. Jim talked about Harper's reaction and the visit he and Ed had made, and nearly everyone seemed to understand that he was getting older and more possessive. They expressed concern that the church keep in touch with him and be as supportive as possible. Jack Reilly, Ed was sorry to notice, said nothing throughout the whole evening.

Finally, it was Ed's turn to share a few thoughts. He decided to clarify where he stood in all of this.

"You know, I wasn't sure I wanted to come to Dinkel Island when it was first mentioned to me a year ago. Sally and I really didn't know much about small town life, and sometimes we're still not sure about that. But then I suspect that's true for people wherever they live, especially if it's a place where they've been sent to stay and function for an undetermined amount of time.

"Tonight I want to tell you that I love all of you. I love your church fellowship. I love your town, and I feel more a part of it than I would have imagined even a short time ago. I think we've just tapped a terrific resource for exciting ministry and growth. However it will only happen if it's real, not affected, and not reactively directed just to keep things the way they've always been— or just to see that they change for the sake of change itself. From where I stand right now, especially after the emotion and faith we've shared over the last week, I don't think I'd trade places with anyone, anywhere."

Ed paused as several people spontaneously clapped, expressing approval. Then he went on, "As I look back now I realize how little my associateship in Richmond prepared me to serve here. It was somewhat artificial because I wasn't in on the ups and downs of how things got done and how decisions were made behind the scenes. I know I've made some mistakes over the last few months, but that's okay, because I've learned from them, and maybe we all have. We'll get over them. We always do, and usually we are stronger because of our mistakes. I will make a pledge to you: I'll do my best to serve you. When fresh ideas or challenges come up, I'll present them to you. I'll take care of myself and my family, but I'll also stay connected with you. That's what a church is—a vital, life-giving connection. I won't take over for you, back off just because things get tough, or ignore your needs or opinions. What's more, I'll expect the same courtesy from you. Have we got a deal?"

"Yes."

"You bet."

"Right on."

The replies, filled with emotion and positive energy, resounded around the table. Ed thanked Jim for calling the meeting, and they shared a prayer then adjourned. As they were leaving, Ed added one last thought.

"By the way, I meant to say that I'm as concerned about Harper as you are. I'll try to be a pastor to him and to love and support him."

"Honey, are you all right?" Stan asked Lillie as they got into her van after the Sunday morning service. "I mean, that guy sat down on your leg awfully hard."

"I'm okay. He startled me more than anything else...I think! I might have a bruise."

They had parked along the street on Seashore, a block-and-a-half from the church. Traffic was heavy, with people leaving the church in all directions. Stan was finally able to get into the flow and head toward Dinkel Avenue.

"Not a good way to get a fresh start on church, is it?"

"Well, I don't know." Lillie mused, "I mean, it definitely was not fake. That old man really was upset, for whatever reason, and he sure didn't stuff his feelings away. And what about that guy up front,"—she chuckled—"the one who yelled out and his wife got mad at him. I mean, that was real."

Laughing with her Stan said, "I guess I was surprised to hear all of that in church."

"Stan! Don't you think people *feel* things in church just like anywhere else?"

"You know what I mean…." The light turned red, and they stopped.

"Yeah, I do," said Lillie. "Remember, I'm the church dropout who got sick of all the pretense about religion. And, being honest, I had a lot of pretense myself. I guess I still do, although you've helped me a lot with that. Still, I've probably always wanted to find integrity and honesty or something at a deeper level in church."

"I hear that," said Stan, accelerating as the light turned green. "But don't you think the authenticity part has to be the personal element people find with God in their own relationship? Am I making sense?"

"Sure. You see, I don't think I'm that different from a lot of people I've known. I don't want to go to church, or do anything else, just to keep up some tradition or appearance. I think sometimes churches have driven people away. What happened, at least for me this weekend, is that one church did something to begin pulling me back."

The discussion was getting deep now. Stan perceived that Lillie was thinking at a deeper level than he had been. Maybe she had been all along. He wanted time to digest some of his own thoughts.

"Well," he offered, "one thing's for sure. Neither of us has ever been to a church service quite like that one."

"And I don't think we will be again soon, but I *am* ready to try going to this church. I think there's something there for me—for *us*."

"You mean, besides a wedding!"

"Yeah, besides that. Our wedding isn't going to be held there anyway. It'll be at the Wedding Pier."

"Right!"

They'd reached the Yacht Club & Marina, with its mirrored exterior walls that enclosed the finest restaurant in town. Stan parked and turned off the engine. He pulled her close and caressed her lightly. They kissed and then got out of the car and walked into the restaurant, shoulder to shoulder, hip to hip, their arms wrapped around each other's waist.

13

<hr/>

Wedding Pier Plunge

*I*t was May 4, and Stan had butterflies in his stomach. Tomorrow he and Lillie would get married. He loved her dearly and wanted this marriage so desperately, yet irrational fears began to play on his mind. Lillie and he had agreed that they would be apart this week before the wedding, so she was in Alexandria finishing up the last details of her permanent move to Dinkel Island and closing up her apartment. He checked his watch—it was 4:30 p.m. She would be coming in any time now. They were due at the Wedding Pier for the rehearsal at five-thirty. He had no time to waste.

Stan's mind raced back to some of his feelings when he got married the first time. *I was so hopeful then, so sure of myself and the strength of Peggy's and my relationship.* He knew Lillie was an *entirely different person and that he was, too, at this point in his life. He knew nothing was the same, yet the fear still surfaced. What if he did this and it all fell apart! What if...* His thoughts were broken by the sound of Lillie coming in the backdoor.

"Stan, I'm here, honey."

He grabbed a towel and went out to the kitchen where he met and kissed her.

"Mmm," she said, "have I missed *you*! I can't wait until tomorrow at this time." She returned his kiss with passion. "We haven't much time. I need to get ready."

They both scurried through dressing and getting her things in from the van and then went over to the Wedding Pier. With a navy blue canopy stretched over curved rods wrapped with garlands of artificial roses the pier took on a whole new appearance. In between each set of rods were flower boxes with petunias in them. A red carpet ran up through the canvas arches to the platform area out over the water.

The area was large enough for a small wedding party and a few close friends or family members to gather.

Stan and Lillie decided they would not invite a lot of people. He wanted to have Marty as his best man, but Marty was not cool with that idea. In fact, he said he wasn't even sure he wanted to attend. The pain Stan felt about his estrangement from his son was intense and deep, especially since he had once devoted a lot of his life to trying to help young people in just such circumstances. But there was nothing he seemed able to do about any of it now, and he stuffed the sadness away inside.

Pastor Heygood and Jenny, the organist, were walking toward them. Stan noticed that there was a man finishing up some work on the canopy out on the platform over the water. He asked Ed, "I see this guy working out there. Do you think everything will be finished in time?"

"I asked that very question over at Town Hall, and Ann Streible assures me it will be finished. We'll just have to trust that she knows what she's talking about. I think it will be fine." As they began walking toward the pier, Ed added, "That guy working out there is Jimbo, the town handyman. They get him to do a lot of jobs around town, including setting up the pier every year."

They all walked through the archways to the platform, and Jenny checked the power on the keyboard. "Is it hooked up? I don't get anything when I turn it on."

"I don't know," Ed replied. "I should think it would be. No one gave me any special instructions for turning any switches on or anything." He turned to Jimbo. "Excuse me, but do you know if we need to do anything special to turn on the keyboard?"

"No sir," replied Jimbo, "it should be all ready to go. It always has been before."

"I'd say it might be the main power switch, but the lights come on when I throw this power switch over here. They are both on the same circuit, aren't they?"

"Yes sir," said Jimbo. "Maybe they's a short in the line. I better check." With that he started to climb over the railing.

"Hold on," said Ed, startled by his sudden action. "What are you doing?"

"Oh, that's all right. Y'see the lines run up under the deck. I hafta crawl in across the supportin' studs and check it out."

"Are you sure that's safe? I wouldn't want you to get hurt. Maybe we ought to wait until morning and get someone from Town Hall to check it out."

"That ain't necessary. I useta wire up boats for Mr. Jake out to Lighthouse Point. I know wirin'."

With that Jimbo disappeared under the pier. They looked at each other and shrugged their shoulders. "I guess I'll practice the music later, if that's all right," said Jenny.

"Sure," everyone agreed. So Ed proceeded to talk them through the ceremony, showing them how to join hands, face each other, and exchange rings. They'd just finished when they suddenly heard "*Ah!*" followed by a splash.

"He's fallen in!" exclaimed Lillie.

"Oh no!" shouted Jenny. "I knew he shouldn't have gone under there!"

"Jimbo!" Ed screamed, leaning out over the railing.

There was no reply.

Stan immediately went over the railing and down under the pier. It was high tide and there wasn't much space between the supporting studs and the water. He saw a broken section of wire and a roll of electrical tape dangling from it. About that time he saw Jimbo thrashing in the water.

"Are you all right?" called Ed.

"He can't swim!" cried Lillie.

"He shouldn't have to this close to shore. Maybe the water's deeper than it looks or something else is wrong," said Stan. He noticed that there were boxlike sections under the pier.

Without another thought, Stan plunged under water and came up where Jimbo was. Holding him up out of the water while he tried to get his breath, Stan could see panic in Jimbo's eyes and a cut on his head. He was trembling, and Stan seriously doubted he had the strength or coordination to climb back up onto the pier. It looked like the only way to get out was to go under the outer divider, which meant taking Jimbo underwater again.

Stan said to Jimbo, who was still sputtering and coughing and seemed disoriented, "Look, we're gonna have to do something that will be frightening, but I need your help. Try to relax and let me take care of you.

Stan had been treading water, trying to control Jimbo, and work him over to the side at the same time. Now they were both holding onto the understructure, and Jimbo didn't want to let go. There was nowhere to go up above that didn't require crawling through the structural beams. Stan didn't want to deal with that. His way was still best, so he talked reassuringly to Jimbo. Suddenly, for some reason, Jimbo just quit fighting him.

"Okay, now close your eyes and take a deep breath. I'm gonna cup my hand over your mouth and hold your nose while taking you down, under, and back up. Let's go on the count of three." Jimbo nodded and sucked in his breath. "One, two, three."

Stan quickly cupped his mouth, pulled him down and under. As they came up, he felt Jimbo's body tense with fear and felt him starting to release air against his hand. And then they were up out of the water, hanging onto the structure again.

"Hey, see how easy that was!" exclaimed Stan. Jimbo wasn't sticking around for small talk. He literally scurried around the pier until he reached the shore where he fell prone. Stan lunged forward with a few swimming strokes until he could find the bottom with his feet then walked out. All the while he heard cheers from the pier and shore and the blast of the rescue squad siren. He felt limp, cold, and physically drained, yet exhilarated. He walked up to the front of the pier where Lillie flew into his arms. Rescue squadsmen came running up. A *Sentinel* reporter's camera flashed.

"Are you all right?" Lillie asked between kisses.

"Oh, yeah…just a little drained and soaked. That man's strong, but he panicked. If he hadn't been so afraid he could have gotten himself out of there the same way without any help. I guess panic is what causes people to drown."

"Well, you saved his life," said Ed.

"I dunno…I guess so. That's the first time I've ever been in a situation like that. I just did what seemed natural at the moment."

Stan knelt beside Jimbo to check on him as the press camera flashed again. A reporter asked some questions, and then everyone dispersed. The squad treated Jimbo and released him on the spot. His cut was superficial. What had almost done him in had been, indeed, his panic.

The next day the wedding went off without a hitch. Someone in Town Hall had the wiring problem corrected so the keyboard played beautifully. Stan was dressed in a white tux, and Lillie had on a flowery dress with a straw bonnet and carried a spring flower bouquet. The reception was held at the Park Gazebo, served by the Wesleyan Brethren Women's Association. During the ceremony, there was one special guest—Jimbo—who had expressed surprise and appreciation at being invited. It was a notable break with Dinkel Island tradition.

14

Heart Attack

*T*he Grayson's spent their honeymoon in Resort City. It was a week of deep bonding that ended much too soon. They left for Dinkel Island Saturday after supper and arrived home after dark, tired but deeply satisfied that the best times were ahead now that they had each other.

～

The Sunday morning sun filtering through the partially opened shades of the bedroom window backlit Lillie's auburn hair as she leaned over to caress Stan's body and invite a morning kiss. As he opened his eyes and looked into her glowing presence, he felt a warm, throbbing response and pulled her onto himself and their lips met. Time seemed to stand still as their passion grew, and they engulfed each other in the newly-wedded bliss of a tender and cathartic sensual sharing. Suddenly, Stan's eye caught the time on the face of the alarm clock.

He sat upright, which shook Lillie from her charmed state of bliss, and she caught her breath. "Stan, what's wrong?"

Stan immediately felt sorry for having startled them both out of their reverie, and he touched the smoothness of her face. "I'm sorry. I didn't mean to break the spell, but I just looked at the clock."

"This is Sunday, honey. Who cares what time it is."

Stan considered that for a moment, but something inside him pushed the idea aside. "I just had a thought," he said. "Why don't we start our first week of marriage worshiping God? You are such a blessing in my life that I want to do that. How would you feel about that?"

More awake now, Lillie thought a moment and smiled. "I think that's a very sweet thought. It's late, and I wouldn't trade this kind of wake-up for anything, but there's still time to get to church. I say let's do it."

When they arrived they were glad they had made the effort. Two of the first people they saw were Cheryl and Bob Drew. After some small talk, Cheryl took a clipping from *The Sentinel* out of her purse and handed it to Stan. The headline read: "Groom Takes the Plunge." A photo showed Jimbo on the ground getting his breath back and Stan, his hair and clothing soaked, kneeling over him. The story went on to describe what had happened. In closing the article mentioned that Stan and Lillie were not only new residents in town, but they would soon be "plunging" into business by opening an art shop in the old Carter building across from the Grande Hotel.

Cheryl said, "Stan, you're the first celebrity I ever met. So tell me, how does it feel to make the headlines? What was it like to do something like that?"

Stan said, "I don't know about the celebrity part. It all just seemed to happen so fast. I don't know what I felt, really. When a crisis happens, you just do what is in front of you. I really don't think it was such a big deal, but I have wondered about Jimbo after all of that. He sure was nervous about standing up on the platform with us, but I give him credit. He did it."

Bob said, "You know drug stores with lunch counters like ours are famous for hosting the latest gossip in town. Well, I've heard a lot of stuff, one being that some people thought Jimbo up on the pier with us was wrong. The folks here seem to have some pretty set ideas about what people should and shouldn't do. At the same time, I heard some people say it was wonderful that you jumped in and saved Jimbo from drowning. Whatever side they're on about him, *you* are pretty much a hero to everybody, Stan."

"You know," Stan went on, "I've wondered about Jimbo being the only black person I ever see around town. That really seems unusual to me. He said he lives out past Crabber's Creek Acres in a small settlement with a bunch of his relatives. Said they all used to live up near the old lighthouse when the guy who owned it was living. Apparently Jimbo provides support for a lot of extended family."

"Oh yes," said Bob. "There are several black families out there. It's a little closed community at the end of a dirt road past the subdivision. There are more people than just his family living there, and I know some of them have jobs in Potomac City. Oh, that reminds me. I heard the other day that somebody from Northern Virginia has bought the old Pointer property out in that same area and is planning to open a furniture craft shop or something. I wonder if that might open up more local employment for some of the folks living out there."

"Depends on how big the business is, I guess," said Stan. "Sounds like something that ought to be good for the whole town. Oh, look at the time. We'd better get inside."

As the organ was playing and people gathered, Stan found himself getting caught up again in the power of the prodigal son window. For a brief, meditative moment, he saw not a jealous older brother in the background but a defiant one, angry and afraid. *People always seem to shrink in the face of change,* he thought, *so maybe the older brother sees something is about to change and feels threatened. I wonder if that's the same thing that will happen with this new company coming into the area.*

Little did Stan, Lillie, or even the Drews realize just how much the incident at their wedding rehearsal really had impacted the local folks. It had turned the focus of the grapevine away from the Weekend Spectacular, which had been the biggest thing to happen at Dinkel Island in decades. That was even true with the Brunch Bunch, as was evident when they gathered after the worship service. Most of the regulars were there, including Harper Jauswell. After that Sunday when he stormed out of church, Jauswell had gone on about his life as though nothing unusual had happened. He hadn't discussed it with anyone, which made everyone uneasy because normally he would have. They figured he would get to it when he felt ready. Today he felt ready.

"That was some spectacle on the Wedding Pier the other week," he said suddenly. "I saw them two that got married in church today, and I wondered how they could have done such a thing—having Jimbo up there like he belonged with them. I tell you, that Heygood is out to upset everything we've got nice and settled here at Dinkel Island. This is just another case of it."

"Why would you say that?" asked Pansy Sprunt. She rarely spoke up, but since she was sitting at the same table with Harper, it just seemed natural to ask an obvious question. "It wasn't the preacher who jumped in the water and saved Jimbo's life, for goodness sake, it was the groom. I'll bet they got together and asked Jimbo to be up there just to make everybody feel good about him still being alive."

"That's a lot of hogwash. That man—what's his name? Stan something—"

"Stan Grayson, and his wife's name is Lillie," Sid Streible interrupted.

"Okay, Grayson. Anyway, he should know that's not the way we do things around here. Heygood was the other person up there—"

Polly interrupted this time, "Excuse me, Harper, but were you there yourself to see this?"

"No, but I heard all about it, and everybody knows Heygood was the one in charge. He should hold to the way things are done. He should have put a stop to it. It's just like Christmas when he went off helpin' Barney Jinks with church stuff, without askin' anybody, like he owned the place—stuff we'd already decided to give to Jimbo and his family. I tell you, it's just another way this man is tearing down our town, little by little. We've gotta do something about him."

This really upset the brunch gathering, and people started buzzing at their tables, while Harper started to feel he was losing control. Just then Jack, who had been busy in the restaurant, stuck his head in the door and said, "Just thought y'all might want to know who just came in the front door. None other than the preacher, and I expect he's headed back here."

Jack went back out into the restaurant, and a few minutes later Ed, Sally, and their children made their entrance. With them were four other people: the Graysons and the pharmacist, Bob Drew, and his wife. It wasn't the first time for the Heygoods to show up at the Brunch Bunch gathering, but since there were usually no other children there, Angie and Billy didn't want to be there either, so Ed and Sally had decided to only go occasionally. This was an occasion because after the worship service Ed was surprised when both the Graysons and Drews asked what they needed to do to become members of the church. Ed was overjoyed and wanted to share this good news with his church family. He wanted to introduce the Graysons and Drews to the Brunch Bunch.

Ed had expected a joyful reception, but instead there seemed to be an awkward silence in the room. They weren't sure what to do since the tables only seated six, and there were eight of them. Polly got up and came over, offering to take the kids over to her table where they had extra places. Ed and the others went to the buffet for food then settled down at their table to eat. Ed stood a moment and tapped his fork on a glass.

"I'll only take a minute of your time, folks, but I want to introduce you to some people you may not know yet." He had the two couples stand as he introduced them, and then he went on, "I have their permission to tell you they all will be joining our church on June third. It's wonderful to welcome new people to share our faith journey, and I know you'll want to express your welcome to them." The response was fantastic with everyone applauding and enthusiastically welcoming them. Everyone, that is, except Harper, who sat rigid and solemn and looked like he had swallowed something that didn't agree with him.

Everyone sat down and began eating and conversing again. After a short while, Harper broke into the celebratory atmosphere. "Just because the preacher came in don't mean we can't continue talking about the business at hand. In fact, it's a good thing he's here so he can get this straight from us."

The room reverberated with the shock and tension Harper's words evoked. No one knew quite what to make of this or what to do about it. They certainly didn't want to be in the middle of a verbal exchange like they had heard happened at Harper's house between him and Ed. Jack had come back in to join the fellowship just as Ed had introduced his guests, and he had sat down with Barb at her table. He seemed as shocked as everybody else and realized someone had to ease the tension.

"Harper," he said. Harper spun around in his direction, startled to hear his voice. "I think I know what you want to talk about, and this isn't the time or place to do that. So I'd like—"

"You *think* you know what I'm going to say? You don't know anything about it. It's obvious you don't listen when I talk to you, so why should you butt into this conversation." It was well known that Jack supported Harper and tried to back him up in most situations. Jack had been pretty reserved and distant during the Weekend Spectacular, and they didn't expect him to change about that. So they were shocked to hear him challenge Harper.

"Harper, I believe there are some things you and Ed need to talk out in private, and this is not the place for that. I'll tell you what, I'll go with you to Ed's office tomorrow, and we can talk about these things. If that suits Ed's schedule?"

"It's fine with me," said Ed. "I agree with you—we don't need to air out our differences in this setting. Let's not ruin a wonderful, joyful occasion. I'm free from ten o'clock on tomorrow."

Harper fumed and couldn't seem to get his words together. He pushed back from the table and got ready to walk out. Jack got up and said to him quietly, "I'll pick you up at nine forty five in the morning. Please go home and get some rest. And pray about all this."

"Ain't nothing to pray about! I'm right, and I know it. And I ain't putting up with no city preacher messing up my church and my town. But I'll be ready, and we'll get this thing taken care of once and for all!" People were up from their tables now, trying to tell Harper they cared for him. He could hear their words, but he couldn't take in the message. He pushed his way past them and went out through the restaurant.

Jack turned to everyone and said, "I'm sorry for all of this. I really don't think Harper has been himself lately, and we need to pray for him and for our church. And we're happy to have you new folks with us here and in our church. The Brunch Bunch isn't usually like this, so I hope you'll come back. Ed, I wonder if you'd pray with us now before we all finish our lunch and leave."

"Sure I will, Jack. I think we all share your concerns about Harper's health and disposition. Let's pray. Oh Lord, we know you are with us, and with Harper, just now. You know us even better than we know ourselves. You know our hopes and our disappointments, our loves and our hates, our joys and our sorrows. By your grace see us through our torn emotions to a redemptive and victorious faith. May your blessings be with us all as we go from here. In the name of our Savior, Jesus Christ. Amen."

After all of this, lunch was essentially over. People began to gather their things and leave. Ed went back to the table and spoke with the Graysons and Drews.

"I don't quite know what to say except I'm sorry that this is your introduction to Dinkel Island Wesleyan Brethren Church. The older man who was so upset is Harper Jauswell. He has been in this town and this church all his life and has a lot of influence in just about every area here. Somehow he has been offended by some things that have happened at church, but he doesn't speak for everyone. I hope this hasn't dissuaded you from becoming members."

"Quite the contrary," said Bob. "I was active in the leadership of my church back in Richmond and saw some of what goes on in the background. Actually, it's refreshing to see someone come out into the open with negative feelings, and that man who stepped in did a wonderful thing. I felt the Spirit of God at work right here. No, it doesn't change my mind at all."

"The same for me," said Cheryl, as did Stan and Lillie.

"Well, I'm glad. Thanks for hanging in here with me today. I'll talk with you later this week, and we'll make all the arrangements for June third."

As the four of them left, Polly brought the children back from her table. Angie said "I'm scared, Daddy. I don't like church meetings."

"Honey, this wasn't a meeting. It was just someone who doesn't feel well and he said some things that weren't nice…kind of like what happens on the school playground when somebody says something that hurts somebody else. But God loves him, and he loves us, and everything will be all right."

"I think y'oughta punch him in the nose," said Billy. "He sounded like a bully, and that's what I'd do to a bully."

"Now Billy, that's not the way things are. He's not a bully, and nobody is going to punch anybody in the nose. He's just not feeling well. He'll get over it, and we want to be his friends."

Billy turned away muttering under his breath as Sally said, "I think we need to get home. I've had enough of the Brunch Bunch today. I really did appreciate Jack stepping in like he did." With that they all left the restaurant.

∾◡◠

Monday morning at ten o'clock sharp Jack and Harper were at Ed's office. On the way over, Jack had tried to get Harper to talk to him so he could smooth things out a little, but Harper was closed up tight and wouldn't talk. When they entered the office, Louise said Ed was expecting them and would be with them in a minute. It was sooner than that when he opened the door and invited them inside the pastor's office. The room was fairly large with an executive desk in one end and a round table and four chairs in the other end. Ed invited them to sit at the table, and he joined them.

"Would you like some coffee? Louise can get that for us, and we also have some doughnuts, if you'd care for one."

"That would be very nice," said Jack. "Thank you."

"Nothing for me," groused Harper. "Don't hold with eatin' doughnuts, and coffee gives me heartburn."

Ed thought he looked like he might be in pain even as he spoke, and he noticed he was sweating. He asked Harper if he felt okay, and Harper brushed him off.

Immediately Harper started to charge in verbally. He seemed to be breathing hard in short, quick gulps. Jack, wanting to calm him down, put his hand on Harper's arm. "Harper, do you mind if I say a couple of things before we start?"

Harper looked surprised with a pained expression again on his face. "Oh, well…okay."

Ed interrupted, "Actually, before we start I think we should pray." He asked for God to be present in their thoughts and words, in their concerns and anxieties, and to calm everyone with his Spirit. "Okay, Jack, what would you like to say?"

Jack looked directly into Harper's eyes as he spoke in a gentle tone. "Harper, you and I have been close for a long time. We've shared a lot of good things. I know you have only the best interests of the church and the town in your heart. But I want you to hear something else. Over the past couple of years, I've seen you not behaving like yourself. I sense a lot of tension in your body, and you fly off in anger over things that never would have upset you as much in the past. I've been concerned about you, and maybe I haven't done my part by speaking up. Actually, I—"

Harper jerked back in his chair and hit the table with his fist. "What the devil are you sayin' to me! You're turnin' on me, ain't ya? I seen it when you didn't meet me at the train station. You didn't stop this fool from embarrassing me and our whole church with some Jumpin' Jack in the sky. And you let that clown of a preacher bring wild animals into the church. You—"

Jack put his hand up, and for some reason, Harper suddenly stopped, red-faced and trembling. "Harper, this is not the way to do this."

Ed said, "It's okay to speak your piece, Harper. I want to hear it—all of it. But you're getting too upset. Let's try to breathe deeply for a moment and get our minds and words in focus."

Suddenly Harper's eyes seemed to roll up into his head. He clutched his chest and doubled over in pain. Jack and Ed suddenly realized what was happening. Jack said, "You call 911. I know CPR so I'll try to keep him alive. Hurry!"

Ed jumped over to the desk and dialed 911. Hearing the commotion, Louise knocked on the door. "Is everything all right in there?"

Ed reached over and opened the door. "We think Harper's had a heart attack! I just dialed 911 and talked to the folks at the rescue squad. They should be here any moment. Jack's giving him CPR. Let's pray for God's healing presence and grace."

Shortly after that the rescue squad crew came in and took over, and Harper was transported to Nor'easter General Hospital in Potomac City.

15

Prayer and Support

When Stan and Lillie got home from the Seafood Pavilion on Sunday, she said, "That whole thing that happened today with Mr. Jauswell's anger toward the preacher bothers me."

"It bothers me, too," said Stan. "He really seems to have it in for Ed Heygood."

"Yeah, that's how it sounded to me, too."

"Well, I've been getting to know Ed, and I think he's a cool guy. I think he had a tough job following Sam Prentiss."

"Yeah, tell me about Sam."

"Oh, he was a trip! The guy just seemed to have this natural talent for comedy. He could get anybody laughing in just about any situation, which was a talent he was very skilled at using. If he'd been there today, I think Harper himself would have been hooting in laughter, and it would have all been different. But you know, I'm not sure the real stuff underneath would have ever been dealt with had that happened."

"Do you think it will be dealt with now?"

"Well, you noticed how the guy who runs the place—Jack I think his name is—seemed to calm Harper down and saw him out the door. They set up a meeting, and, yes, I think Ed will get to the bottom of whatever is hidden. Jack was pretty smart the way he set that up. There has to be at least one person other than Harper and Ed there, because Harper could just use the meeting to crucify Ed on the grapevine, no matter what came out of their talk."

"I think you're right. Ed seems to have some good ideas. Yes, he does seem to be making some changes, but I don't think they're just for his personal benefit. They're changes for the good of everybody. I've learned in my life that if I don't change the way I do things sometimes, I get stale and things go sour."

❧

As soon as the ambulance left with Harper, Ed followed in his car. At the hospital he found that Harper was still in the cardiac emergency room, and they had scheduled him for a heart catheterization. The receptionist told him he could go in for a brief visit. Ed wasn't sure what he would find and was sensitive to the danger of his presence upsetting Harper, but he was his pastor, and he would have to be careful how he approached him. When he stepped into the cubicle, however, Harper seemed either to be sedated or asleep. He decided he would simply offer encouragement and prayer. If he saw Harper getting upset, he would leave.

"Harper, this is Pastor Heygood. I've come to offer a prayer with you and offer you the comfort of God's Spirit."

There was no response. Ed was glad Harper wasn't reactive but also wondered what was going on with him at this point. So Ed said, "I'm going to take your hand for a moment while we pray. I know if I were in your place, I would have a lot of questions and maybe be afraid, but I would also want to remember that God is with me and he is greater than any situation I might face. I know that's how it is for you, too. So I will pray that you can relax in your spirit, put everything else out of your mind, and let God and the doctors take care of you."

Again, Harper did not respond, so Ed offered his prayer. After he finished he said, "I'm going out to the waiting room, and I'll see you again a little later. Being here for you is the most important thing I have to do today. May God's healing grace be with you."

Ed decided Harper's nonreactivity was normal in this situation. He couldn't read what all the things on the monitor behind his bed meant, but he had noticed there were no sudden or sharp changes in the lines or the beeps going on. He trusted Harper would receive whatever he was able to receive from this visit. He also hoped it would give Harper reassurance knowing that he was going to wait at the hospital until there were some answers. Ed found a phone booth and called home to tell Sally he would be at the hospital all afternoon, and possibly until late that night. She said she understood. They were all fine and Patty Swank had offered to drive them somewhere if they needed her.

The receptionist handed Ed a beeper and said she would let him know as soon as there was any news about Harper. He went to the car where he had a couple of books he had been trying to read. He had no sooner returned than the beeper went off. At the desk he found out Harper had been taken in to the operating room for bypass surgery. Ed went to the waiting room and settled in to read and wait. An hour later he looked up to see Jack Reilly and Jim Swank coming through the door. He got up and motioned them over to where he was. The first thing they wanted to know was about Harper's condition, and Ed explained what was going on.

"I'm glad you guys were able to come up here," he said. "I'm not sure how much Harper is hearing or taking in since he has been unresponsive, at least when I was with him, but your voices could reassure him that he has friends who are with him. I called the church and asked Louise to find out how to reach his sisters. She called back and said Fanny had the numbers and she would take care of it. Neither sister, of course, is able to travel, so he has no family here. Louise said his sister in Florida had been concerned about him because he seemed so depressed and preoccupied the whole time he was there last winter. We'll need to call them back after we know what's going on with him."

They found a more private section of the room and sat down. Jack said, "Since those two sisters are his only living relatives, Jim and I think it's really important that folks from the church visit, call, and stand behind Harper. It must be tough to be his age and going through a crisis with no immediate family nearby."

"I can understand his sister's concern. I've been puzzled about Harper for some time," said Jim. "He never was an overly joyful person, but he wasn't the bitter, angry person he has become lately—at least not in my experience."

"You're right about that," said Jack. "Barb and I feel especially close to him because he was the person who helped me get the loan to start my business. He came around a lot and encouraged us. As we got to be more involved in the church and community, he brought me into leadership, and it was because of him that I became treasurer. It's been hard to watch him change lately."

"That's helpful to me," said Ed. "I haven't quite known what was going on with him. There was an incident years ago when he apparently created some problems for Clara Jasper. I found something about that in the office and shared it with Jim. He sounded, at least in that situation, the same as he's been sounding lately."

"Well, he's always had a tendency to go that way," Jack said, "especially when he felt threatened or when he really wanted something he thought was good for the church but felt people were blocking him or not taking him seriously. But he didn't persist in it and stay on something like he has recently."

"We were talking about this driving up, and we both agreed that you have done a fantastic job in dealing with him," said Jim. "You've been firm yet open to him at the same time. I don't know how you do it."

"It takes prayer! His harsh words and actions have been very difficult for Sally, and the children feel it, too. I have wanted to keep a door open to find out what's really behind all this and get it resolved. Yesterday Billy thought he was a bully and wanted to punch him in the nose." They all laughed. "I told him Harper wasn't really a bully and there were better ways to deal with him than punching him in the nose. I hope Billy understands that as he grows up."

They both nodded, and Jack said, "Harper has a deep fear of things changing that he's worked for all his life. We know he didn't have a very happy marriage. I don't know what that was about, but I know he was actually more married to the church and town than to Annabelle. You know, his father was the founder of Liberty Savings and Loan, and Harper was mayor of the town at one time. He seems to have inherited a deep distrust of people who live in cities, as well as strangers in general. It's almost like he needs to feel in control of everything in order to feel safe and secure. He's a very complex person."

"That's really helpful, Jack. You're answering some of the questions Sally and I have been asking. You know, I hope he comes through this surgery okay and that it becomes a time for some softening of his spirit and calming of his anxieties. I am praying that he can make that change and have a few more years to enjoy life from a more positive perspective."

"Amen to that," said Jim.

"Ed, I owe you a personal apology," said Jack. "I let myself get so wrapped up in Harper that I haven't really given you a chance.

I apologize to you right here and now. I hope you'll forgive me and let me know how I can be supportive in your ministry. I think you really do have the best for Dinkel Island Church in your heart. I'm not sure whether I agree that the Weekend Spectacular should have been done, but it *was* done and the church leadership worked hard for it—and there seem to be some positive results. So I want to help take things forward from here positively, if you'll let me."

"Of course I'll let you! I deeply appreciate your apology, but you don't owe me that. You were honest and true to where you thought things stood, and I respect that. And sure, I welcome your support. I don't know what's ahead, but I know God has blessings to share, and we all need to be woven together in faith and trust for it to happen."

All three of them found things to read and settled down to wait out the surgery. After two more hours, the waiting room attendant came over to them and said Harper was out of surgery and in recovery. The doctor would be coming out to talk with them in a few minutes. The three of them joined hands and offered a prayer of thanksgiving. Ed looked at his watch. "Wow, it's been three and a half hours since they took him in. I wonder how long he'll be in recovery?"

About that time a doctor came in, still in his scrubs. "Are you all family members?" he asked after the attendant directed him to them.

"No, I'm his pastor, and these men are members of his church and very close to him. As far as we know he has no relatives living in the immediate area. My secretary at the church has been keeping in touch with his sisters in Michigan and Florida."

"Well, let me share this with you. Mr. Jauswell is very fortunate to be alive. He had a massive heart attack, and we had to do four bypasses. Things went well, but he will need some recovery time and as much freedom from stress as possible. Do you know if he's been under any kind of stress lately?"

"Yes," said Ed, "He's been upset over some things at the church and hasn't seemed able to reconcile himself to some changes that have happened."

"That could create enough stress to contribute to his heart attack, perhaps along with some other factors. Does he get much exercise, watch his diet?"

"We wouldn't know about that," said Jack. "He does have a housekeeper who cooks for him and sort of looks after him. Maybe we could talk with her about that."

"Before you leave we'll give you some information to share with her," said the doctor. "Meanwhile he will be in recovery for an hour or two then transferred to Cardiac Intensive Care. Visits there will be limited but could be very helpful to him."

All three men shook the doctor's hand and thanked him, and he left the room. It suddenly felt kind of anticlimactic, and then Ed said, "Looks like its supper time. Are you both staying to see him when he's in his room?"

"Yes," they both said.

Jim added, "We made arrangements to be here as long as needed."

"Then let's go to the cafeteria, and maybe after we eat we can get more of an idea when he'll be back in his room."

News about Harper's heart attack spread quickly around Dinkel Island. Cheryl called Lillie during the afternoon and told her Bob had heard about it in the store. Lillie called the church office and Louise told her what she knew. Lillie in turn called back to Cheryl and filled her in.

"Bob and I said we knew something was seriously wrong with that man when he was so upset at lunch Sunday. Does he live alone? There didn't seem to be anyone with him Sunday. Bob says he's well known in town and apparently has a lot of influence. We hope he's going to be all right."

"Louise said he had a heart attack right there in the pastor's office when he and another man came to talk about whatever was bothering him yesterday. I don't know how old he is, but a heart attack could change a lot about his life. Louise says he's in surgery now, so we hope he comes through okay."

"You know," said Cheryl "we really ought to pray for him. I mean, not just now, but throughout the day. I believe God hears and answers our prayers. And when we pray, I believe we should expect God to answer. Would you mind if I offered a prayer right now while we're on the phone?"

This was something totally out of Lillie's experience. She felt awkward, yet wasn't repelled by the idea. "Sure." She closed her eyes and bowed her head as Cheryl offered a prayer for Harper's surgery and recovery. "I've never done that before, but it feels good to do it. Thanks, Cheryl."

They talked a few more minutes about some other things then hung up. Stan was outside, and Lillie started for the door to tell him about the phone call when the phone rang again. This time it was Sarah Jones.

"Mrs. Grayson, this is Sarah Jones. I'm the president of the Women's Association at church. One of our older members, Harper Jauswell…well, you were at the Brunch Bunch Sunday, so you know who I mean—the older man who seemed so upset…"

"Yes, I know who he is."

"Did you know he had a heart attack this morning?"

"Yes, as a matter of fact, I just had a call about that and have talked to Louise in the church office."

"Good. Well, we in the association want to be supportive to Harper, and we've decided the best way to do that is to have a prayer vigil at the church. It will be at seven o'clock tonight in the sanctuary. We hope you and your husband can come."

"Yes, I'm sure we can. Thanks for the information. We've been concerned about him."

Lillie went outside and told Stan what was going on, so after supper they drove around to the church. There looked to be about fifty people gathered. Sarah Jones was in charge, along with Polly Allmond and Barb Reilly. Louise had printed up an order of service that included some prayers, scriptures, and hymns from the worship book. At the end of the service, they all stood and formed a circle, joining hands around the room, then offered one last prayer. Polly led them in singing "Alleluia" softly as they prepared to leave.

On the way home, Stan and Lillie agreed that the service had a very warm feeling to it and was a very positive experience. They both felt this kind of fellowship and support was something they had been missing in their lives. They were glad they had gone and that they were connecting with Dinkel Island Wesleyan Brethren Church. They had a lot to learn and experience, but it gave them a sense of peace and wholeness. They both hoped Harper Jauswell would come out of surgery and the hospital with a fresh sense of life and maybe some of his rigid, argumentative nature would be changed through this. It was certainly worthy hoping and praying for.

16

A Knock on
the Door

One thing in the background of Harper's heart attack had occurred just two weeks earlier, and nobody in Dinkel Island knew anything about it. He had received a very troubling phone call from his sister Hattie in Florida.

"Harper," she had said, "I'm so confused. A man came to my door and said he was my son. I thought you said all of that was settled years ago and he would have a good family and never know about me. How could this happen?

Harper felt panic rise up within himself. *What in tarnation is this about?*

"I did take care of that!" he said. "I told you all about it. How did this guy find you?"

"He says his middle name is Jauswell—Mark Jauswell Howard. He's from California."

The California part connected, as did the last name. *I paid good money for this arrangement.* Harper fumed. *Why'd they go and tell him who his mother is?*

"He wasn't ever supposed to know anything about you or me. He wasn't supposed to have the Jauswell name at all."

Harper felt enraged. *All I wanted to do was keep my sister from having an abortion and find a good home for the baby. You can't trust anybody! I'll sue them!*

Heaving a sigh and calming down a notch, Harper said, "How did he find you?"

"He said he had wondered where his middle name came from but always got vague answers when he asked. Then his parents were in an accident, and before his mother died, she told him who I was."

"She wasn't supposed to know who you are!"

"Well, somehow she did. He knows who you are, too, and says he's coming to see you."

"That's all I need," said Harper.

"What?"

"I'm sorry. It's just that I've got a lot of trouble up here right now, and I don't want to have to deal with this on top of it.'

"He seems so nice," said Hattie, her tone softening. "He dresses well, drives a fancy black car that looks expensive, and says he's an accountant. He's also a Christian and went to church with me."

"Humph! You didn't give him any money, did you?"

"He didn't ask for any money. He just wanted to get to know me. He's my son."

"So he might be. If he comes up here, I'll grill him and get to the bottom of this."

"He's on his way there now. I'm sort of glad to get to know him. I never should have given him up. I should have found a way to keep him."

Harper could hear Hattie going soft on him. He got her off the phone as soon as he could. His body felt tense and his thoughts were racing. The last thing he wanted was for this old scandal of his sister's affair with a married man to surface in Dinkel Island and put a blot on his reputation.

It was nearly midnight when Ed got home from the hospital. When he left, Harper had been stable but he wasn't having an easy time of it. Nobody knew what his prospects were for a full recovery. One thing Ed was sure about was that he had a lot of changes to embrace or he ultimately would not live through this.

The next morning Ed and Sally tried to catch up on things and deal with the fact that he had to take the car back to Potomac City again. He thought they should talk to Steve Tyrone and see if he had some old car that was fairly dependable on the lot that they might be able to buy. "I don't want to put more pressure on us, honey," said Ed, "but every time we have a situation that takes me to Potomac City day after day, you're stuck here and *that* puts pressure on us. I'll stop by Steve's dealership and mention it after I drop you at school and before I leave town this morning. Maybe we can get back with him in a few days and work something out."

"Thanks, honey. I didn't get to tell you yesterday, but there's a rumor we will lose an English teacher at the high school this summer. I'm making sure my name is in the pot if that happens. A full-time position would mean more intense work but certainly less financial stress for us. Let's pray about all of this today, okay?"

"Absolutely! In fact, let's start right now asking God for guidance and clarity of judgment." After they prayed together he took her to the high school and then stopped by Tyrone Chevrolet. Steve was in his office. When he heard it was Ed who wanted to see him, he came right out.

"Ed, good to see you. What's up? You're not ready to turn in that old Plymouth for a real car, are you?"

"As a matter of fact, that's what I want to talk about. I don't have much time now since I need to get back to Potomac City to check on Harper—"

Steve interrupted, "Yes, how is Harper doing? We heard he had a bad heart attack. Is he recovering okay?"

"I can't really tell you how he is today. He had a rough day yesterday, and he is in intensive care and very sedated. That's why I just wanted to ask you to think about this so maybe tomorrow Sally and I can talk with you."

"That's fine. What do you have in mind?"

"We *don't* want to trade in the Plymouth," said Ed. "I know it's getting old, but our problem is trying to handle all the demands on my time and Sally's and the children's needs when I'm away so often and so unpredictably. We were wondering if you have something old that's been traded in yet is in fairly good condition, and not too expensive. I know that's asking a lot."

"No, it's not any particular problem for me to do that, but it might bring you a new set of problems. So far you've been fortunate not to have breakdowns or repairs on that car. What is it, a seventy-nine?"

"Yes, it is. What kind of new problems?"

"Well, if you're running two older cars, you have double the chance for major breakdowns and repairs."

"Oh, yeah, another added expense. We have thought about the extra costs involved with having two cars, but we missed that one."

"What would probably serve you better would be to buy a new car that has a three-year, thirty-six thousand mile warranty on it. Then use the other one strictly as a spare, so you reduce the chances for major problems."

"Oh, I know you're right about that, but this is already a stretch. We can't possibly afford a new car right now. Maybe we can in another year, or sooner if Sally happens to get a permanent teaching position at the high school."

"Okay, I understand what you're saying. But before you go, let me just give you something to ponder. Let me show you one of the new Malibu's and show you the sticker price so you at least have all the information when you and Sally are talking."

"Really, I have to go."

"I know. I'll walk you to the parking lot, and on the way I happen to have a blue Malibu on the floor that's in the medium-price range. At least look at it on your way out, and we'll talk tomorrow or whenever you're ready."

"Well, okay, since it's right here."

Ed looked at the Malibu. It was roomier than the Volare, a four-door sedan with a small V-8 engine. He noted the price and said he and Sally would be back in touch. Then he left and drove up to Potomac City, thinking all the way up about how much more comfortable a ride that car would have. Then he chided himself for thinking that way, reminding himself that caution was necessary. They would have to insist on an older, cheaper car.

When he got to Harper's room, not much had changed. Harper was still heavily sedated, and Ed could not interact with him. He did ask Harper, if he heard and understood him, to squeeze his hand. He thought he felt a very light squeeze. Ed knew that often comatose patients took in more of what people said around them than others realized, and that could either help or hinder the recovery process. So he chose his words carefully and prayed briefly with Harper. He told him about the prayer vigil that had been held at church and that he had many friends who were praying for him constantly. It may have been his imagination, but Harper's hand seemed to relax ever so slightly. Ed left, promising to visit again the next day.

That night he told Sally about his conversation with Steve and his suggestion that they consider a new, middle-of-the-line Malibu. He told her about glancing at a car like that in the showroom as he was leaving but said he really thought this was out of the question.

She seemed receptive as they talked about it some more.

The next morning Steve showed Sally the same car in the showroom and let them both test drive it. It seemed just right, so Ed said, "Okay. Let's do it." Sally seemed relaxed and cheerful as she drove home in a brand new car, followed by Ed in the old one. When the kids got home from school, they couldn't believe it, and the whole family went out for a drive.

Later that afternoon, Ed drove his old car up to Potomac City and found Harper showing some improvement. He still had all the equipment hooked up and wasn't talking, but his eyes were open. Ed did not see any signs of fear or anger in his eyes. He seemed calm. It was like he was a different person. Ed complimented him on making some improvement and prayed with him that God's miraculous healing power would continue to work in him and that Harper would be open to God's Spirit. When he finished and was ready to leave, Harper actually squeezed his hand. Ed felt relieved and thanked God for what he saw happening.

Out in the waiting room were several people from the church. He talked with them for a while and thanked them for their faith and support. As a pastor Ed had been able to go in to see Harper regardless of visiting hours, but these folks had to wait for the appropriate time. They had been going for brief visits two at a time. There was a very positive feeling among them, and they expressed faith in God's healing presence. They also told Ed there was another shift of folks coming for the evening visitation. Ed felt refreshed and inspired at this caring initiative among his congregation. When he got home, he told Sally about all of this, and they prayed again for Harper and for their congregation before they went to bed.

Fanny heard the doorbell ring and went to see who it was. There on the porch stood a handsome man with dark wavy hair and a mustache, dressed in a dark suit. Looking past him she saw a shiny black car in the driveway. She nearly panicked at the thought that Harper had died and this man was from the funeral home. But she pulled herself together and opened the door.

"Hello! My name is Mark Jauswell Howard. I am Mr. Jauswell's nephew. Is he in?"

Fanny tensed up immediately. She'd never heard Harper speak of having a nephew. The man in front of her was soft spoken and seemed unthreatening, but she didn't budge from the door frame or ask him in.

"Forgive me, ma'am. Here…" He pulled out his wallet, which contained his California driver's license with his picture. It certainly was the same person she was looking at.

"You say you're from California, and I see you are, but how did you get here? Why didn't we know you was comin'? I've been Mr. J's housekeeper for a long time, and he's never mentioned you. How come you show up here all of a sudden?"

"I understand your questions. I would feel the same way if I were in your shoes. I've just come in from Florida where I spent a few days with my mother, Hattie. I left there three days ago and took a room at the Grande Hotel when I got into town. What a nice town you have, and this house…what a gem."

"I've been talkin' to Hattie every day since Harper's been in the hospital, and she never mentioned you once."

"Uncle Harper's in the hospital? Why? What happened? When did he go in?"

"What happened is he had a heart attack day before yesterday. He had surgery and is in the Nor'easter General Hospital up in Potomac City."

"A heart attack! Oh! I'm so sorry. Is there something I can do?"

"Well, I think the first thing you can do is explain yourself more to my satisfaction. I'm goin' to call Miss Hattie. You stay right here on this porch while I go in and do that, and then I'll get right back to you." With that she closed the door and went to the phone and called Hattie. "You don't have anything to be afraid of with Mark," said Hattie, "just please don't let him go to visit Harper at the hospital, and don't let word out about who he is."

That seemed strange, and it was a tall order, since nobody kept secrets like that at Dinkel Island, but she would try. She wished she knew what was going on and decided she would offer Mark supper there at the house. Maybe she could find out a little more about things.

Fanny went back to the door. "I'm sorry I put you through that," she told Mark, "but I had to be sure, especially with him in the hospital and all. Miss Hattie says you are who you say you are, and she said you left before she got the call about Harper's heart attack. She also said she thought if you visited him it might upset him, so to ask you to not go to the hospital to see him. Maybe if we give this a few days he will be stronger and ready to see you when he gets home."

"Oh, that's a disappointment, but I understand. I certainly will respect your wishes."

"I appreciate that. Thanks."

"You're quite welcome. You said you don't know much about me, so let me tell you a little more. I'm an accountant by profession, and I'm in the process of relocating here, so I'll be looking for a job and a place to settle. Since I can't see Uncle Harper right now, I think I'll take a few days and drive up to Washington, DC, and see if I can get any leads on a job. Finding a job will help me know where to settle down."

"Well, you do what you need to do, and thanks for honorin' Ms. Hattie's—I mean your mother's—request. I think she knows what's best right now."

"I do want to pray for him," said Mark. "That's the best visit we can make—to pray with and for each other. Do you mind if I do that right now—if we do it together?"

Fanny blushed. She was shy about praying out loud and told him so, but he said he would do the talking if they might join hands and let her spirit be connected with God's Spirit as he prayed. She agreed. He offered a beautiful prayer for Harper and for her, too. After he finished, Fanny invited him to come back to the house for supper. He said he'd be there.

Back at the hotel, Mark undressed and carefully hung his suit in the closet, then showered and freshened up before taking a nap. He called room service and ordered a bottle of wine. He really felt like a stiff belt of whiskey would prop up his courage, but that didn't seem to be a good idea in a small town where everybody probably knew everybody else and what they did. Wine would do and probably wasn't noteworthy for gossip. This was a critical time in his visit. *Wish I'd known about this heart attack earlier,* he thought. *I could have gone right to the hospital first.* He drank a glass of wine then lay down for a nap before dressing and preparing to meet with Fanny again. *She certainly is a unique character,* he mused, *kind of what I always pictured long-term family service staff people to be like. And she is very loyal to Harper. I've got to handle her very carefully.*

Mark arrived at the Jauswell house right on time at six-thirty Fanny had set the dining room table for two and had prepared a meal the likes of which he had only read about in books. The menu consisted of a tossed salad made with fresh produce, roasted Ribeye of beef au jus, a baked potato, freshly baked rolls, squash, butter beans, and iced tea. It was more food than Mark had seen at one meal in a long time. This was a whole different world from eating in restaurants. Fanny herself actually looked charming in a skirt and blouse with a sweater, modest heels, and fresh makeup, with her hair combed and modestly styled. She was a little stout and appeared to him to be in her early forties and probably had a rather restricted social life. With Harper in the hospital, Mark figured she had probably been eating alone in the kitchen and even one guest in the house was an occasion to really fix a meal.

"Fanny, this is about the best meal I've ever had! I'm surprised you went to so much trouble just for one person."

"Well, like you told me, you're not just *any* person. You're Harper's *nephew*, so I wanted to treat you like family. Besides, I needed an excuse to use up some of the food."

"All my life I've heard about southern hospitality. I guess this is what that's all about."

They ate at a leisurely pace, and then she served him peach pie a-la-mode and coffee. When they finished he offered to help her clear up all the dishes and clean up the kitchen. At first she was reluctant then let him help her. They talked about life at Dinkel Island, about her history and how long she had been at the Jauswell's, and about Annabelle. Then they went into the living room and continued their conversation. They seemed to find a lot to talk about, and suddenly Mark realized it was after ten o'clock.

"Look at the time, Fanny. This has been such a delightful time. Thank you so much for the delicious meal and for letting me help clean up afterward. You have helped me to feel like I belong here, and I appreciate that. I hope you're more at ease now with my suddenly showing up."

"Yes, I think I am. I've enjoyed this. It was such a nice change from the usual."

"Well, I must get back to the hotel and get some sleep. I want to leave early for Washington tomorrow."

When he got in his room, he drank a glass of wine and thought back over how his plan was working. Things looked promising!

Then he thought, *Maybe on my way out of town I should drive around a bit to get more of a feel for this place. Maybe I should go around to Harper's church and get to know the preacher. If I get in good with the reverend, I'll have a much better time of it with everyone else.*

17

Foot's in the Door

The next day Mark called Fanny from Washington and said he had a line on a possible job. He said he'd be back in town later in the afternoon, and he was anxious to find out how Uncle Harper was doing. Fanny said she had just had a call and Harper might be released the next morning. Mark thanked her and said he would check in with her when he got back.

The job possibility was better than he could have ever hoped for. A regional insurance agency with an office in Dinkel Island had a bookkeeping vacancy occurring there in July. Although Mark presented himself as an accountant and had some forged documents to back up his claim, his actual experience was in bookkeeping. The persona he took on was convincing enough that he got the job.

When Ed got to the hospital Friday morning he found good news. Harper was going to be released later that morning, and he was like a different person. He had actually welcomed Ed's visit on Thursday, and they had enjoyed a very positive conversation. Today he was even more positive.

"Pastor Heygood, thank you for being here these last few days. I'm not sure how you could do it after the way I've treated you."

"You can call me Ed, Harper. I prefer that. It's more personal. As your pastor I want the best for you, and I hope we can relate on a friendship level. I'm here because God's love is here, and he has called me to make that love visible to everyone I can."

"I've heard words like *grace, love,* and *forgiveness* all my life, but I haven't really let them sink in," said Harper. "These last few days have made a difference in me. Can I tell you what happened when I was in surgery?"

"Sure! If you want to talk, I'm happy to listen."

"Well it was like I had died and wasn't even in my own body. In fact, I seemed to sort of expand. I was aware of what everybody around me was sayin' and even what they were feelin'. I felt *connected* with them. I could look at myself and see what was goin' on, but I seemed not to be a part of it. Does any of this make sense? It's really hard to put into words."

"Yes, it does. I have heard of people experiencing such things. Please, go on."

"Okay. Well, it seemed like all of that faded and a bright light began to fill the space around me. Suddenly I seemed to be in a kind of tunnel. And there was an overwhelmin' feeling of love, forgiveness, and acceptance. I didn't feel I had to explain myself but all my sins and shortcomin's were just there, along with the good parts of my life. Like somehow I had entered a whole different *kind* of life. Then all at once, I saw Jesus. He was there, just like that. He called me by name and said he loved me, and he told me everything I was experiencin' was yet to be, but this wasn't quite the right time. He told me I would recover and be all right, and I would come back there later. He said I wasn't finished in my earthly life."

The emotion in Harper's voice and his whole body was apparent. Tears of joy kept filling his eyes. He had an almost radiant look as he told this story. It was a man Ed had not seen, and he wondered if anyone who knew him had ever seen this side of the man.

"What a fantastic experience, Harper! What a wonderful assurance of God's grace and his promise to you. You have had a wonderful privilege to experience this."

"I start to feel like there must be some mistake. I don't deserve this. Then I remember his words—such *clear* words—that I don't hafta *earn* his love. I already have it. All I have to do is *trust* him to take care of things and show me the way."

Ed was almost beside himself with joy at these words coming from the same man who had cursed him and run him out of his house just a few weeks before—who had been stirring distrust and confusion in the congregation. *Only God can do this*, he thought. Then he said it out loud, "Harper, this is a miracle. It's a miracle of God's love, the kind of love *only God* can do. The kind of love that *changes* people from the inside out."

"Yes, it is! And that word *change*. I've hated it and feared it all my life. I realize all of a sudden that I've *said* I had faith, but it was just words on pieces of paper that I said I believed in. But I didn't really have faith deep inside. Now I want to get it, and I want you to help me. I did say awful things to you and about you. *I'm so sorry*. I mean that."

"I know you mean it, Harper. I more than accept your apology."

"That might have been how I felt *then*, but it was wrong. I don't feel that way now. I want to get to know you and for you to help me learn to trust God, instead of myself, in everything. I tell you, when you've been where I was a couple of days ago, you just feel different about everythin'. God has given me a chance to get this right, and I wanna do it. I was always afraid of change and tried to do everything in my power to stop it, but now *I want to change!* Please help me."

All the tubes and wires had been disconnected from him, and Harper was sitting up in a chair. Ed went over and put his arm around his shoulder and said, "Let's pray, right now. Let's give thanks and put you and me and everything else strictly in God's hands."

"Okay," Harper said. He reached out to take Ed's left hand in his, so they prayed hand-in-hand.

As they finished they heard movement, and a voice said, "Mr. Jauswell, I'm Doctor Maxwell." Harper and Ed looked up."

"Mr. Jauswell, we're ready to release you. Do you have some-one here to take you home?"

"I can call my housekeeper, and she'll get someone to take—"

"No need for that, Harper. I can take you home," said Ed.

"Oh, well, that would be great."

"Okay, then," Dr. Maxwell went on, "I'll need to have a few words with you privately to go over your stay here and what you need to do as you go home—what you can look forward to."

"Can Ed stay? He's my pastor, and that's as good as family to me. I might need to have a second pair of ears to remem-ber everythin'."

"Well, I guess so at your request. And we will give you written instructions to take with you."

"Okay."

Dr. Maxwell filled Harper in on the details of his condition and what to expect during recovery. Then he asked, "Do you have someone to help you get around if needed?"

"I have my housekeeper, Fanny," said Harper.

"He also has a church family with lots of folks who will help out," said Ed.

"Good. Don't hesitate to call me if you need anything."

Shortly after the doctor left, Harper was discharged, and Ed took him back to Dinkel Island.

Ed called Fanny before they left the hospital so she would be prepared for Harper's return. "You can expect some changes in Harper. He came into the hospital with a heart attack, and he's coming home with a changed heart."

"What do you mean?"

"You'll see when he arrives. Just be prepared for some pleasant surprises."

"There's a change here that I need to tell you about," said Fanny. "Harper has a nephew from out in California who has come to town to see him. He was here the other day then went up to DC, and I think he'll be coming back to see Harper tonight. You better warn him. He gets pretty upset over things like that."

"Okay, what's his name?"

"It's Mark. Mark Howard, I think."

"Don't worry about that. I'll talk to Harper, and I believe everything will be fine."

On the way home Ed mentioned this. Harper said, "Oh, I forgot about that. My sister Hattie called from Orlando just before I had my heart attack. It's a long story, but I got upset with her. I'll need to make amends for that. As for Mark, I've never seen him, so it will be good to get acquainted." Then he told Ed the whole story about Hattie and how he paid for an adoption. "I've got a lot of fences to mend, don't I?"

"You do, God being your helper. Remember, you don't have to control it or do it on your own. God is greater than any problem or need we have, and he already has the solution. Just stay connected with him through Christ, and trust him."

❧

Mark called Fanny when he got back into Dinkel Island. She told him Harper was home but he needed rest and they had a lot of things to do learning to take care of him, so it would be best if Mark came in the morning. Mark agreed. He felt relieved that Harper was back and things seemed positive. As he went to bed later he said to himself, *Okay! Foot's in the door! First step accomplished!*

18

Golf and Going Forward

When Ed visited Harper on Saturday he found him cheerful, positive and excited about his nephew. "I would like for you to meet Mark," said Harper. "I'll give you a call when he comes by later."

"I'll look forward to meeting him, but I can't do it today. I do have some time Monday morning," said Ed.

"Oh, that's fine. If that doesn't suit him, I'm sure you can find another time. Mark has found a job and will be settling in here. I'm sure you'll see plenty of him in weeks to come. You know, it's just a miracle: in the last week I've had a heart attack, almost stepped into heaven itself, then as I'm getting a new chance in life, I discover a relative I hadn't remembered, and he's even planning to live here. I can't tell you how much all that means to me."

"It's amazing what can happen when we step back and let God control things instead of trying to do it all ourselves, isn't it?"

"If anyone had told me I'd be sayin' this two weeks ago, I'd have jumped all over 'em, but what you say is true. I'm just beginnin' to learn to trust God, and already he's worked miracles I couldn't have imagined. I can't wait to see what else he has in store for me."

"A word of caution, though. Bad things still happen, and hard times aren't erased by God. But now you *know* God's in charge, even when you can't see it directly. You know that when you suffer, God suffers with you. He goes through the pain as well as the joy with you."

"Thanks, Ed," said Harper. "I've got a lot to learn, but I'm into learnin' it now, and I'm a better man for it."

Ed met Mark when he introduced himself as he was leaving after the worship service on Sunday.

"Good morning, Pastor Heygood. What a great service! I'm Harper Jauswell's nephew, Mark Howard."

"Well, it's good to meet you, Mark. Harper's really been excited about having you here in town. Did you spend some time with him yesterday?"

"I sure did. I hear he's a different man since his heart attack. I hope he and I will be good for each other."

"I'm sure you will. I understand you moved here from California. What were you doing out there?"

"Oh, I grew up in LA then moved to Laguna Beach after college. Until now I've always lived in California. I was adopted, you see. Before she died my mom told me who my real mother was and connected me up with Uncle Harper. It just seems natural to stay here now where I have family."

"There's nothing like family ties! By the way, Harper tells me you've gotten a job here. When do you start that?"

"Not until July first, which gives me some time to get better acquainted with people here in town."

"So where will you be living?"

"Right now I'm staying at the Grande Hotel, but that can't go on much longer. Do you know of any places that might be available?"

"You know, Harper has a pretty large house. Perhaps he'd let you stay with him until you get settled into a place of your own?"

"Well, that did occur to me, and I need to talk to Uncle Harper about it. I'm sure I could be of some help to him, but then he has Fanny. She seems pretty capable."

"I believe you'll work things out. It's good to meet you." Ed went back to his office. He was surprised when Mark knocked on the outer office door then poked his head inside. "Pastor Heygood?"

"Oh, Mark, I thought you'd left."

"I did, but I was thinking. I belong to an independent community church back home and I'm going to want to be in a church here. I really don't know much about the Wesleyan Brethren denomination. Do you have something I could read about it?"

Ed gave him a couple of pamphlets and said, "I will be offering a membership orientation class week after next. Maybe I could include you with that class?"

"Hey, that would be great. Praise the Lord! Thank you."

With that, Mark left again. Ed mused to himself, *That's an interesting man, but he seems a little too quick to step into things. I'll have to keep an ear out about him.*

❧

Monday morning Randy Adams from Mammoth Baptist Church called Ed and asked if he'd be interested in playing nine holes of golf at the Grande Hotel course on Wednesday. Ed hadn't played in years but decided it might be a chance to connect more positively with Randy, so he said he'd do it. Ed had actually forgotten about his old clubs stored out in the parsonage garage. They met at the golf course as agreed. The weather was perfect, in the low sixties with a clear sky and subtle breeze. It was a nine-hole course. The tee boxes, greens, and fairways were well kept. Clusters of trees sporadically bordered the fairways, and a view of the water made the course interesting. The longest hole was 425 yards, and the shortest 95 yards. Randy and Ed loaded their clubs in the cart and went to the first tee box.

Randy, who played the course frequently, led off with a beautiful, straight shot. Ed stepped up and tried to deliver a relaxed swing that would let the club do the work. Unfortunately, he was too tense and sent a short, low drive that sliced off into a wooded section less than a hundred yards down range.

"As you can see, I really am out of practice," he told Randy.

"Who wouldn't be after not playing for…how many years did you say?"

"I'm not sure, but at least seven or eight."

"Well, I think you have a lot of courage to come out and try. It'll come back to you. Just give yourself a chance to get into the feel of the game again."

"I don't like being in those trees down there. Let's go find the ball."

It was a rough start, but with that behind him, Ed felt his body relax a bit more. His game didn't improve much, although he did gain some experience chipping out of sand traps. Randy outclassed him with his game, but they both laughed about it. Randy said it was all about fellowship anyway, so what did the score matter?

It did turn out to be about more than fellowship. As the two men talked during the course of the game, Ed found out what was on Randy's mind. He had been hearing a lot of talk about the mistake Ed had made by including Jimbo on the platform of the Wedding Pier.

"I know that was a brave thing the groom did by jumpin' in and savin' Jimbo from drownin', but that shoulda been the end of it. It's not my place to criticize anyone else's judgment or actions, but I thought you might not know how the locals feel about these things. I expect Mr. Jauswell in your church has probably spoken to you about this by now, too."

"We had a conversation," Ed replied.

"Oh, I understand he had a heart attack and is back home now and expected to do well. He's always been a pillar of this community so we all feel like we know him personally. I'm glad he's doing okay."

"Yes, Harper is doing very well. Actually, we're all surprised at how resilient he is, and he has a more positive and relaxed mood than I've ever seen him have."

"You're kidding! He's a fine man, but everybody knows how his temper can flare. I don't think I ever heard anyone speak of him as relaxed, either. That's quite a surprise!"

"I think the heart attack really got his attention," said Ed, "and I know his doctor had a talk with him about adjusting his lifestyle to avoid stress. I just think Harper was probably scared by this—who wouldn't be—and it really got his attention."

"Well, that's great. We'll keep him in our prayers."

"I'm sure he will appreciate that. Now, Randy, about Jimbo—"

"Oh, you don't have to tell me about that," Randy interrupted.

"No, I don't *need* to, but I want to clarify something for you. Stan Grayson talked to me about asking Jimbo to stand with him and Lillie, and I encouraged him to do it. I knew some people might get their feathers ruffled, but that happens easily with many issues, so I don't play to that. It seems to me the gospel clearly calls us to love unconditionally, as Christ loves us. I don't think race, nationality, gender, or social class has any bearing on that. Jimbo didn't really feel comfortable, but he finally agreed to it, and that was between him and the bride and groom. I supported that all the way and make no apologies for it."

This was like a bombshell going off with Randy Adams. Ed wasn't sure what his deeper thinking was, but his practical attitude seemed obvious—don't offend anyone, and don't transgress on tradition. That was not Ed's way of doing ministry, so he thought he might as well get that out up front.

Randy said, "Oh, don't get me wrong. I'm not looking for apologies. You did what you thought was right, and I admire you for taking your stand. But you gotta keep in mind where the locals stand on things if you want to succeed at Dinkel Island."

Ed decided to sidestep that comment, and said, "Randy, I've enjoyed the golf. Thanks for the invitation. Hope we can do this again, maybe even invite a couple of other guys, too. And I thank you for speaking directly to me about what was on your mind. I hope we can always have that kind of clarity."

"Yes, well, you have a great week, and we'll get together again sometime." With that they both left the golf course.

When Ed got back to his office, he had a phone message from Jim Swank. He said he had a couple of things he needed to talk over and wondered if Ed had some time that afternoon. Ed told him to come on to the office as soon as he was ready.

Jim arrived an hour later and got right to the point. "First, I just want to express my gratitude, and I think that of most people at church, for the way you have worked with Harper these last couple of weeks. I've never seen such a change as there is in him. I know you didn't do that, but you certainly did hang in there when things were tough and keep the door open."

"I appreciate your thoughts, Jim. I'm as much overwhelmed with Harper's change of heart as anyone. He seems to have had a truly deep spiritual experience that is impacting his whole life. I'm sure he's going to tell us about that himself one of these days when he's ready."

"Well, I hope so," said Jim. "The second thing I wanted to say has to do with the Weekend Spectacular—"

"Oh, I'm glad you're bringing that up," Ed interrupted. "I've been wanting to get back to that issue."

"I think we need to measure the results and see what steps are needed to make that experience have some lasting impact," said Jim.

Ed thought about that a minute. "You're right. We need to look at what has come from it and what might yet come from it. Harper's heart attack did get our attention sidetracked, and we need to get this back in focus. Got any ideas how to do that?"

"What about having a meeting this Sunday afternoon? It's short notice, but I can reach everyone by phone and most of us can probably meet for a while. Maybe do it right after the Brunch Bunch."

"Hmmm. I get the impression the Brunch Bunch kind of guides the decisions around here—"

"Well now, I'm not sure I'd go that far," Jim interjected.

"That's okay. I'm just saying I know how things work here, so I'm wondering if we can't pick up on that in a positive way—like maybe combining the board meeting with the Brunch Bunch gathering, opening discussion to everyone there and seeing where it goes. If something comes out of that where a vote is needed, have just the board members vote. That keeps it legal, and everybody has a chance to feel heard. You know, if I'd have known about the Brunch Bunch earlier and we had taken this approach, I'll bet we wouldn't have had as much reactivity to the Weekend Spectacular. Or who knows, we might not even have done it!"

"Actually, that's sort of how things are done now, but it's not an open process. I don't go to the Brunch Bunch gathering regularly, but sometimes when I've been there, a discussion has taken place about something the board is planning to vote on. They get into a discussion and build a consensus from peoples' comments that they take to the board meeting later. What you're talking about is another way of making that same thing happen. So yes, I guess it could work. I could call the board members and explain the idea to them and see how they feel. If they agree, then I'd say let's do it."

"Okay, then. I'll wait to hear back from you after you talk to the board members."

"Actually, I'll put Sarah Jones on the calling detail," said Jim. "She loves to do that kind of thing, and she'll do it faster than I could."

∿

Within two days Sarah had talked to everyone and the idea had been enthusiastically received. When Sunday rolled around the Brunch Bunch was better attended than it had been in weeks. The level of chatter was high, and the atmosphere seemed positive. Harper Jauswell wasn't able to attend but he had talked over his thoughts with Ed, Steve, Jack, and Jim. He was pleased they had offered him the opportunity to have some input. When an appropriate time came in the discussion, Ed shared Harper's feelings.

"Harper said to ask your forgiveness for his outbursts—those are his words—when y'all talked about the Weekend Spectacular. He said he's had time to reflect on a lot of things lately and he had to admit he had missed the whole point of why we did the program and what it could mean to people other than himself. So he wants you to know he's in support of whatever we plan as a follow-up. His main concern was that we not delay but get right into this. He said to tell you he's been reminded that life is too short to get sidetracked by petty disagreements. We need to have a vision for the future and go forward with God's help."

The others who had been with Ed and Harper nodded their agreement that Ed was right on target about Harper's sentiments. Several around the room commented to one another about what a change this was. Then somebody asked, "Have there been any real results from the weekend—anything measurable?"

"If you count six new members who will join our church next Sunday as measurable, then yes, there have been," Ed responded.

"Who are they?" someone asked.

"I don't think that's confidential information, so I'll tell you." He named a couple who had just moved into Crabbers Creek Estates, plus the Graysons and Drews.

"The Graysons and Drews are a direct result of the Weekend Spectacular. In fact, Lillie said it was pivotal in her willingness to join a church at all. So these are definitely measurable results."

The group discussed this then Jim Swank said, "Isn't this a little off from the kind of results we wanted? I mean this is about measuring numbers and statistics, but I thought we wanted something deeper than that to happen in our church. I think that hope stood behind lots of us pitching in and making this happen."

"Well, there's nothing wrong with getting new members," said Jill Upton.

"No, of course not," Jim Swank agreed, "but there has to be more to it. We have to not only look at what new people might bring us in strength, talents, and money, but don't we also have to look at what we're offering them? What is there, past an exciting weekend that was really different, that we have to offer newcomers? Maybe we should be thinking *spiritually* about this."

"Do you mean we should have more prayer meetin's and such?" asked Polly.

"Not necessarily," answered Jim. "Maybe nothing quite so formal. I'm not sure what I'm talking about, but that's why we're putting our heads together today—to figure out what we want and what we do next."

Ed stepped into the conversation. "I like the way we're thinking here, and I wonder if it might help to consider what our church is really all about. Surely it's not all about a building, music, Sunday morning worship, Sunday school, vacation Bible school, Women's Association, bake sales and such.

If that's all it is, what's different from the Ruritan Club or the Kiwanis? I think Jesus calls us to examine ourselves in his presence and make changes in our lives with his help. Then he calls us to reach out to other in his name.

The Palm Sunday experience gives us a way to reach some folks who might never hear the message of Christ in a life-changing way. We're called to open our fellowship so we can share a common journey into God's love that puts him at the center of what our lives are about."

There was complete silence for a few minutes, and then people began to buzz with individual conversations around the room. Finally Jack said, "I think that's exactly what we need to be doing. I guess I didn't see that in the beginning. I was opposed to it because I thought it was just another program, and an expensive one at that. I think Harper was upset about it because he thought it was something that would change our church into a club instead of a church that he thought was doing what it was supposed to do. From what he says now, this discussion we're having is more where he would want us to go. So what kind of things can we do from here on to build spiritually on the foundation of Palm Sunday?"

This launched some lively discussion, and finally Jim called things back to order. "Why don't we form a committee? We'll call it the 'What's Next?' committee to explore this whole issue and bring some ideas back to us for discussion three weeks from today."

That idea struck both positive and negative chords. On the negative side were a couple of grumbles about "No, not more meetings! That's what we always do is form a committee, and it ends there."

The positive response was stronger, however, with several people beginning to mention things the committee could talk about, or things they had done in the past, or things they had seen or heard in other churches. Finally Jim was able to get a consensus that this committee should be formed and put to work right away.

"Now the question is," said Jim, "who wants to serve on this? Who wants to step forward and make this work?"

Usually it was hard to get people to serve on committees, but this time several jumped right in. Sarah Jones offered to chair the group, and she was immediately accepted for the job. Jim made a list of all those who volunteered and gave it to her so she could get things organized. I think we need to honor the way we said we'd do this, folks. We're all agreed about this, but I think we need a formal vote, so let me ask the board members who are here to take that vote." They did, and it was unanimous. Jim thanked them all for taking time to be there and wished them God's blessings in their tasks. Ed closed the meeting with prayer, and everyone left.

19

What's Next?

Sarah called Lillie Grayson. "I hope I'm not pushin' y'all with what I'm gonna ask, since y'all just now joined the church, but that's why I called right away. I'm in charge of a committee that's tryin' to find out how to keep the spirit of the Palm Sunday Weekend Spectacular alive and growin'."

Lillie said, "That sounds like a good idea."

"What I'm callin' about is to ask y'all to be part of the committee." Sarah was often criticized for being too blunt, but she usually got results and her bluntness saved a lot of time.

Lillie asked Sarah to hold on a minute while she told Stan what Sarah wanted.

"Why not?" said Stan without hesitation. "We're part of this church now. Let's get involved. What do you say?"

"I say let's do it! You're right about getting involved."

So Lillie told Sarah, "Sure, we'd be happy to help out. Will you be meeting soon?"

"Yes, we don't have much time to get some basic ideas together. Come on over to my house Tuesday night, seven o'clock."

"We'll be there. By the way, I know someone else who might be interested."

"Oh, who is that?"

"Cheryl Drew. We were all together at the Weekend Spectacular, and we've become friends. She and Bob were as impressed as Stan and I that the church stepped out and did something like that program. You can tell her I suggested you call her."

"We had thought about asking her, so yes, I'll do that. Hope we see all of y'all at the meetin' Tuesday." With that Sarah hung up. A little later Lillie called Cheryl, and they both felt a stirring of fresh excitement.

∾

The Graysons and Drews weren't the only ones feeling excited on this Sunday evening. Mark had been invited to Harper's for supper. He had again enjoyed Fanny's cooking and, he had to admit to himself, her presence. She was different from any woman he'd ever dated—or even known. In his California world, the women he met were more on the wild side, partying a lot, with seldom any depth to their conversation. Fanny was totally opposite of all that, and he never would have thought he could be the least bit interested in someone like her.

Mark knew how to play a good role and how to win people's confidence. At first that was how he had approached Fanny that day he showed up at the Jauswell house. It had been the invitation to supper that evening and the time they spent talking afterward that had sparked something inside him he had never felt before. As he came to supper that spark was still there, even somewhat intensified.

After supper, just like after the first supper invitation, Mark offered to help Fanny clean up the dishes and the kitchen. Harper must have sensed the chemistry that was going on, because he said, "That's a great idea. Let this fella help you, Fanny. You deserve it."

They went into the kitchen and, like last time, found they worked easily together and were soon finished. A short time later, Harper said he felt tired and went to his room. Mark and Fanny went out onto the porch where there was a swing hanging from the ceiling.

"I sometimes come out here on summer evenings if there's nothin' else I need to do, and I love it," said Fanny. They could hear the muffled sounds of people farther down the street and at the beachfront. The air teemed with the sounds of tree frogs, children's voices, cars, laughter, an occasional dog barking. It created a comfortable ambience of life in another time and place for Mark. Fanny seemed relaxed. They swayed forward and backward on the swing, the chains creaking at the strain against their ceiling anchors. The moon glowed brightly above them.

Some rather high boxwood screened the porch railing in front of them providing intimacy, and a light breeze caught Fanny's hair. A few strands blew across her face, causing her to wrinkle her nose. Without thinking Mark reached out to catch the hair and then felt very self-conscious. She seemed to sense his feelings and took his hand in hers and said "Thanks!" They continued to hold hands and then both pulled back a little in awkwardness. Fanny said, "We really don't know each other very well yet, but I want you to know I'm glad you found your uncle and came here. His heart attack seems to have really softened his moods. I've never seen him this relaxed and easy to get along with, and I think you've helped that happen. So I want to say thanks to you."

"Please, you don't need to thank me. I'm glad I found Uncle Harper and you. Oops, don't get me wrong. I'm not trying to be fresh or something, but you're a great cook and you're different from any woman I've ever met. I'm glad to get to know you."

"You don't have to apologize for saying that," said Fanny. She turned a bit and faced him as she continued, "You've been good for Harper and for me. You wouldn't have any way to know this, but Harper had gotten almost impossible to be around. He was always fussin' about somethin', never satisfied with anythin', always against somebody or somethin', and I felt like I had to walk on egg shells. About the best times I've had were the months when he'd go visit his sisters, but then I still had this whole place to keep up with and nobody here. So it got very lonely. I probably shouldn't say this, but sometimes I thought I'd rather die than go on like this, but I kept on goin'…" She paused. "Oh, I'm sorry. I do go on."

Instinctively Mark put his arm around the swing seatback and touched her shoulder. "Thanks for sharing that with me. I know about being lonely, too. You might not believe this, but you can be lonely in the middle of a bar with a floor show going on and all kinds of people gathered tightly around you. It can feel like you're lost, just going through motions to keep from…I don't know, collapsing, I guess."

She reached out and took his hand. "I can imagine that. But somehow you don't look like you belong in a bar."

"Sitting here with you right now, I wonder if anybody belongs in a bar. It's kind of like something we had to do, like after work that's where everybody went. That's where you made your contacts with people you needed in order to do your job or get ahead. The booze and the women and the talk flowed freely and you just got lost in that. I mean, I never thought about it that way until now. It really is lonely because nobody connects on a deep, personal level."

"I've seen those things on TV and in the movies, and I know that's how life is in places like where you've lived. I can understand how that must have been for you." Fanny took Mark's hands in hers and looked into his eyes. "The person I see here is different from that. I like this person!"

"Thanks," said Mark softly as he pulled her closer to himself. Fanny did not resist. For a few moments they looked deeply into each other's eys, each searching for the soul of the other. Their cheeks brushed as they leaned closer. Then she pulled back.

"Let's not go too fast, Fanny said softly. I can't tell you how much I'm enjoyin' being with you. Thanks for bein' honest with me and sharin' your feelings. I want to have more times like this, okay?"

"Me, too," said Mark. They stood up from the swing still holding hands and walked back to his car in the driveway. "I don't mean for this to come across wrong, I mean—this feels awkward—anyway, I've been waiting until Uncle Harper was stronger to ask him if he would let me move in here with him—"

"Don't feel awkward. That's a perfectly normal thing to ask." They stopped at the car and Fanny looked up into his eyes. "Actually, he's been thinking of asking you to move into one of the upstairs rooms according to what I heard him sayin' yesterday. This is a big ole house, with three bedrooms besides Harper's upstairs and two bathrooms, so it needs more life in it. Mr. J's probably gonna ask you about it himself. And don't feel shy about it because you and I like each other, and I live here, too. Once people know who you are, it won't look strange to anybody."

"Oh, I wasn't thinking about anything looking strange. I was just thinking here we are discovering we like each other and I wouldn't want you to think I'm trying to—"

Fanny cut him off, "Don't say any more. I know what you're thinkin', and it'll be okay. I think I know you a little bit now, and I trust you. And I know we can trust each other."

That being said, Mark started to reach for his car door when Fanny impulsively pulled him back toward her and leaned toward him, saying, "I guess one little kiss won't hurt!" They kissed, lightly, but it was charged with electricity. Then she pulled away, he got into his car, saying "Good night. Pleasant dreams."

In his Dinkel Island hotel room Mark felt upset with himself for getting too close to Fanny and spent a long time going back over all that had happened. *I don't know what to make of this,* he thought. *Fanny's so fresh and different—there's nothing fake about her. I've never met anyone like her. The trouble is, I really like her.* He went to sleep perplexed yet with a kind of inner contentment he had never before experienced.

20

Give God a Fresh Chance

The "What's Next?" committee met at Sarah Jones' house on Tuesday night with a dozen people present. Everyone Sarah had invited was there except Harper—and Jack Reilly, who had gotten tied up at the restaurant but hoped to drop in later.

Sarah served refreshments, and then began the meeting. "As y'all know, the Palm Sunday Weekend Spectacular back in April was a big success. In fact, it was just about the biggest thing I've ever seen at Dinkel Island, and I've lived here all my life. We're meetin' tonight to figure out what to do next to follow up on that. I'm gonna turn this all over to the preacher."

They were seated around Sarah's living room. As she spoke, Sarah leaned back in her chair and Ed leaned forward. "To define our task a little more, we want to figure out how to keep the energy from the weekend experience charged up. How can we see Hew Sterling's work with us not as an end in itself but as a foundation on which we can build a more vital church?"

"Well, I think we already *are* a vital church," said Polly. "That's why we were able to put on this show."

"I hear what you're saying, Polly, and we *do* have a lot of vitality. The weekend program served to charge up our energy, so it's a question of looking farther down the road and planning how to use that energy spiritually to make us better disciples of Christ. What will we do now for our church to make an ongoing difference in our community?"

Sarah said with obvious anticipation in her voice, "Are we gonna do some other kind of spectacular thing?"

"I don't know, Sarah, that's what we're here to discuss. Personally I'd like to see us think more in terms of spirituality, not programs or events, although that may involve some kind of program."

"You mean like a revival?" said Steve.

"Maybe, but let's think more creatively than that. To help us do that, I'd like for you to divide yourselves into three groups of four each then discuss some questions I have for you. From that I think we can work out what we need to be planning."

They quickly rearranged their seating to create the groups, and then Ed handed out some papers with these questions:

What one thing stands out in your mind from the Weekend Spectacular program?

How was this an experience of spiritual growth for you?

How can we at Dinkel Island Wesleyan Brethren Church have a fresh, positive influence on the life of our town?

What is the next thing we should do to grow forward from here, and when should we do it?

Soon the room was abuzz with bustling excitement. People's feelings gushed forth like water from a burst dam, then receded into a more ordered flow of ideas. It was nearly an hour before Ed could unify the three groups for the purpose of sharing the results from their discussions. Once they got started, a consensus emerged about two things. They affirmed that people had talked to each other about their faith at the Saturday program, and those discussions had continued after they left the campground. They also affirmed that people had been awakened to their spiritual hunger, which happened during the services at church following the afternoon program.

Responding to these insights, Ed said, "This is the spark that was ignited on Palm Sunday. What can we do to make it into an enduring flame of God's grace in our town? Think about it. We did this program on Palm Sunday, which commemorates the excitement and enthusiasm when people shouted 'Hosanna' and welcomed Jesus into Jerusalem. A few short days later those same voices that affirmed Jesus and cheered him on became cries to *crucify* him. In other words, the positive tone of response can quickly turn into indifference or outright hostility in the human spirit. Our Weekend Spectacular was our 'Hosanna.' How can we keep that alive instead of letting it deteriorate into a crucifixion of what we just celebrated?"

"That's kinda heavy, preacher," said Jim Swank. The group chuckled. He added, "And we probably do need to wade into the heavy stuff instead of just skimming the surface. It's easy for church goin' to become such a comfortable habit that one day it just fades out of our lives, so we have to grow in our faith on a deeply personal level. I sometimes think about what my relationship with God means in my decisions and actions when I meditate on the stained glass window in our sanctuary." The prodigal son window had such dominance in the sanctuary that everyone saw it in their minds as Jim spoke and related to his thought with their own meditative experiences.

Jim went on, "In a lot of ways, I guess we in the church can be just like the prodigal son. We say to God as he said to his father,

'Give me what I want!' God gives us a savior in Jesus Christ. And what do we do? We build a monument to God and call it a church and fill it up with rituals and rules and then almost turn it into the same religious system Jesus came to call us away from."

This ignited a stir of emotional wordiness as people reacted to Jim's words, and then Lillie spoke up. "You asked me here because Stan and I are new in the church, and I take it you want to hear our thoughts, so here are mine. What Jim just said is what has kept me out of the church—not out of faith, mind you, but out of the church—for most of my life. What brought me back was the very transcendence of this attitude that I sensed in Hew Sterling and the Weekend Spectacular. I responded to the honesty and directness of his approach and that's what Jim has offered us now—honesty and directness. We have to put *that* at the heart of our faith and our lives."

Steve Tyrone stepped into the discussion. "I guess it's time to share Harper's words when we asked for his thoughts and feelings about all of this. His answer seemed strange to me at the time, but I just got what he meant. He said, 'It's amazing what happens when you stop trying to make things happen.' Those were his words. He was asking us to let go of trying to manage or control our church, our lives, our world. When we step back and trust God it will be amazing what God will do. Think about it. Look what God has done with Harper since his heart attack. That's a miracle!"

Jim agreed with him. "Let me finish my thoughts about the prodigal son window. What happened to the son was what happens to us when we try to take everything into our own hands—it all went sour. So the son came home and was ready to endure punishment for his misuse of his father's trust, but his father welcomed him with a loving embrace and a great celebration. Our Weekend Spectacular was the embrace of God's grace that gives us fresh insights, power, and hope. That's what we need to share from the heart of our lives and our church to make what we did Palm Sunday have lasting meaning."

"We have to grow," said Jill Upton. "We have to expand our minds, our experiences, our relationships, our hopes, and our fellowship. We don't have to plan another big program. We have to let the Holy Spirit live in us and through us. What we felt at the campground was just a fresh presence of the Holy Spirit, which continued in everything we did that weekend. Let's focus on that!"

"If Harper was here," said Sarah, "I think he'd say we heard what he meant for us to hear. Now I'm somebody who needs to be active, plannin' stuff and doin' stuff—but maybe y'all are right that God has the plan, and we need to shut our mouths and open up our minds and give God a fresh chance with us, and with our church."

"Trust God to lead us with his Spirit!" said Jenny, and several said "Yes!"

Cheryl said, "Maybe we could take a slogan and a challenge to the Brunch Bunch meeting instead of a program, something like 'Give God a Fresh Chance!' Maybe make posters up and put them around town and encourage people to keep talking like they were after the campground event—somehow make spirituality real in our daily living."

Finally Ed called the group back together. "It's exciting to hear y'all really getting into this, and I've been making some notes. Here are some of the things I've heard you say: put honesty and directness at the heart of our lives and church; see what amazing things happen when we stop trying to make them happen; trust God; receive God's gifts of grace, insight, power, and hope; focus on the Holy Spirit, and the suggestion of a slogan: 'Give God a Fresh Chance.' Does that about cover it?"

They agreed it did, but Sarah asked, "How do you make that into a church program?"

"Perhaps we don't need a program so much as a spiritual recharge," said Jenny. "Maybe if we do that we will find what else God has for us to do."

Such was the flavor of discussion that produced a two-pronged approach beginning the second Sunday in July. Ed would preach a series of sermons on the theme of "The Spirit-fired Life," based on the planting of a brand new faith in a hostile world after the apostles were filled with the Holy Spirit at the spectacular event of Pentecost. Special music, involvement of children and youth, and an outdoor service on the church lawn with lunch on the grounds afterward would give the sense of a homecoming and a revival all rolled up together.

The other prong was to ask every member of the church to become personally involved in some form of missions effort, either in the local community or beyond. One of those opportunities would be a free lunch on Saturdays at the church for anyone who came. Sarah Jones said she would organize that. They would also establish a food pantry at the church, a volunteer transportation pool for older folks who couldn't drive, and other things they would work out as time went on. To launch the whole thing they would call the entire congregation and ask them to go door-to-door handing out flyers throughout town on the July Fourth weekend.

This plan generated a lively discussion among the Brunch Bunch and a unanimous vote by the board. They invested their faith, energy, and prayers to see what new thing God would do at Dinkel Island.

21

Amazing Grace

"Hey, Jimbo!" Stan called out as he entered the Grayson-Plume Studio/Gallery building where renovation work was in progress. "Take a break, man. It's lunch time."

"Oh! Hi, Mr. Grayson," said Jimbo as he looked down from the drop ceiling area where he was installing light fixtures. "I'm almost done with this. I'll eat my lunch when I finish."

"Sure you can't stop now? Lillie and I ordered some pizza, and we've got more than we can eat. Come on, and join us. That work will wait."

Jimbo looked embarrassed. "It wouldn't be right."

Stan walked over to the ladder. "It's not a question of right or wrong. We're all working on this thing together, and we'd like you to have lunch with us." Stan waved his arm. "Come on down."

Hesitantly Jimbo stopped his work and came down the ladder. "Don't nobody ask a handyman to eat with 'em, Mr Grayson. What ain't right is you askin' me to do that."

"Jimbo,"—Stan paused and put his hand on Jimbo's shoulder—"why don't we call you by your real name. When you gave us your employment information, Lillie and I noticed that your full name is James Irwin Brown. That's a great name. Why do you go by Jimbo?"

"Jimbo's just a nickname. It's the way everybody knows me."

Stan could see he was nervous. "Well, I want to call you James. Is that okay with you?"

"I guess that's up to you."

"Come on into the backroom, and take a lunch break." Reluctantly Jimbo went with him. Lillie joined them and as they ate, she expressed her gratitude for his workmanship.

"You know, we don't want to tell you what to do, but Stan and I think you could have a good business as a carpenter. Have you ever thought about something like that?"

"No, ma'am. I'm just a handyman, thas all."

"Somebody taught you a lot more than that, James," said Stan.

"Yessir, I learned a lot from Mr. Jake when he was buildin' boats up to the lighthouse."

"Well, he taught you well," said Lillie. "You know it's because of your skill that we're going to have this place ready to open on time. We'd like to help you turn your work into a real business."

"People wouldn't stand for it, Miz Grayson. I don't like to stir things up. I get along okay like things is."

They talked more as they ate and then went back to work. At the end of the week, Stan brought the subject of a carpentry business back up.

"I was designing our business cards the other day, James, and just for the heck of it, I made one up for you if you were to have a carpentry business of your own. Wanna see it?

James took the card and his face lit up. "*James Irwin Brown Carpentry*," he read. "I can't believe that's me. Do you really think people wouldn't get mad about this?"

"Oh, some might. Some people get mad about most anything. But that doesn't matter."

"It does if you're a black man!"

190

"James, I know that's how things have been, but it's time to change that. Things don't change unless you do something to make it happen. This is something you can do, and we'd like to help."

"But why, Mr. Grayson?"

"Hey, please call me Stan. We're equal, you and me. You're doing some work for me, and I'll pay you for it. But I'd also like to be friends with you. Friends call each other by their first names, so I want you to call me Stan. Okay?"

"Okay, Mr.—I mean Stan. I still don't know why you're doing this."

Stan thought a moment. "Do you attend church, James?"

"Yes, our church is out in the country."

"Well, Lillie and I have been getting involved in church lately, and we think we have to do more than just say we believe something. We feel like we have to act on what we believe."

"I hear that!"

"One thing we believe is that all people, no matter who they are, or what race they are—all people are God's creation and every one of us counts. We're all on the same ground. God loves us all and he wants us to love and respect each other.

"We believe God can change peoples' hearts through his love," said Lillie. "That's why we're interested in helping you build your own business. Does that help?"

"I guess it does," said Jimbo. He studied the floor then looked Stan in the eye. "I told the missus what you done told me and she said, 'what's in it for Mr. Grayson? People don't do stuff like this lessen they gets somethin' outa it.' I explained it to 'er jest like you told me, but she still been given' me grief."

"I'm sorry to hear that. Believe me, Lillie and I don't want anything out of this except what's going to help you an your family. You don't have to do this to satisfy us. If you want, we'll just drop the whole thing. It's your choice."

Jimbo turned away and paced the floor then turned back to Stan. "I done asked the Lord about this, too. I think he's been tellin' me to do it--so I will."

Stan reached to embrace Jimbo. "Good man! I think this will turn out well for you and your family. God bless you."

Mark and Fanny's relationship continued to deepen. After her assurance that Harper would be open to his living in the Jauswell house, Mark went ahead and mentioned it.

"Uncle Harper," he said one Sunday afternoon, "we've really only known each other a few short weeks, but I feel such closeness to you and this place, and Fanny…that, well…it's the family I've always wanted. I'll be starting work with the insurance agency soon, and I need to get out of that expensive hotel. You have such a wonderful house here, and you and Fanny have made me feel like I belong in it, so I was wondering if I might rent one of the bedrooms upstairs for a while—until I get back on my feet and can get my own place. I don't want to be out of line, but, well, I just thought it wouldn't hurt to ask."

Harper responded with warmth that took Mark by surprise. "Don't say another word. You find the room you want, and it's yours. And none of this rent stuff. You're family, and I want you to live right here. I've wanted to invite you and just hadn't found the right time to bring it up. I wasn't sure what plans you were making for housing."

Mark was amazed at his own depth of emotion at Harper's words. He felt overwhelmed at being offered what he wanted without any hesitation. In the world he'd always known you had to fight for what you wanted—grabbing, pushing, shoving before somebody else took it from you. He was at a loss for words.

"Thanks," he heard himself saying to Harper. It came from somewhere deep inside himself that he hadn't even known existed It came out softly, with richness of tone, the words rolling as if on a velvet carpet. "Thanks for your faith in me and your love for a relative you'd never seen. I can't tell you how much that means to me."

That evening Mark went back to his hotel room early to begin packing up his things and move out. Fanny offered to go along to help him with packing and moving. He felt hesitant at first, not being accustomed to relying on anyone else or trusting anyone with things that were personal. His heart was flooded with warmth in her presence, so he said, "Sure, why not. Thanks!"

The hotel room was not neat when they entered it, as Mark hadn't expected this to happen so quickly. His dirty clothes were piled up and books and papers were lying around. As they came in the door he made a quick mental inventory of where anything might be that was really private and decided all of that was secure. At least he thought he did a good job at that, however, Fanny uncovered an empty wine bottle and looked at him with a puzzled expression.

"I didn't know you drank wine, Mark. Harper won't allow a drop of that in the house. He never has!" Fanny seemed hurt and became somewhat distant.

Mark said, "Oh, that? I don't drink all the time or anything, but sometimes I enjoy a glass of wine in the evening. I'm not an alcoholic, if that's what you're thinking." He reached for her, and she did not resist. He pulled her close to him so that the warmth of their bodies resonated with his words. "Having a drink now and then has been a choice, but I can just as easily choose never to drink another glass of wine. I love you, darling, and I don't want some suspicion from an old wine bottle in my room to come between us. Let's just throw that bottle in the trash and forget about it. Okay?"

Fanny's tension eased and she looked deeply into his eyes then kissed him and said, "Okay! I believe you, and I trust you. I'll not mention it again."

When they got back to the house they carried Mark's things up to his room as quietly as possible. "Until I see you in the morning," Fanny said as they kissed good night and went to their separate rooms.

The next morning Harper and Fanny were already at the table eating breakfast when Mark came downstairs. Fanny's face lit up when she saw him, and with a warm smile she said, "How about some scrambled eggs, bacon, and toast? Or would you like somethin' lighter?"

"Bacon, eggs, and toast will be fine," said Mark. She poured him a cup of coffee and went back to the kitchen. Harper said, "I see you moved in okay last night. How does it feel to wake up in a new place this morning?"

"It feels great, just the way being with family ought to feel."

"Well, Mark, I want you to feel like this is your home now. I hope you will be comfortable here."

"Thanks!" said Mark. "Home—that has such a good feel to it!"

"I guess you have more than one good feelin' this mornin'," said Harper with a very serious expression on his face.

Mark's face flushed as he said, "Excuse me? I mean...what are you talking about?"

Harper's countenance softened, and he laughed, "Don't think I can't pick up on the vibes around here. It don't take a wizard to see what's goin' on between you and Fanny. Y'all've got a thing for each other. I can see it in your faces."

Mark smiled sheepishly. "I guess it must be pretty obvious. Yes, we really do care for each other."

"Ain't nothin' wrong with that," said Harper. "Fanny's been here cookin' and carin' for the house for many a year, and I know when somethin' about her changes. I can see somethin's definitely changed. I'm happy for both of you, and I hope you continue to grow closer."

At that moment Fanny walked into the room with Mark's breakfast and looked puzzled. "What y'all talking 'bout, Mr. J?"

"Just sayin' how pleased I am to see that y'all two seem to have a likin' for each other. It couldn't happen to a better couple."

Fanny and Mark were playful with Harper throughout breakfast, and then she had her work to do, and Mark had some things to take care of. Harper settled down to read the newspaper and catch up on the news on TV. "Welcome home, Mark," he muttered to himself. "I wish I felt totally settled about you. Don't you go hurtin' my Fanny. She's more like family to me than you are."

Mark felt overwhelmed and totally confused. He had fallen in love with Fanny. *Fanny!* She was so different from any woman he'd ever known. He hadn't counted on anything like this ever happening in his life. All of a sudden money and material things didn't seem so important. Two human beings, Fanny and Harper, were suddenly more important to him than even his own life.

A note of sadness hit the Wesleyan Brethren congregation in July when a prominent older woman in the congregation died of a sudden heart attack. The funeral was held on a Saturday at the church, with burial out of town in Nor'easter Memorial Gardens. After the burial the family received friends and loved ones in the church social hall where Sarah and the Woman's Association catered a spread of fried chicken, ham biscuits, potato salad, deviled eggs, and other delicacies created in the kitchens of Wesleyan Brethren homemakers.

Fanny asked Mark if he would go to the funeral with her. "She was my Sunday school teacher once, and I always loved her fried chicken. In fact, she's the one who taught me to fry chicken."

"Hers had to be good, then," said Mark, "especially if it was better than yours, because yours is the best I've ever eaten."

"You're just sayin' that," said Fanny playfully, "but don't stop. I like to hear it!"

That evening after Harper had gone to bed, Fanny and Mark sat out on the porch swing and cuddled and talked. Fanny said,

"You know, funerals are sad, and it's hard to lose someone, but they also remind us that it ain't all about what's here and now. Life's about what's to come. When a good person dies it reminds me that God has a plan for us. Don't you agree?"

The question hit Mark right in the center of his struggling soul. He had tried hard all his life not to think too much about what happens after death, so he didn't know what to say. When his parents or friends died, he just felt more driven than ever to get all he could for as long as he was here. He didn't see anybody taking any treasures with them when they left this life, so he felt an urgency to enjoy it all now. That is, he had felt that way until these last couple of months when he got involved with the Jauswell family and then met and fell in love with Fanny. Now he was confused. He said nothing, but simply held her.

Fanny squeezed his hand and gave him that flirtatious smile that always turned him on.

Swinging together with the moon casting a mellow glow around the yard, they felt a closeness that exceeded anything either of them could have imagined. They began to kiss passionately, their emotions fired by a renewed sense of the brevity of life and the spark of human spirits entwined with each other.

"I love you!" Fanny said softly.

"I love you too," said Mark. "I've never felt as fully alive as I do with you right now."

The next morning Mark and Fanny resonated with a glow of affection that made Harper comment, "Y'all two are somethin' else!" They ate breakfast, and the three of them went to church together.

After church they spoke to Ed as they were leaving.

"I hear some whispers that you two are gettin' kind of serious with each other. I think that's wonderful," said Ed. "You're a beautiful couple."

"I didn't know we were a topic of conversation," replied Mark.

"Oh, don't let it bother you. It just means people care about you, and when we die we are remembered for who we were, so it's good when people are taking mental notes about us. We preachers wouldn't have any way to know what to say at a funeral if it weren't for those mental notes we can tap from others."

"You always seem to know the right words," said Fanny.

At that moment someone walked up and asked Ed a question and he walked off. Fanny said, "Oh, Mark, isn't it wonderful to be people of faith? How do people ever deal with loss without faith?"

Mark didn't say a thing; he just smiled and squeezed her shoulder.

22

Testimony and Flight

Summer enveloped Dinkel Island with sunshine, fishing forays, backyard-hammock escapes, golf outings, picnics, beachfront badminton, bingo at the gazebo under the Chinese lanterns, and numerous nuptials at the Wedding Pier. The Grayson-Plume Studio/Gallery opened with much fanfare and added a new dimension to the community profile. Life felt good in general, and there seemed to be no wrinkles to upset the fine balance between leisure and labor. The only exception to this was the frenetic activity of the Wesleyan Brethren folks who spent their summer taking flyers around town, putting up posters, bringing in singing groups, and generally blowing the trumpet of excitement Sunday through Saturday every week. With their "Give God a Fresh Chance" slogan no one could ignore them. The Baptists and Episcopalians, however, wished the Wesleyan Brethren folks would pull back onto their own turf.

That was certainly the message Ed received when he got another call from Randy Adams. "Hey, Ed," said Randy in his good-old-buddy tone of voice, "What's all this new excitement I've been hearing about at your church? Have you got another parachute preacher comin' in? You know we talked about that last time and you said maybe we could all get together for something like that the next time."

"No, Randy, it's nothing at all like that. We're just having a revival all summer. You know, special music and activities and an emphasis on the Holy Spirit in our worship services—stuff like that."

"So what's with all the flyers I've been hearin' about?"

"The flyers are about the Saturday Free Lunch we've started serving and also about our new food pantry. I'm sure y'all have some special things like that going on, too."

"Oh, sure, sure we do. All the time," Randy said. "I should think you would've heard about 'em. But, I mean, spreadin' flyers around seems like you're tryin' to pull folks from other churches into yours, and we need to talk about that."

"No, nothing like that," Ed assured him. "We're looking for people who don't go to any church on one hand, and on the other, we welcome support for our missions program from anyone who wants to give it. It's not about what church you attend. "It's just about serving Christ."

"Well, we got plenty goin' on, too," said Randy, "and it's all for the kingdom, right? Just keep in mind we all need to work together."

"Sure thing, Randy. You have a great day, and I'll talk with you later."

∾৹

One Saturday in August, Harper asked Mark when he was going to join the Wesleyan Brethren church. It puzzled him that Mark kept making excuses and putting it off. Finally, Harper said, "Son,

I just don't buy what you're sayin'. You talk about your church back in California, but you're living here and ain't going back there, and you say you love Fanny and feel a part of this place. It just don't make sense that you don't go ahead and join up with our church."

The question hit Mark's deep confusion like a bullet. Thoughts raced through his mind. *What can I say? I only went to that church in California to learn how to act like a Christian so I could come here. But now things have changed.*

"I guess I just haven't made a point to do it," Mark said. *Will he accept that?*

Harper's eyes bore into Mark. "I don't believe that. You're not an indecisive man. There's got to be something else goin' on. I just want you to know you can talk to me about it."

He's got me! "I guess I do need to talk about it," he said. "The truth is, I did attend church out there, and I wanted to believe what it was all about, but somehow I never could quite take the step to join."

"Kinda like now, eh?"

"Well, not really. I mean, I've been attending Pastor Heygood's classes, and I think I'm ready to do that now. I probably needed somebody to push me."

"I can understand that. It's a commitment. It means something about who you are and how you live your life. Most people have to struggle through that kind of thing."

"I know you're right," said Mark. "I guess it's time to make that commitment." *There! I said it! I really do want to do this!*

Making that decision opened up another decision that had been swelling like a wave ready to break. He decided to ask Fanny to marry him. That evening he took her to the Seafood Pavilion for supper, and afterward they sat on the porch swing and embraced. Mark felt a deep, inner warmth and closed his eyes, envisioning her again at supper in the romantic glow of a candle that had been on their table. *I can't believe this is happen-*

ing, he thought. *I don't deserve a woman like her, but I need her—we need each other.*

"Penny for your thoughts," Fanny said. All the discord of his life was banging around inside Mark's head, but he couldn't turn away from the moment.

Mark held her hands and looked into her eyes. "Fanny, after being with you these last few months, my life can never be complete without you. I began to fall in love with you that first time you invited me for supper, and I felt a spark between us."

Fanny squeezed his hand and returned his gaze. "I know what you mean—I feel the same way."

It just came out then. "Will you marry me?" asked Mark

They slid closer together and Fanny kissed him. "Yes! Yes, I will."

In that moment Mark knew that with her he could become a genuine person instead of a fake. He knew in his heart he had to let go of all the things that had held him back and trust God.

The next week Harper added to the complexity of things when he called Ed over to the house. Sitting in the backyard under the massive oak trees, sipping iced tea, Harper said, "Ed, I'm a changed man. You know that, because you've been with me through this change, but I feel it's time for me to share my personal testimony with my church family. I'd like to do it this Sunday, if that works into your plans."

It was an astounding development. The old Harper had railed against such things as being fake. Now he had met his Lord and been told he had another chance to get his life straightened out. Now he knew he had to be honest, and he had to make a public witness to the Lord and his faith.

Ed was elated with this news. "Harper, I can't think of anything I'd rather do than give you time to share your faith journey with the congregation. And it works so well with Mark joining the church the same day. Yes! Of course. You can plan on it."

On Sunday the church was packed. Word had somehow gotten out that Harper was going to talk about what had happened to change his life so much. Ed saw a bigger picture than just Harper Jauswell's penitence and redemption. He saw the opening of a door through which other people could share what was happening in their own faith so they could pray for and support one another. One of those people was Clara Jasper who let her friends know that she was doing better now, and it was time for her to get back into church. Ed saw Clara and Phil seated right up front. She was almost radiant, overflowing with peace and joy. She and Phil seemed harmonious together. Ed was thrilled.

"I've decided to start a new feature in our worship services," Ed announced after the choir had sung. "A lot of folks have been experiencing new insights and growth in their faith, as we're saying this summer 'fired up by the Holy Spirit,' so I want to take a few moments each week for what I am calling Faith Sharing. I'll be asking who has something that is happening in their lives by the grace of God that they'd like to share with us. We'll bring a microphone to you. This morning I want to start with Harper Jauswell, who has asked to share his faith journey with you today."

Harper stood up. "I have been a fearful, self-centered, controlling man most of my life, as all of you who have known me over the years can attest. Now don't shake your heads, 'cause I know what I'm sayin' is true. I've heard the gospel all my life and have been here in this church from the first day my momma could bring me out of the house. You know I've given money for many things here, but I always had strings attached to it so God didn't have a chance to really get into any of that. It was all for *me*, to make *me* feel good, and look good, and have power and influence over people."

Harper paused, then went on. "I didn't consciously know that was what I was doin', but I knew it in my soul. I put a big, dark lid over my soul so I wouldn't have to deal with what I knew was true. In other words, I played a game with my life, and that's all anybody or anything was to me—just part of the game.

"Annabelle was a wonderful woman, and I loved her but for the wrong reasons. I loved her for myself—to possess her, and I was married to my own ego more than to her so I didn't treat her well. She made a life for herself out of her garden, and when she died, I refused to keep up that garden, and it all went to weeds and brush."

Harper continued, "Oh, how sorry I have been for that, and how I've prayed for God to forgive me."

"I've also prayed for forgiveness for the ways I've offended and hurt many of you as I tried to puff myself up at your expense. I see Clara Jasper over there. Clara, I'm glad you're here…" Harper's voice broke, and his eyes clouded with tears for a moment. He went on, "Clara, I hurt you by maneuvering behind the scenes to get the official board to double your rent when you and Phil was livin' in the old parsonage, and I know you knew I was behind it. It was senseless and mean of me, and I want to apologize to you today, these many years later, and ask your forgiveness. God has forgiven me, but he has told me I need to ask you to do the same."

The emotional charge in Harper's words set off lightning bolts of soul-wrenching energy in the congregation. Eyes darted back and forth between Clara and Harper. Clara interrupted, "Harper, that's okay. That's all—as the saying goes—water over the dam. It's gone. Yes, it hurt, but God's love has been healing that. Like you, I didn't let him get too close to me until here of late. Now I've opened the door and found God was right there all the time, waiting for me to accept his forgiveness. You are my brother in Christ, Harper, and I love you and forgive you. And thanks for being bold enough to say what you did."

There was dead silence for a moment, and then a ground swell of applause filled the room, and people shouted, "Praise God! Thanks be to our loving God." When things quieted down again, Harper continued his testimony. He told about his heart attack and the out-of-body experience and said, "God has changed my heart and given me a fresh chance to get things right in my life. He has healed my spirit so completely that all the anger, swearing, meanness, and rage that lived within me for so long has simply disappeared. So today I want to share this with you and to say I'm praying for this church that has been such a part of my life, and for Pastor Heygood, and all the staff and the leaders, and I'm praying for you—each of you."

As Harper spoke, Mark felt an inner wrenching. Harper was describing the real person inside him that he didn't want to acknowledge. Those words, *fearful*, *self-centered*, *controlling*, described him to perfection. He had learned to play the parts he thought would keep him safe and in control of things. He was afraid of what he couldn't manipulate to his own advantage. He had always been the center of his own universe and fit everyone and everything else into his design by whatever means necessary, with little regard for appropriateness or legality. Until these last few weeks, he had never allowed himself to admit to this inner distortion of his life. Now, through the very presence of Fanny and Harper in his life, he couldn't keep these conflicting pieces of himself hidden.

It was when Harper went on to express his deep joy at having his nephew from California, whom he had never seen in his life until the time of his heart attack, become a part of his family that Mark just about lost his composure. Harper wanted everyone to know how grateful he had been to Fanny. She had stayed with him, cooking and keeping up his house after Annabelle died, when she certainly had every right to leave a grouchy old man. Finally he expressed gratitude that Mark would be joining the church later in the service, and he thought Mark and Fanny might even have an announcement to make. That statement made Mark feel so uncomfortable that he could barely sit still.

After people applauded Ed thanked Harper for his faith and honesty and went on with the service. His scripture was Galatians 5:16-25 where the Apostle Paul contrasts the works of the flesh with the fruit of God's Spirit. In the midst of Mark's inner struggle, the words of this passage jolted him like an electric shock, every syllable striking a note of conviction:

> Live by the Spirit, I say, and do not gratify the desires of the flesh. For what the flesh desires is opposed to the Spirit, and what the Spirit desires is opposed to the flesh; for these are opposed to each other... Now the works of the flesh are obvious: fornication, impurity, licentiousness, idolatry, sorcery, enmities, strife, jealousy, anger, quarrels, dissensions, factions, envy, drunkenness, carousing, and things like these.
>
> Galatians 5:16-25 (NRSV)

The words so penetrated the dark cover Mark had riveted over his soul that he scarcely heard the positive fruit produced in the lives of the faithful through the Holy Spirit: love, joy, peace, patience, kindness, generosity, faithfulness, gentleness, and self-control.

It was as if a brilliant light suddenly broke through his spiritual darkness. In an instant, after a lifetime of desperately trying *not* to believe, he found that he *did* believe. A flooding sensation of certainty surged through his brain. He *did* believe in Jesus Christ. He *wanted* salvation. He *wanted* to live in the strength of God's Spirit. But here he was caught in the web of his own malignant purposes and counterfeit relationships, a web of lies and deception. His very being was shaken by all Harper had said followed by the scripture Ed had presented. He absolutely did not know who he really was.

A spiritual earthquake rubbing the plates of Mark's conflicted natures together caused vibrations that charged his brain with a sudden resolve—he could not go through with anything that was in front of him He needed space, time, and a chance to become complete again.

While Ed was still preaching, Mark knew he could not sit there and listen another minute, much less stand up and profess his faith and join the church. He leaned over to Fanny and gave her hand a long, firm squeeze. When she looked in his eyes, she saw pain and tears, and he whispered, "I love you. Forgive me." He got up and walked toward the social hall entrance and left the sanctuary. Fanny was puzzled, but seeing him go out that particular door, she thought he was going to the men's room and wanted her to forgive him for stepping out during the service. She was a little uneasy but not overly so until he didn't come back. After the sermon when Ed was calling those who were joining the church up to the front, Mark still wasn't there. Harper leaned over and said, "Where is Mark?"

"I thought he went to the restroom," replied Fanny.

"Me, too," said Harper. "I'll slip out there and see if he's all right. I hope he's not sick."

Ed had seen Mark leave and wondered when he didn't see him return. He noticed Harper go out as well, and then Harper came back in, slipped back into the pew and whispered to Fanny. It was time to receive the new members, so he decided to call them forward and begin with those who were there and maybe Mark would appear. When he came to Mark's name he said a few words about him, then noticed Harper motioning to him. He stepped away and met Harper between his pew and the chancel.

"Something's wrong," said Harper. "Mark's not here."

Noticing the expression of puzzlement on Harper's face, Ed said, "Where is he? What's going on?"

"I don't know. I thought he went to the restroom, but he's not there."

Ed scanned the sanctuary quickly, checking the doors for some sign of Mark. "Do you think he's coming back?"

"I don't know. Maybe he's sick. This isn't like him."

"Well," said Ed, "I think the best thing to do is to receive the other members and simply say it has been necessary for Mark to leave and we'll receive him at another time.

∿

When Mark faked his trip to the restroom, he literally ran out of the church and all the way back to the Jauswell house. He grabbed some of his things, charged out to his car, and sped out of Dinkel Island as fast as he could go. He had no specific plans other than to get away and resolve the confusion in his soul. He couldn't stand to tell another lie and didn't know how to deal with the mess he'd made. He had to get some time and space for himself. He had to talk to God. He was afraid.

The words of scripture Ed had read hit him deep in his gut. He had gotten up and left while Ed was preaching because he couldn't listen any more. He felt a frenzy of guilt and shame in his soul, and he thought as he sped along the highway that it would be so easy to just run headlong into a tree and end it all and burn in hell, he was sure, for all eternity. He needed God now. He needed this fire in his soul to be put out with grace and hope and peace, but it wasn't happening. Where was God?

He drove until he reached Richmond where he found that most businesses were open and busy, unlike Dinkel Island where nearly everything was closed from noon Saturday until Monday morning. Just ahead he spotted a small used car dealership with a sign that said "Cash for Your Car." That was just what he wanted, and without giving himself time to think, he charged into the parking lot and screeched to a stop in front of the office. A seedy-looking man came out with a perplexed look on his face.

"What are you runnin' away from?" asked the man.

"Why would you ask that? I'm just a man who wants to sell his car. Is what your sign says for real—cash for your car? What will you give me for this one?"

"You want to sell *this* car? It's almost new, and it's high class. Is it hot?"

"Do you think I'd tell you if it was?"

"Yeah, you'd better, 'cause I ain't takin' in no hot cars."

"Look, I've got the title right here, and I'll sign it over to you. I bought this car in California and came east, but my plans have changed so I need some cash, and I just want to sell the car. You can take me up on this and buy it, or you can tell me to get off your lot, but if you do, I'll just sell it to your competitor."

"Okay, okay," said the man. "I'll give ya eight thousand for it."

"That's all?" said Mark, feeling insulted. He'd paid well over three times that much for it not a year ago. He argued back, but the dealer said that was his best offer, take it or leave it. Mark signed over the papers, took the money, and got a cabbie to take him to the bus station. Before nightfall he was headed west. He decided he needed to mix things up. He knew it wouldn't take long for Fanny and Harper to report him missing and when the nature of his exit was known, the state police would be looking for him.

When the bus stopped in Harrisonburg, Mark got off with his bags and took a cab to the nearest truck stop on the Interstate highway. There he went in and hung around watching the truckers come and go and listening to their conversations. He finally picked up on a guy heading to Cleveland, so he went over and asked if he could bum a ride with him.

"No, buddy, I can't pick up no strangers or hitchhikers. It's against company policy, and I could lose my job for that. So get lost."

"Maybe I could offer a little incentive," said Mark as he handed him five one hundred dollar bills. The trucker's expression changed. His eyes lit up, and then he looked hard at Mark.

"You runnin' from the law, bud?"

"No!"

"How come you're so generous?"

"Well, it's not the law I'm running from. It's that chick I knocked up, and her old man is out for me. I gotta git myself far away pronto. I don't want no shotgun wedding, y'know what I mean?"

"Yeah, I guess I can git ya outa that jam. Come on, but don't make it obvious."

It was a long ride, and the trucker talked until Mark couldn't listen anymore. When they got to Cleveland, he rented a car under an assumed name and drove southwest to Columbus. There he found a cheap hotel on the outskirts of town, rented a room under a false name. Then he went back out to the car, took his things, locked it and called a cab from a phone booth.

"Take me to a hotel near the airport," he said. The cabbie did as he requested, and Mark again registered in a hotel under another false name. When the desk clerk seemed suspicious, he winked and said, "If a really stacked blonde comes in here looking for Max Richards, tell her he checked out, but don't send her to my room. I know, you think I'm nuts, but her husband's onto us, and I don't want any trouble."

"Sure, I understand," said the clerk when Mark handed him a fifty dollar bill. Mark went to his room and for the first time in two days fell into a deep sleep.

23

Penitent Return

Back in Dinkel Island, Harper and Fanny had walked the short distance to church. As they came out after the service, it had turned hot and humid. That along with their anxiety over Mark had them sweating and out of breath when they reached the house. Harper had been making a marvelous recovery from his heart attack, but when he came in the back door, he immediately sat down at the kitchen table and took a nitroglycerin tablet to settle the pain in his chest. Fanny sat down next to him. She took his pulse and blood pressure, and tried, in spite of her own tears of confusion, to calm him.

With his car missing from the driveway, it was obvious Mark had come back to the house and then left. After Harper was stabilized, Fanny went upstairs to Mark's room and found he had hastily grabbed a few things, dumped the clothes he had worn to church on the bed, and taken his shaving gear from the bathroom. As she went back downstairs, her emotions overtook her and she burst into tears. "What's happening?" she wailed. "Why did Mark do this? Where has he gone?"

Harper was alarmed at her outburst. "What did you find in his room?"

"It's not what I found. It's what I didn't find. He dumped his church clothes on the bed, but his shaving gear is missing," said Fanny through her sobs. She flopped down into an easy chair, threw her head back, and clenched her fists. "Mr. J, somethin's really wrong here. He must be sick or somethin'. We gotta find him."

Harper said, "Call Chief Thompson at the police station, and tell him I need him over here right away. Don't use 911. We don't want a lot of noise and attention. I'll see what Charlie thinks of this and what he suggests. His nonemergency number is on the calendar on my desk."

The chief was out so she left a message that Harper needed him to come to his house right away. Within five minutes the chief was there.

"What's going on, Harper?" he asked as Fanny ushered him in. "Are you okay?" Charlie and Harper went back a long way to Harper's term as the town's mayor, and they had a kind of rapport that undercut officialdom.

"You met my nephew, Mark Howard, didn't you? A couple of months ago?"

"Yes, I did. What's going on with him?"

"Well, we don't know, which is why I called you over to see if you can help us figure that out." Harper and Fanny went on to tell about Mark leaving church and their coming home to find his car and some of his personal things missing. Fanny told him how Mark had squeezed her hand and what he had said when he left the pew. She told him they had just become engaged and she thought they had an ideal relationship. She knew he was from California, but as far as she knew, that had nothing to do with his life now in Dinkel Island.

"Would you mind if I took a look at his room?" asked the chief. Harper said to go ahead, and Fanny led him upstairs. It was obvious Mark had not planned to leave, Charlie said, and it was equally obvious that he had only taken a few basic things with him. There were some papers from work on a table he used as a desk, along with some small sticky notes to himself, but nothing suspicious.

"It looks like he left unexpectedly and in a hurry," said Chief Thompson, "It also seems he must have had a plan because he took things that might give us a clue to what's going on, so I wonder if he's in some kind of trouble."

"But why would he jump up and leave during the church service?"

"That's a good question. Normally we couldn't do anything with this until he'd been gone over twenty-four hours, and then we could file a missing person on him and put out an alert. But I'm feeling something is going on here that is a lot deeper than we can see on the surface. I can't say what I mean by that. It's just a gut feeling."

They went back downstairs, and Charlie told Harper, "Tell you what, I'll send our forensic guy over to dust for fingerprints in his room. If you haven't heard anything from him by tomorrow morning, I'll run a check on whatever prints we pick up. I'll also try to find out if he's had trouble at work. Sometimes people mess up and get fired, but they can't talk about it, or don't want to admit it, and they'll run away or behave in some unusual manner. Anyway, I'm sure we can come up with some clues that will help find him with a little time."

"We appreciate that," said Harper. "Can't you run a check on his car? He has only been here a few months and still had California plates and registration on it. I just told him the other day he needed to get that squared away soon."

"That's a good idea, Harper. I'll see if we can get the state police to put out a low-profile alert for his car." With that Charlie left, Fanny went to the kitchen to fix lunch, and Harper, feeling chest pains again, took another nitroglycerin and closed his eyes.

"Oh, Lord," he prayed, "what's goin' on? I know your love and power are greater than anything we can face, but this is beyond imagination. Please bring Mark back safely to us and help him to resolve whatever is troubling him. Amen."

～⌘～

It was nearly ten o'clock the next morning when Mark awoke in a strange room. He blinked his eyes, shook his head, and suddenly the whole thing came flooding back to him. He felt panic and fear. What had he done? *Fanny! Oh, God…Fanny! What was she going through? And Harper…they must be frantic.* He got up, shaved, and showered and went down to the hotel café for breakfast.

As Mark picked at his scrambled eggs and bacon, mental images floated through his mind from his and Fanny's times together, as well as his almost constant panic at the emotional attachment that had developed between the two of them. *He closed his eyes and could practically see her face and hear her voice. And Harper! How much he has done for me!*

Then there was the faith he had always snubbed, except when it might fit his purposes to mimic it—a faith that had begun to take deep root in his soul so that he was in conflict with himself and his entire world. He remembered the words Ed had read from scripture about living by the Spirit of God instead of the ways of the flesh. No wonder he couldn't go through with joining the church—he had too much baggage in tow, too many contrary issues he hadn't resolved. *Now look what I've done! I've cut myself off from two people who mean so much to me. I feel like I'm falling down through a cold, dark shaft with warmth, love, goodness, and true satisfaction falling behind me.* The inner pressures suddenly felt so oppressive he had to physically move or he felt he would suffocate.

At that moment it struck him that after two days there might be a warrant out for him and he'd better protect himself or he might never have a chance to get anything in his life back together. As he paid his bill and left the café, he noticed a stand in the lobby with newspapers from several major cities. The thought struck him that his picture might be out as a missing person. He scanned through the papers but found nothing. He went back to his hotel room and began to shake with anger and remorse, sitting on the edge of the bed, his head in his hands. His breath began to come in uncontrollable gasps as his body was wracked with deep sobs. He began to cry out in pain and fell onto the floor.

"Oh, God, help me!" he cried. "I believe in you. I'm so sorry for all I've done that was wrong. Help me, please!"

Just then the hotel door opened and he heard a startled gasp as the maid started to enter his room. She dropped the towels she was carrying as she put her hands to her face in alarm. Realizing he had forgotten to put out the do not disturb sign, Mark stammered, "Hold it! Don't come in. I'll be out in a few minutes."

As suddenly as she had opened the door, the maid slammed it shut. Mark's tears suddenly turned to panic as he jumped to his feet, hastily gathered his things, and nearly ran to the elevator. In the lobby the desk clerk gave him a quizzical look as he checked out. He caught the hotel shuttle to the airport and entered via the US Airways terminal where he asked about flights to Richmond, Virginia. There was a flight leaving in an hour, but all the coach seats were sold out.

"Do you have anything in first class?"

"Yes, I have three vacancies. Do you want one of those?"

"Sure. How much is it?"

The ticket agent told him the price for a round trip ticket, and Mark clarified that it was only one way. He paid for the ticket and got his boarding pass and the gate for the flight. Then he got some quarters and went to a pay phone and called Ed Heygood.

Ed picked up the phone. "Hello?"

"Pastor Heygood, this is Mark—"

"Mark! Where are you? Are you all right?"

"No, I'm not all right, but I am getting better. Look, it's a long story, and I need to ask for your help."

"Okay. Tell me what's going on. Why did you walk out of church and leave town when we were about to receive you into membership?"

"I'll tell you what I can, briefly, then I'm going to call Fanny, and I want to ask you to go over there and be with her and Harper when they get my call."

Ed thought about that a minute. "Maybe you'd better tell me what this is all about."

"The first thing you need to know is that I'm *not* Mark Howard, but I knew Mark. He and I shared an apartment after we had served our parole for a crime we had committed. I'll explain more when I get back there."

Ed was shocked. "Hold on a minute… What did you just say?"

"I'm not Mark Howard. My name is CJ Crumbold—"

"*CJ Crumbold?*"

"Yes. I took Mark's name for a purpose I'm not proud of, and I want to tell you about all of that—"

"Yes, you need to do that! Wait a minute. You say you're not Mark, but you were in prison with Mark? Does that have something to do with your having claimed to be Mark?"

Mark filled in a few details and added, "Since I'm calling from a payphone, I can't go into more detail now. The real Mark Howard died in an auto accident, and I took his identity to try to steal Harper's money. But that was the *old* me—before I came to your church and found out who Jesus Christ really is and what a life of faith and trust and honesty is about. Before I met Fanny and fell in love for the first time in my life. And before I met Harper and came to care about him as a person."

CJ paused a moment. "Pastor Heygood, I am sorry for all that I've done and the pain I'm causing everybody. I really need your help so I can start my life over with faith and integrity. I'm in Columbus, Ohio, and I'll be leaving on a plane to Richmond within the hour. As soon as I can get back to Dinkel Island, I want to meet with you, Fanny, and Harper."

"You know the police are looking for you, don't you?"

"I thought they might be."

"They found where you sold your car and traced you to a bus station, but I don't know any more than that. I am going to have to tell them about this phone call."

"I understand, I'll just have to take my chances on getting there before they arrest me. Actually, I want to turn myself in. I know there will be consequences I'll have to face, and I'm ready to do that. If you want to tell them I'm coming back, that's okay."

"Your three minutes are up." It was the operator interrupting their call. CJ put in more coins, and then said, "Whatever happens next, I am going to trust God to get me through it. Right now my main concern is not to hurt Fanny and Harper any more, and I need for you to be there with them."

"Are you sure it's the best thing for you to try to talk to them right now? This is very heavy stuff you're dropping on them, and I think it might be better if I go over and break this to them without you calling just yet."

"Oh,"—CJ paused—"Maybe you're right. I guess I was thinking of my need to hear Fanny's voice and feel connected with her."

"Maybe you'd better change that around and think of Fanny and Harper first. And if you're going to really trust God, and are sincerely penitent, you need to totally let go of things here and deal with yourself. God is greater than this situation, and he will be with you if you stay connected to him. But you can't dictate the terms."

There was silence on CJ's side for a few moments, and then he said in a resigned tone of voice, "I know you're right. It's hard, but I caused all this so I'll just let go and let things take their course."

"Remember, your end of this is to have faith and integrity, so you need to be on that plane when it lands in Richmond, and see where God takes you next. I'll go over to Fanny and Harper and tell them what's going on—"

"Your three minutes are up," the operator chimed in again.

"You need to go, Mark—I mean CJ. God be with you." Ed hung up and CJ dropped the receiver back into its cradle, then left the phone booth.

Ed sat in his office for a while and played the conversation over in his mind. He took a note pad and wrote down some basic details so he could keep them straight. Next he called Sally and told her a brief summary of his talk with CJ and that he was headed to Harper's house and might be late for supper. She wasn't happy about it but said she understood and for him to please be home as quickly as he could. Ed left his car at the church and walked the short distance to the Jauswell house.

When he got there, he found Chief Thompson's cruiser in the driveway and knew he was already behind in the scenario that was unfolding. He said a quick prayer as he walked up to the house and knocked on the door. Fanny answered his knock and the instant Ed stepped inside she threw her arms around his shoulders and began to cry. "I'm sorry," she managed to say between sobs. "I'm so glad you've come. Something terrible has happened, and Mr. J is so upset. I'm afraid his heart can't stand this." Ed gave her a reassuring nod and stepped into the living room.

24

Redemption

The moment he entered the room, Ed felt the overwhelming tension. Harper was pacing the floor, obviously enraged. His face was red, his expression harsh, and he seemed to be back in his old persona. "That sorry excuse for a man came in here and tried to take my nephew's identity," yelled Harper. "To think I *trusted* that idiot! And to make it worse, he tried to mess up my housekeeper's life, too—"

Charlie Thompson interrupted. "Now, Harper, there's no sense going on like this. We've known each other a long time, and I've seen you get upset before, and it never does you or anybody else any good. I need for you to calm down so we can get to the bottom of this."

"Get to the bottom of it, my foot! You get yourself out of here, and go arrest that skunk." He began to cough and grabbed his chest and sank into a chair, yelling for Fanny to get him a nitroglycerin tablet. When he saw Ed he said, "Preacher, this whole thing just hit me so hard, I can't hardly handle it."

Chief Thompson spoke to Ed, "I was telling Harper and Fanny that the fingerprints we took came back from the state police with a criminal identity. This man, who called himself Mark Howard, is really someone named Clarence James Crumbold, who apparently goes by 'CJ.' He has a record in California where he served time for possession of drugs with intent to distribute and accessory to murder. Our suspicion is that he targeted Harper for some kind of extortion."

"Yes, I know," said Ed. "He called and told me his real identity over the phone. He said he'd answer all our questions when he gets here."

"So he's coming back here?" said Chief Thompson.

"By his own choice. He wants to turn himself in."

"Well, I'll be... That's a twist on things."

"Don't you trust him!" yelled Harper. "That snake's got something up his sleeve."

Ed spoke up, "I believe he regrets what he's done and wants to make amends."

"When will he get here?" asked Fanny.

"Sometime this evening, I expect. He's on the way now."

"We'll get him picked up as soon as he gets off the airplane," said Chief Thompson. "Is he armed or dangerous? Do you think he's a flight risk?"

"No, none of those things," said Ed. "The content of his call to me is confidential except that he wanted me to share with Harper and Fanny that he's coming home."

"What's going on," said Harper, "is that he's trying to rip off everything I own!"

"Now, we don't know that for certain," said the chief. "We just know he took your real nephew's identity and came here under false pretenses. We know he owned the car he sold in Richmond, and he's been spending his own money, nobody else's, at least up to this point and that he has been using your nephew's Social Security number.

"What did he tell you that you can share with us?" asked Fanny.

"Fanny, he told me how much he loves you and how bad he feels for having hurt you."

"Bunch of horse manure!" spat Harper.

"No, I don't think so," Ed replied. "And he also said he loved and respected you, Harper, and was coming back to take the consequences for what he has done. He wanted me to tell you about this before anything broke open, but obviously that has already happened."

Ed looked intently at each of them, and then said, "Chief, you'll find that Mark Howard died in an auto accident some while ago." There was a sudden gasp from Harper, but he didn't get ruffled. "Clarence does go by the nickname CJ. He and Mark were both convicted of felonies back in the seventies when they got mixed up in a gang of druggies. They both served time and were released on parole, which they completed successfully. After their parole they moved to Laguna Beach where Mark was an artist, and CJ did some kind of accounting work. He took care of Mark's finances for him, which is how he had access to his Social Security number when Mark died. He told me I could share all of this if it would help."

Fanny nervously twisted the napkin in her hands and said, "You know, Mark told me a little about his lifestyle out there in California. He said when he got here, he found life with a goodness he had never imagined." She hesitated a moment, swallowed hard, then added, "I'm still having a hard time thinking that this CJ person is the Mark that I know. It seems so weird."

Chief Thompson stood up, reached for his uniform hat and a notebook he had brought in with him. "We'll need a complaint from you, Harper, to pick him up. We could do it on the basis of his fingerprints revealing his false identity. Until you came in, Pastor, that's all we really had. It's up to you, Harper, to initiate a complaint for criminal impersonation with intent to defraud, so we can arrest him. That should be our first step, and then we'll see what happens at the arraignment."

"I'll sign that complaint, Charlie," said Harper.

As soon as that was completed, the chief left. Ed sat down to try to help Harper and Fanny work through some of the issues they were facing. With the chief gone, Fanny began to let out more of her own emotions.

"Darn it!" she said. "I thought I had found a man with real integrity who loved me. He seemed so gentle and understanding, and all the time he was just trying to get Harper's money! I'm sorry. Excuse me for blowin' off steam."

"Go ahead, express yourself," said Ed. "You can't keep those feelings stuffed inside, or they will get you down. I believe God understands the anger we feel when things happen that hurt us. After all, think of God's own pain in the crucifixion of Jesus. Just get it out, and make room for God's grace to comfort you and strengthen you."

Fanny seemed to fall back as though her energy was spent, and she wiped away the tears and blew her nose. Then she said quietly, "Last Sunday I went to church thinkin' everything was perfect, feelin' completely at peace. Then all this happened, and I've just been losing it." She looked at Ed with determination in her eyes and said in a stronger voice, "But I can make it through this! At the same time, there's such a deep hole in my heart where Mark has been. I wonder if I will ever see him again or if I even *want* to see him, but of course I'll have to see him if he comes back here. It's so confusing."

Harper had been visibly shaken by Fanny's grief. "I know I've blown off my steam. I've been hurt by Mark, too, but that's no excuse for carryin' on like I did. Please accept my apologies, both of you."

"You know, God forgives us before we forgive ourselves, but we don't feel forgiven as long as we hold onto the shame," said Ed. "It's when we believe that God is forgiving each of us—even

CJ—that we can begin to forgive ourselves and give God's Spirit the freedom to work within us and give us peace and hope. We have to step back so *God* can make something positive happen."

As a pastor dealing with such a heavy situation, Ed felt like a pilot in a snowstorm flying strictly on instruments. His instruments were the things he had learned in courses in seminary and continuing education, and the truths he found in scripture. He asked God to nudge his spirit with the directions to take, but he could not clearly see exactly what to do or say because he lacked the experience of a seasoned pastor. But he knew how to pray, and he prayed with each thought and word that transpired as he worked with Harper and Fanny.

Ed looked in Harper's eyes and said, "Harper, I'm thinking back to your testimony in church Sunday. You gave us a glimpse inside your own soul, at a struggle no one saw until there came a time when something had to happen. If I hear Mark correctly, I think he's been going through a similar struggle, only it's been in a much shorter time frame. Sunday in church was the time when something just had to happen. I don't think he could take the vows of church membership without resolving his own inner battle, and I don't think he knew how to tell you that. Somehow I believe panic hit him, and he just ran until he was far enough away to stop and let reality sink in."

The hardness and the pain in Harper's eyes seemed to melt somewhat as Ed spoke to him. "Thanks for your words, Ed, that all means a lot to me. Puttin' things that way, I can imagine a little bit of what Mark's been going through. It's just hard for me to imagine somebody thinking the way he did or actually trying to do something like stealing my money. I can't understand how criminals think or how they live with themselves. I guess if they have any sensitivity at all, something can happen inside them to make them change. After all, I was a harsh person, in a different way—not as a criminal—and God made a change in me. So I guess I can see how Mark wants to come back and try to make things right."

"We all have parts of ourselves that are incomplete," Ed offered, "and the crime he was trying to commit came originally from a harsh, spiritually deadened brain that hadn't been nurtured with love, truth, kindness, generosity—any of the things God can bring out within us through his Spirit. In order to find that part of life and make it a part of us, we first have to make an intentional break with the old self. I think that's what's happening with Mark, and it took a lot of courage for him to come back and come clean."

This direction in the conversation seemed effective as both Harper and Fanny lost the hypertension that had been rampant within their bodies. Wanting to build on this inner release, Ed suggested they pray together. In the course of the prayer, Harper and Fanny each asked God's forgiveness for their reactivity. They asked for the wisdom and strength to go wherever God would lead them as CJ returned home.

Ed closed his prayer with a petition he often used in times of grief. "Lord, thank you for all you have given us, for all you have taken from us, and for all you have left us, for we know that it is in this process that we become complete persons. In the name of our Savior, Jesus Christ. Amen."

After their prayer time, Ed asked Harper and Fanny how they felt, and they each said, "Relieved!"

"I don't think CJ's coming back here expecting everything to be just like it was before," said Ed. "I hope all of us can listen not only to his words but also to his spirit when we see him—and that we can each let God show us how to respond. From talking with him, I think this house and the two of you are the healthiest family he's ever known. In a strange way—yet maybe not so strange either—he's actually coming home like that prodigal son in the window at church. If we keep our faith strong and trust God, he will show us each step we need to take. Forgiveness and restoration are possible, but they take time, so let's all keep ourselves centered in Christ."

∾

With calmness restored Ed felt it was time for him to go home to his family. Fanny went to the kitchen to fix supper, and Harper fell asleep on the couch. When Ed got home, Sally was just serving supper, and she and the kids were elated to see him.

"What kinda 'mergency was it, Daddy," Billy asked. "Were the police there and the firemen? Is everything okay?"

"Yeah," Angie said, "can you stay here for supper or do you hafta leave again?"

Sally said, "Come on, kids. That's enough. Let your daddy get ready for supper so he can sit down at the table with us."

"That's okay," said Ed, "It wasn't that kind of an emergency. Just some people in the church who had something very hard they had to figure out, and they needed some help to talk about it and pray about it. So that's what we did, and God will take care of it."

"Oh, is that all?" Billy said. "I thought it really was something big. I'm sure glad you didn't have to miss supper for *that*."

"You know," said Ed, "so am I! Now, let's say grace and enjoy this wonderful supper your mom has made." After supper they spent an ordinary family evening together, and after the kids were in bed, he and Sally sat and talked a long time about what had happened. He often confided in her because he valued her insights, and they both felt it was their partnership in ministry.

Sally said, "That's a huge step for Harper and Fanny to take in one afternoon—getting past that much anger and pain and even being open to hear about CJ. I hope they can hold onto that."

"I think they will," said Ed, "especially Harper because he's already been through some huge spiritual changes. We need to just keep them all in our prayers."

"Did they pick CJ up this evening? Have you heard anything more from Chief Thompson?"

"No, I haven't heard anything more, but I expect I will tomorrow, probably quite early. Boy, you never know what's lying in wait for you in the ministry! It's a privilege to be able to be with people through things like this," said Ed, "but it sure can wear you down."

~⁀↩

CJ went over his plans for what to do when he deplaned. He would rent a car and drive to Dinkel Island. He was sure Ed Heygood would have prepared Fanny and Harper for his visit. He figured it was just a question of time until they traced him back to California and discovered his criminal record. He hoped he could avoid arrest and maybe negotiate some kind of plan to regain the trust of the two people he had almost swindled. He especially hoped he could regain Fanny's trust and restore his relationship with her. In retrospect he knew it had been foolish to run, but that's what he had done. He had to somehow go forward and try to make amends.

Upon entering the terminal, he was approached by two state police officers who suddenly stepped up and showed him an arrest warrant from Nor'easter County and asked him to accompany them quietly to their car. He did not resist. During the long ride to Potomac City, it became clear that he would not have a chance to talk to Fanny and Harper, much less go to their house. The consequences of his actions began to sink in. He knew from his experience in California that he would likely be arraigned, and he would have to have a lawyer. He felt depressed.

At the Nor'easter County line, he was transferred into the custody of the county sheriff's deputies who took him to the courthouse and a hearing before a judge. At the arraignment he was charged with impersonation with intent to defraud based on a complaint signed by Harper Jauswell and further evidence from the Dinkel Island police chief. The judge advised him of his rights, and since he had no permanent residence in the area, he was ordered to be held over at the jail until a preliminary hearing could be arranged.

"Mr. Crumbold," said the judge, "you will need an attorney to represent you. Do you have someone in mind?"

"No, sir. I don't know any lawyers here. Can you recommend someone?"

"You appear to have some resources," said the judge, "so I would suggest you speak to one of the gentlemen in the back of the courtroom."

A man who had been standing in the back with several others came forward, put out his hand, and said, "Mr. Crumbold, I'm an attorney practicing here in Nor'easter County, with offices in Dinkel Island and Potomac City. May I be of service to you?"

CJ accepted his services. They discussed the details and then CJ was was taken to the jail for the night. The next day CJ asked his lawyer to arrange a meeting with Pastor Edward Heygood from Dinkel Island.

～∾～

The next day Ed went to the jail to visit CJ and was ushered into an interview room. When they brought CJ in, Ed was struck by the change in this man who had always presented himself as enthusiastic and self-assured. His face was drawn. His movements seemed jittery and tentative. An aura of shame enveloped him. Ed wondered whether it was humiliation at haveing been found out, or the humility of a penitent heart that he saw in CJ. He decided to focus on the penitent heart unless CJ indicated otherwise.

"CJ, I'm glad you came back. I know this has been hard for you. It took a lot of courage to turn yourself in." He extended his hand. "Let's sit down."

They sat across from each other at a wooden table in the center of a sparsely furnished room. CJ looked Ed in the eye. "Thank you for coming."

He seemed to search for words. "This is really hard--facing you I mean."

Ed nodded reassuringly.

I'm not sure how I can face Fanny and Harper. What must they be thinking of me now.

"They were both deeply hurt by the suddenness of your running away, and then finding out who you really are and about your fraudulent intentions." CJ shifted in his chair, nodding with understanding as Ed spoke. He didn't try to interrupt or challenge Ed.

"Amazingly, Harper seems to have softened toward you," said Ed. "I think he might be willing to work something out to drop the charges. I have passed that information along to your lawyer."

CJ breathed an anxious sigh. Ed continued. "Fanny is another matter. She is a very sensitive woman who has been hurt by men in the past. She trusted you deeply and needs a lot more time to get past the hurt she feels. It would be good to give her space and let her decide when she's ready to talk with you."

The two men talked for a few more moments during which CJ seemed to take hold of his situation more positively.

"Thanks for helping me. I'm sorry I've made things so hard for Fanny and Harper, and I hope to earn back their respect and trust."

"All things in their time, CJ. There will be opportunities to work on restoring your relationships." Ed looked searchingly into CJ's eyes. "The first thing you have to do is work on your relationship with God. He'll take you forward."

"I know. What I did--running away like that--was because I couldn't live with myself. I know I have to make some big changes. I want to feel God's forgiveness and to be baptized. I want to make a commitment to Christ."

Ed reached across the table to CJ. "I believe what you say. I will be available to help you take those steps." He felt CJ's tension release, offered a prayer, and then left.

∾

At the preliminary hearing, CJ's lawyer requested that they entertain a plea bargain. "My client has told me if this case goes to trial he intends to enter a guilty plea. He has been fully cooperative in revealing his background, motives for what he did, and his own remorse. He has made it clear that he no longer wishes to defraud anyone, least of all Mr. Jauswell who has requested that the charge be dropped. It is my belief that pursuing this case further will result in unnecessary investment of time and resources for the state. Therefore I would move for a dismissal of all charges."

The judge asked CJ to speak for himself. When he finished the judge raised his eyebrows and looked across the rim of his glasses. "What does the state have to say?"

The commonwealth's attorney said, "I have known Harper Jauswell for many years. If he wants to drop the charges, and the defendant admits guilt and has experienced the change of heart my colleague suggests, then I would concur in the request for dismissal."

The judge gave everyone a hard look. "I will honor your request with one stipulation, that Mr. Crumbold be fined $1000 for putting the Commonwealth to the trouble and expense of this proceeding. Case dismissed!"

When CJ had paid the fine, court costs, and his attorney's fee, he found Ed Heygood had arrived to take him back to Dinkel Island. "You have been richly blessed by this outcome, CJ, and you have Harper Jauswell to thank," said Ed. He wants to meet with you as soon as you get settled back in town. Oh, you asked me if I could find you a place to live. I have found a furnished room down on the Town Hall Square that you can move into today. I used our petty cash fund at church to put a deposit on it. You'll owe that money back to the church."

"That's fantastic," said CJ. "I'll give you back the money today. I want to look for a job and begin getting my life straight as soon as possible."

"you asked to be baptized and received into the church. I have planned a private ceremony that we can do as soon as you're ready. I believe taking this step is an essential part of establishing your new life."

"Thanks. Anytime is fine with me."

"We'll have a ceremony at the church altar, and Harper and several church leaders want to be present to witness this and to offer you their prayers and support."

"Who will be there?"

"In addition to Harper, there will be Jim and Patty Swank, Jack and Barb Reilly, Steve and Jenny Tyrone, plus two of our new members Stan and Lillie Grayson, who heard about your situation and asked how they could be supportive."

CJ fought back tears and a lump in his throat as he recognized those names of people offering him undeserved forgiveness. Never in his life had he known such love and acceptance. He felt overwhelmed.

25

Turnaround

$\mathcal{E}$d went by to visit with Harper the day after CJ was settled back at Dinkel Island. Fanny seemed distant and reserved when she let him in the front door. Motioning toward Harper's office, she said, "He's expecting you."

"Thanks. How are you doing now?"

"I'd rather not talk about it. I've got a lot of work to do." She turned and walked away toward the kitchen.

Ed went in and found Harper behind his desk, engaged in some paperwork. When he started to get up, Ed said, "Stay seated, Harper. I'll just sit over here. You look busy today!"

"I am, I am," said Harper. "All that has happened with CJ Crumbold has made me realize I really need to go over my assets and decide how I want things to be distributed at my death. Nothin' like a heart attack to bring you a dose of reality!" He gave a short laugh. "You know, I'm willing to work with CJ because I have a clear sense that this is what God wants me to do, and I have to also think about Fanny and her needs. She is takin' all this very hard, and I can understand that—she was in love with the man. Now she can't get over what he did."

"It's going to take her some time, and realistically, she may never get over it."

"Yes, I know." Harper seemed pensive for a moment. "I think that underneath everything, CJ is a basically good person who just needs some guidance to get his life on track. That's the only reason I dropped those charges against him. I still have to fight feeling angry about it…"

"That, too," said Ed, "is something that takes time, perhaps a lot of it. But your heart is in the right place, and you're doing some admirable things here."

"Yes, well one thing I can't do is allow any part of my estate to be available to him. I've been setting up a codicil to my will that will direct a portion of my estate to my two sisters, and the remainder, after a one hundred thousand dollar gift to the church, I will leave, along with the house, to Fanny Morris."

"Harper, that's a wonderful gift for the church, but please make sure you put the others first. I believe God works through many channels, including family support."

"Don't be concerned about that. Fanny has been loyal to me over so many years. Annabelle brought her here, and the two of them always worked well together. Then when Annabelle needed her, Fanny was always dutifully present. She's done the same for me. She has no family of her own, you know, so I consider her part of my family. She will not squander an inheritance. I can assure you of that."

"I'm sure you're right, Harper, and I admire your wisdom in this."

"Now, what I want to do while you're here is to talk out all of this with CJ. Where's he stayin' now?"

"I found him a furnished studio apartment down on Town Hall Square that he can rent a week at a time. It's nothing fancy, but he's okay with that for now."

"Let's let that be for a time. Maybe sometime later if I feel settled about it I'll ask him to move back in here, although I will have him pay some rent, which frankly I'll use to give Fanny a raise. This sounds strange, I know, but when he was here, there was life in this house, and it needs to be that way again. He got himself into this mess, and he'll have to get himself out of it. I know he's motivated, resourceful, and energetic. He can get a lot accomplished when he puts his mind to it. I've prayed about this, and I keep getting the same answer: love him in Christ, support him, but don't enable him to get back into the old kind of thinking."

"Only you could do this, Harper. God has equipped you by saving you from your own inner demons. When he does that, he usually asks us to help someone else get rid of theirs. Oh yes, CJ says he's ready to be baptized and make his commitment to Christ and the church, so when does it suit you to do it?"

"How about Sunday afternoon, if there's nothin' going on at church then?"

Ed checked his calendar. "That works fine this week. I'll get Louise to call the others and set it up at, say, three o'clock? That way everybody can have lunch after church and then come back."

"Let's do it," said Harper. "Before you leave, let's pray over this thing. I'm doing this for the Lord, and he's working in me at the same time." So they prayed, and then Ed left to make some other pastoral visits.

On Sunday afternoon everybody who was involved gathered at the baptismal font with CJ. Ed said, "I want to thank each of you for giving up some time to be witnesses to the baptism and confession of faith of Clarence James Crumbold. We all know the storm of temptation he has gone through. He has decided to make a fresh start in his life by beginning with Jesus Christ.

Through your loving acceptance and support, CJ has acquired a sense of who God created him to be. This has been a huge step of faith for him, and he has asked to say a few words." Ed turned to CJ and motioned for him to speak.

"I am overwhelmed that you are here, and I thank you," CJ spoke with a voice that was both soft with sincerity and strong with authenticity. He looked each person in the eye, moving his gaze from one to the other. He continued, "Not very long ago, I had no belief in God and no purpose associated with my life except to get all I could as fast as I could while I had a chance. At one point that led me to be involved with a gang where drugs were worshiped. A crime happened that I had nothing to do with, but I was convicted with the others in the gang, and I served my time. I learned to leave drugs out of my life, but I didn't learn to put God into it. I confess to you that I played a role in your lives that was false and totally self-centered. I have come to understand that God forgives me, and I'm learning how to forgive myself. Now I need your forgiveness as well. Thank you for your love and your faith. Please help me to grow in my own faith from here on out."

Everybody in the group embraced CJ and spoke encouragingly to him. Ed called them back to order. "CJ, do you renounce all evil in your life, confess your sins before Christ and this fellowship, and accept Jesus Christ as your savior?"

"I do," said CJ.

Ed proceeded to ask the rest of the questions involved with confession of faith and church membership. CJ answered affirmatively to each one.

"Do you now desire to be baptized in this faith?"

"I do!"

Ed had him kneel before him as he reached into the font, cupped water in his hands, placed it on CJ's head. "Clarence James Crumbold, I baptize you in the name of the Father, and of the Son, and of the Holy Spirit. Amen.

"Clarence, you have confessed your sins to Almighty God and been baptized as a disciple of Jesus Christ. Do you now pledge to go forth seeking to follow the commandments of God and to walk in the same as a member of this congregation of the Wesleyan Brethren Church?"

Again CJ answered affirmatively, and Ed placed his hands on his head. "I confirm you in the faith and fellowship of all true disciples of Jesus Christ, and welcome you into the membership of this Church."

When CJ arose, his face had a radiance that only God could create. It was as though his very soul was visible. His eyes flowed with tears of joy. He would later say he felt a warmth that plunged through his body from head to toe and back. He was indeed a new person, redeemed by the Lord, and set on a fresh path.

All those who witnessed the ceremony were elated and tearful with joy. They embraced CJ and spoke their wishes for God's blessings in his life. Ed noticed the afternoon sun hitting the prodigal son window in just the right way to enhance the figure of the son in his father's embrace. He turned to CJ and said, "Look at the window, CJ. God is sending you assurance of his grace this moment."

When everyone else had left, Harper turned to CJ. "I forgive you, and I love you in Christ. I trust God to guide your new life. In a few weeks, after we've all gotten our feet back on the ground, so to speak, I want you to come back to my house and take your old room again. I want to graft you into my family. I hope you will accept."

CJ was overwhelmed and broke down in tears. "Are you sure?"

Harper said, "I wouldn't ask if I weren't sure."

"Then yes, thank you, I would be honored to do that. You, Fanny, and this church have been the only real family I've known. When you are ready, I will count it a privilege to be there, and I won't disappoint your trust."

"I believe you," said Harper. "One word of caution—I'm afraid Fanny hasn't gotten to the point of forgiveness yet, so you will need God's grace and guidance in relating to her. That's one reason I want to wait a few weeks, to see if she is able to make that step of forgiveness before you return."

"I understand. I deeply love her and miss her, but I know I have hurt her. I will pray for her healing even if it doesn't include a restored relationship with me."

Harper and CJ embraced and left the church to walk into the next chapter of their lives.

26

A New Day for James

Fall found CJ getting settled into his new life in Dinkel Island. The dismissal of charges in Nor'easter County did not settle the issue of his having used Mark Howard's Social Security number fraudulently. He went through another hearing from which he emerged $2500 poorer but with no jail sentence and a period of probation. Harper helped him with the services of an attorney. CJ didn't know much about carpentry, but he was a willing and able worker. James Brown hired him to help with some renovations at Stan and Lillie's shop. During those few days, Lillie learned about his accounting experience in California. She and Stan needed someone to handle their books and to be a part-time clerk. Lillie offered CJ the job, and he accepted.

In September a new business opened out near Crabber's Creek Acres. The Fashion Flair furniture craft shop specialized in high-end, handmade, custom wood furniture. Fashion Flair had the latest in equipment and design capability and hired a number of local people including James Brown, who needed what he called a day job to keep things together in between his carpentry jobs. James was only on the job two weeks when the owner called him into his office.

James was scared. It felt like the old times at Dinkel Island when he had been called before someone in authority and told to keep his place. Stan and Lillie hadn't been like that, and in recent times neither had Harper Jauswell.

James entered the office hesitantly. Hank Angelo, the owner, greeted him warmly. "Hi James. Come on in and have a seat. I just poured myself a cup of coffee. Can I get you one?"

James said "No, thanks" to the coffee and then sat down.

"James, I've been impressed with your knowledge and skills in the shop. You know more about working with wood than most of the people I've hired over the years."

"Thank you, Mr. Angelo," said James stiffly.

"Hey, you don't have to be so formal. We're all just one big happy family here at Fashion Flair. Just call me Hank."

"Okay, Hank."

"Now, the reason I called you in is to ask if you'd be willing to take over the foreman's job full-time?"

James was flabbergasted. He said, "I've just been working part time to help support my family while I get my carpentry business going—"

"I realize that's why you came here, James, so let me tell you that I'm prepared to pay you a fixed salary, with bonuses when we complete projects that bring the company extra money. We'll pay for hospitalization insurance for you and your family, plus you will get two weeks paid vacation every year. In return I'll expect you to pull out all the stops with your knowledge and skills and keep those boys on the production line working. I'll want your feedback if we plan a project and you see problems with it or have suggestions for a better way to do things. And we'll deduct your taxes and send them in for you instead of you having to do all that for yourself as a self-employed person. James, you can give us something we need to make this company top-notch. I think we can give you security and a future like you've never had before. So, what do you say?"

James didn't have to think about it very long. "Okay," he said, "I'll do it. When do I start this new job?"

Hank got up, walked over, and shook James's hand. "Glad to have you aboard! You can start the minute you walk out this door. I'll take you out and introduce you to your workers and set you up. Let's go!"

So it was that James Irwin Brown, who'd been called "Jimbo" in town and manipulated to keep an illusion of racial balance, became a man who felt liberated and proud of himself. Things went well for several weeks, and then one Monday morning, three rough-looking men stormed into the company office. They shut the door and a large man, who seemed to be the leader, leaned over the desk and shook his fist in Hank's face.

"You ain't welcome in Dinkel Island," he said. "You can take your big-city ideas and go back where you came from. We'll help you find your way out of town."

One of the others stepped up and said, "Where do you get off comin' in here and upsettin' things that have been accepted for generations?"

Hank didn't flinch or speak. His face was blank except for the fire in his eyes.

The third man stepped up to the desk then. "What right have you got to take our handyman, Jimbo, and puff him up like he was somebody? Jimbo's already got a job, see?"

"Yeah, he keeps things repaired and runnin' all over town. Our old folks and women folk depend on him. Now they got nothin'."

The first guy made a move toward Hank, not knowing that he was a former marine and a Vietnam war veteran with a Purple Heart and a Bronze Star. Hank got up from behind his desk, rose to his full height of six foot five. He spoke in a voice that thundered. "What the devil do you mean barging into my office telling me a sorry mess like that. What goes on in this company is none of your business. If you ignorant goons think you're gonna come in here and shake me up, you just better think again. I'll mop the floor with your sorry butts, and when I'm through, I'll turn you over to the sheriff. I'll press enough charges against all of you that it'll take an army of lawyers to keep you out of jail. What you just did by threatening me is against the law in this country. That's a law I fought and bled to defend, and I live by it. So will you. Now get off my property, and don't you or anyone else threaten or harm any of my people. You got that straight?"

The three men who had come to threaten Hank Angelo felt lucky to get out of his office with their skins intact. When they talked things up around town afterward, they found few people willing to stick around and listen. James was liked and respected by most townsfolk, and they were more than happy to see him succeed at the furniture shop. There were a lot of veterans around town, too, and they backed up one of their own. As a result the racial issue seemed to die or at least to slide into the dark shadows of the town's fringes.

Ed heard about the incident when Jack Reilly called to get his take on things.

"Have you met the guy who has started that new furniture business out on the highway yet?" he asked.

"No," said Ed, "but I need to. He moved in from Northern Virginia, didn't he? Bob Drew told me he lives out in Crabber's Creek Acres."

"Yeah, that's right," said Jack. "He seems to be a pretty tough guy, somebody who doesn't get pushed around easily."

"Is that so?" Ed sensed something was hidden behind Jack's words. "So what's going on with him?"

Jack told him what had happened. Ed said, "Well, that sounds like an old, familiar story to me. Maybe it's good for us to have somebody like Hank around. Sometimes a little change is a good thing."

"Well, it's just that Jimbo has had a certain place in this town," said Jack, "and now he's working as a foreman out there plus running a business of his own. It all seems to go back to the influence of Stan Grayson on Jimbo, and I'm not sure how to deal with all that."

Ed gave him a quizzical look. "Jack, I don't know what there is to deal with. I mean, here's a man with a strong conscience and the guts to back it up who stands up for his employees, and it seems we should be thanking him. As far as Stan is concerned, he got to know James when he saved him under the pier last spring. He's taken a few lumps for that, but he believes in the dignity of every person and wants people to reach their potential."

"But that's just my point. Guys like Angelo and Grayson go around meddling in things that affect other people. Everything works best if everybody just tends to their own business and leaves other people alone."

Ed could not believe the attitude he was hearing. It brought back to him Harper's reactivity at the time of the Weekend Spectacular. He thought, *Like you're minding your own business right now.* "Jack, it sounds like this is a little too deep to deal with on the phone. How about coming over to my office, can you do that?"

"Well, I guess I could. When? Now?"

"I can make time now if you can make it. Come on over." Ed said.

When Jack arrived he and Ed sat down for what became a very uncomfortable conversation. Ed let Jack elaborate on what he'd said over the phone. He listened until Jack was finished, then offered his thoughts.

"Jack, I'm surprised we're having this conversation. God loves James Brown just as much as he loves you or me or anybody else. James allowed himself to be pushed into a mold that kept everybody from looking at the issue of race relations realistically. When Stan encouraged him to step out of that mold, he did, with wonderful results. As followers of Jesus Christ, we should be celebrating this whole thing. Justice is being done, and prejudice is being overcome. That can put us all one step closer to the kingdom of heaven."

Jack was obviously upset. His facial features were set like a brick wall. He wasn't letting Ed's message filter through his anger. *This isn't like Jack. I wonder who or what's behind this?* Jack spoke again. "Preacher, I thought you were an okay guy, but it seems I've misjudged you. You seem to be one of those liberals who turn everything upside down. I'm sorry I came over here, so I think I'd better get back to work."

"Okay, if you need to leave, that's fine. But I'm puzzled. I remember when you brought Harper Jauswell over here to talk things out when he was sounding an awful lot like you're sounding right now. And you were with Jim and me at the hospital when Harper's life was changed. You've been a strong leader in the church dealing with those issues. So I don't quite understand this. Let's do something. Let's both agree to pray about these concerns centered around James Brown and examine our own thinking. Let's step back and let God show us the way forward."

Jack softened a little and seemed a little less sure of himself. "I guess I hadn't considered praying about something like this, like prayer was just for illness and large problems. I'll think about it. I really will."

"I'm glad to hear you say that." Ed offered a brief prayer with Jack. After he left Ed decided to go over to the gallery and talk to Stan Grayson. As he entered the store a little bell tingled. Lillie said from back beyond the display walls, "Be with you in a minute."

"Hi, Lil! I came by to talk to Stan a minute. Is he around?"

"Oh, sure," said Lillie, recognizing Ed's voice. "He's out back in the storage area."

Stan was packaging some pottery for shipping. "Hey, Ed, what's up?"

"I just want to run something by you that I'm trying to figure out."

"Shoot!"

Ed told him about the conversation about Hank Angelo and James Brown and the prejudice he heard was floating around in the community. "I really care about this town and I wonder who or what is behind all of this. I think it's pretty scary."

Stan stopped what he was doing and put his hands on his hips. "Somebody's really scared of something if the old status quo is broken," said Stan. "I might have thought it was Harper Jauswell in the past, but not any longer. We may never know who it is. It seems evil is always around. We just have to recognize it for what it is and fight it when we can."

"Those are my thoughts, too," said Ed. "With time the person or persons behind that threat toward Hank will come into the open. It'll happen because Hank isn't intimidated."

"You know, my freshened faith has changed my heart, my thinking, my values—my very life. Maybe we have to share the power of God that comes through faith.

"I think you're right. We need to find ways to build sensitivity about persons and not roles and institutions. We need to make Christ's healing of lepers and calling of tax collectors constantly visible. When God touches people, people touch each other, and that's when things change. Yes, you're right. Thanks, friend. I knew you had something to help me with this."

"Hey, not me," Stan said, laughing as he pointed upward. "He's the one with the answers. He'll give us what we need to deal with this."

Jack called Ed at home on Christmas Eve, and asked to talk with him at the church. When they met Jack plunged right in. "Pastor, I can't face myself or my family and proclaim my faith tonight and tomorrow if I don't get something off my mind."

"What's going on?"

"I thank you for listening to me when I spouted off all that stuff about Jimbo and lost hold of my faith. I was wrong. Those are not the things I really feel or believe in my deepest soul. I let other people and their words poison me. I want to confess that to God at the altar now with you present, and I want to renew my walk with Christ."

"Sure, Jack. I understand."

"I couldn't sleep the last few nights, tossing around with turmoil raging in my brain. I felt God telling me to get this turned around before I celebrated the birth of his Son. Will you forgive me? Will you pray with me at the altar?"

"Of course," said Ed. "I certainly forgive you, as does God. And you are right about making your confession because once you've done that you will feel forgiven and be refreshed. Let's go do it right now."

Ed and Jack went before the altar of the church, and Jack felt his soul cleansed and a fresh presence of God's design for his life surging into his consciousness. As he left to go home, Ed said, "Merry Christmas to you and through you to every person you meet."

27

Change of Heart

Harper was unprepared for Fanny's reaction when he told her he had invited CJ to move back into the house.

"How can you do that?" Tears of outrage flowed from her, and she clenched her fists. "After what he done to me and tried to do to you, I can't believe you'd do this."

He tried to ease her anger by speaking softly. "Fanny, I'm sorry to upset you, but the man is honestly penitent. You'll feel differently with a little time."

She was not to be assuaged.

"Mr. J, I believe that heart attack must have shut down some of your brain! I've worked with you and Mrs. J, when she was livin', through good times and bad. Even when I didn't like somethin' you said or the way you said it, I always supported you. But this is somethin' I can't support. If he moves in here, I'm movin' out, and I mean it. I will quit workin' for you." With that she retreated to her apartment in the back of the house for the rest of the day.

The next morning at breakfast, Harper said, "Fanny, I know you've been hurt by CJ. That was insensitive of me to spring that on you yesterday. I would hate to lose you here, but I won't stand in your way if you need to leave."

Things were tense for a few days, but Fanny stayed on. Harper knew she had no idea where to go or how to quickly find another job. He tried to be sensitive and to give her time for her inner wounds to heal.

෴

After a few weeks, CJ moved back in. It was both a joyful and a painful experience. It was joyful because he was still overwhelmed by Harper's forgiveness and graciousness toward him. It was also painful because there was such a huge wall between him and Fanny.

"Fanny," he said one morning when he stepped into the kitchen, "I never meant to hurt you. I was so confused that I couldn't help myself."

Fanny froze and stared straight ahead.

"I love you," said CJ. "You have meant so much to me. Without you I never could have made the changes that I have."

Fire flew into Fanny's eyes. Her gaze bore into him as she said, "You don't know what love is. Love is trust and honesty. Love is commitment. I trusted you! I never trusted a man before in my life, until you. Look what it got me!"

O Lord, how can I reach her? Will I ever be able to make amends? "You're right," he said. "I did betray your trust—and Harper's trust, and Ed's trust, and God's trust. I am sorry."

"Sorry might do it for God and Mr. J, but it don't do it for me."

CJ didn't know what else to say, so he turned to leave.

"CJ, this is *my* kitchen, and I don't want to see you in this room again. And one more thing: I won't clean your room or do your laundry. You might live here, but it has nothing to do with me."

CJ left the kitchen and tried to avoid conflict with her after that. *It's what I deserve*, he told himself. *Lord, I pray that some day, some way there will be a crack in that wall Fanny has put up between us.*

After he had worked part time at the gallery for a couple of months, CJ was able to buy a car and attend counseling sessions with a psychotherapist Ed had found for him in Potomac City. The therapist helped him work through his guilt, shame, and conflicted emotions. He learned healthier ways of thinking and behaving and gained a more honest sense of himself than he had ever known. Where he had always rationalized things to support his intentions, he learned to accept contradictions and to see with a deeper vision. In a word, he became a more complete person who was in the process of becoming healthy and whole.

Parallel with mental health came spiritual health. With Ed's help, CJ began to study the Bible and learn about the faith he was embracing. He began to hear a small, inner voice nudging his consciousness with fresh perceptions. He was fascinated by the story about Saul being blinded along the Damascus Road through which Christ called him to become the leader in taking the gospel to the gentiles and gave him a new name, Paul, in the process. One day he said to Ed, "I'm intrigued that God gave Saul a new name to fit his new life. I tried to take a different name for a sinful purpose, but lately I've been wondering if I should take a new name as a Christian to mark my new life."

Ed discussed that feeling with him and said, "I wonder whether it's a new name, or a new identity, that you really are seeking."

"Well, I have a new identity in Christ through my faith, don't I?"

"Of course, but are there other dimensions where you need to express that identity? I wonder if that isn't something you need to explore with God in your prayers."

CJ began to pray about it. He borrowed books from the church library with stories about how people had been transformed by their faith. He studied the face staring back at him in the mirror when he shaved and looked for a clue as to who or what God wanted him to be in his life. He talked about this with Stan and Lillie, and they told him about their own struggles and discoveries in their faith. He talked about it at the supper table and other times around the house. Over the months between Christmas and the season of Lent; there was much tension in the Jauswell household—a good kind of tension where the soul of a man who had been a stranger to himself was touched by his Savior who lifted him to a new sense of life and purpose.

It was Ash Wednesday and the season of Lent that finally resolved CJ's inner searching and pointed him in an entirely new direction. He began attending the weekly Lenten services, and using a daily devotional guide with his morning Bible study. Week by week he grew in a sense that God had a redirection for his life.

Finally he shared this inner experience with Ed. "I'm not hearing voices or angelic music or anything like that," he said. "It's more like a constant sense that there's something just out of reach to which God is calling me. I almost hesitate to say the specific direction that keeps coming to my mind because I'm totally unqualified to even think of it."

After listening some more, Ed said, "CJ, I think you do know what God wants for you. Sometimes you can hear what God is nudging you to discover by telling someone else what you think it is. I'm here to listen, I won't be judgmental, and you can trust me as a prayer partner and as your pastor. CJ, exactly what do you think God wants you to do?"

CJ inhaled deeply, then looked Ed square in the eyes, and said very simply, "He wants me to be a pastor."

"So you're feeling called to the ministry!"

"Yes!" said CJ. "But given my background, I can't do that. I must be hearing something wrong."

Ed reached over and put his hand on CJ's shoulder and said with obvious conviction, "The call doesn't surprise me. That's how

God brings servants into the fold. What bothers me is that you still feel so unworthy."

"Why do I feel that way after all of the love, acceptance, and support I've received through you, Harper and the church?"

Ed said, "Because you *are* unworthy. We *all* are unworthy. None of us deserves God's salvation or calling. We don't earn God's love or forgiveness. It's offered to us by his grace through Christ."

"Yes, I believe that."

"If God has something for you to do, he will keep nudging you. If God wants you in the ministry then it doesn't matter who you are or what you've done. God will call you until you respond, and then he'll continue to call you every day *because* you responded. I know because I've been there."

"But I'm so unqualified. I don't know how to do that. I'm not someone who would naturally draw people to God or know how to help with their spiritual needs." Even as he spoke those words, he felt they were contradictory to what he knew was God's truth. CJ paused then said, "I guess I can learn all of that, and God will make me qualified. Right?"

"Exactly," said Ed. "You could learn all the things to say and do to be a pastor, but if the Spirit of God is not in you, none of it will mean anything."

"I know you're right. What do I do about it?"

"Well, we start right now with prayer." He took CJ into the sanctuary, turned on the soft altar lights, and they knelt at the communion railing. Ed prayed: "Oh Lord, it's us, CJ and Ed, and we hear you speaking to us. Help us to hear you clearly and open your path before us. CJ feels you calling him to a whole new direction in his life, Lord, and he's scared that he can't make that change. We ask you now to overcome his fears with confidence through your Spirit."

When Ed looked at CJ, he saw his face streaked with tears and an expression of complete calmness and peace. CJ then spoke his own prayer, "Yes, Lord, yes! I will go where you lead me and do what you ask. I don't know how to do it, but I know you will show me. Thank you for your forgiving love. I commit the rest of my life to your service. Amen."

As they stood up Ed looked CJ in the eye and said, "My friend, God has truly changed your heart. What a blessing!"

"Okay, I'll trust God to show me what's next," said CJ as he started down a totally new path in his life.

∿

Ed, Sally, Stan, Lillie, Fanny, and CJ were Harper's guests at the Seafood Pavilion. Fanny had come only because it was Harper's request. When they had finished eating and were sharing in some small talk, Harper made an announcement.

"Friends, I'm glad you honored an old man by accepting my invitation to supper tonight. Now I want to tell you why I invited you. I think CJ has a something special to share."

Everyone, except Fanny, had their eyes fixed on CJ as he said, "I guess the only way to say this is to just come right out with it. I have a new purpose in my life." Fanny looked up, startled, and everyone else had expectancy in their eyes. "You all are the closest people I have on earth. You have helped me through some huge changes, and now God has called me to a path I never expected. God is calling me into the ministry."

There was a shuffle of excitement among them. Fanny seemed to turn pale and had a look of disbelief in her eyes.

"I talked with Ed about this a couple of weeks ago, and he has helped me see my way forward. I thought I was unqualified, and he reminded me it is God's grace, not what we do or say, that qualifies us for his blessings. And this *is* a blessing."

Everyone except Fanny applauded. "When God changes a heart," said Harper, "he changes other things with it. Somehow I think God always did have this in mind for CJ, and he let us have a part in helping CJ find his calling. I think we should pray right now."

They all bowed heads and joined hands around the table as Harper, Ed, and CJ each spoke a brief prayer.

"I'm so pleased with this," said Lillie after the prayer, "but not really surprised. Since my own heart was changed, I've come to expect God to do unexpected things. Congratulations, CJ. I believe you will make a wonderful pastor."

"Thanks. I hope that's true. Anyway, it's in God's hands."

Fanny seemed to gradually warm up. CJ was shocked when she finally turned to him and said, "CJ, I'm glad to hear this. I will pray for you."

CJ started to reach for her hand but thought better of it. "Thanks," he said, "I will pray for you, too. In fact, I do that every day."

Tensions began to ease around the Jauswell house after that. Right after Easter there was a special program at Mammoth Baptist Church with a gospel quartet. Randy Adams sent out an invitation to the other churches in town for their people to attend. It was on a Saturday night and included supper in the fellowship hall. Randy asked Ed to offer a prayer during the opening of the service. Ed agreed and encouraged the Wesleyan Brethren folks to attend, including Stan, Lillie, Harper, Fanny, and CJ who all went together.

Southern gospel music was something CJ had never experienced before. The group went by the name Four for Hymn and had a vibrant harmony as they sang some hymns CJ knew, like "Love Lifted Me," "Rock of Ages," and "I'll Fly Away." They also sang many songs he had never heard, like "Steal Away," "Jesus Hold My Hand," and "Gone at Last." CJ loved the message and the harmony in this music.

At the close of the service, an invitation was given. Randy said, "If you have a problem or a special need that only God can resolve, I want you to raise your hand. While everyone bowed their heads, CJ felt Fanny raise her hand next to him. He instinctively reached over and took her other hand in his. She did not resist.

Afterward he said to her, "I apologize if I offended you by holding your hand during the prayer at the end, but I just wanted to be supportive. I want you to know I meant nothing else with that gesture."

Fanny looked at him with an expression that said more than her words. "I understand," she said. "Thanks for the prayers, and I was not offended."

Then it happened! That crack in the wall that CJ had longed for actually happened right there in the concert.

Tears filled CJ's eyes as he looked deeply into Fanny's face, seeing an expression he had wondered if he would ever experience again.

"Thanks!" he said.

"It finally hit me," said Fanny. "I guess if God can change Harper's heart and then yours, he can change mine, too. I forgive you, CJ."

CPSIA information can be obtained
at www.ICGtesting.com
Printed in the USA
LVOW04s2057120816
500060LV00016B/268/P